SUSPICIONS

"You know better than I that the police are right a hell of a lot more than they're wrong. But Ann and Frank want me to look. If there's nothing there in the next few days, I'll pack it in."

"Probably a waste of time," Al Thompson said.

"Yeah, I figured you might tell me that," I replied.

"But," the former police chief said, "I also know it's hell on the family. Aaron deserved a whole lot better."

"What would you look for in a situation like this?" I asked.

"If it were me, I'd look for something tangible to give you a lead. Sometimes you look for motive first. This case, you've got a dead college student. Tough enough to figure out the life and motives of a live kid that age. It might be a whole lot easier to begin sorting things out by finding a witness, the gun, the helmet, the reason the bike broke, something like that."

"So you think there's something there for me to find?"

"I doubt it. But as much as I love this part of the world and the people in it, I'd be the first to tell you that there are a lot of strange goings on out there."

DEAD LOW———
———*TIDE*

Jamie Katz

To Bob,
    Hope you enjoy
the book,
        Jamie Katz

HarperPaperbacks
A Division of HarperCollins*Publishers*

HarperPaperbacks
A Division of HarperCollinsPublishers
10 East 53rd Street, New York, NY 10022-5299

This is a work of fiction. The characters, incidents, and
dialogues are products of the author's imagination and are not to
be construed as real. Any resemblance to actual events or
persons, living or dead, is entirely coincidental.

Copyright © 1998 by Jamie Katz

ISBN 0-06-109711-X

Cover illustration © 1998 by
Chris Gall/Carol Chislovsky Design Inc.

First printing: December 1998

Printed in the United States of America

Visit HarperPaperbacks on the World Wide Web at
http://www.harpercollins.com

❖ 10 9 8 7 6 5 4 3 2

For my mother and father, for their support and the love of books they passed on; for Lee, who proves each day the power of dreams; and for Cynthia, who has taught me all there is to know about courage and has helped me every step of the way.

DEAD LOW ———

TIDE

CHAPTER ———

ONE

"Hey, you old fart," a voice called from behind me. I tried to step backward but my legs were buried almost to my knees in wet sand. Two kids were piling more on while another one splashed me from the shallow water at the edge of the beach. I twisted around as best I could. Higher on the beach stood Aaron Winters, nineteen years old and just over six feet tall, in tight black biking shorts, a bright orange and blue skin-hugging shirt, purple wraparound sunglasses, and an iridescent-blue biking helmet. Nobody else on the beach wore anything more than a bathing suit.

"Wanna ride?" Aaron asked.

"Who you calling old?"

"Anyone who can't keep up with me." He flipped a long stray lock of brown hair that had escaped from his helmet off his forehead.

"What's my reward for beating your butt?" I asked.

"Tell you what," he said, "you just stay in the same time zone with me, I'll take you to a cool place. Not many people know about it."

"Piece of cake."

"Let's go. I'll make sure we have a wheelchair for when you get back."

I extricated myself from the sand and the clutches of the small builders. After leaving the beach and showering off the sand, I changed into blue jean shorts and a T-shirt.

We took off down a long dirt driveway, leaving behind a cottage. At the end of the driveway we met up with Ann and Frank, the owners of the cottage, who were headed off, buckets in hand, to pick wild blueberries.

"I know Aaron talked you into biking with him, but you don't have to," Ann said to me. "You just got here, so if you want to hang out at the beach, just relax, that's fine."

"I—"

"Come on, Ann," Frank said, cutting me off. "You think he can't handle a short ride in the country with Aaron? You think he'll get tired just sitting on a bike for a couple of hours? Not our Dan Kardon, athlete extraordinaire. He'll ride poor little Aaron into the ground."

"Frank, don't be obnoxious," Ann responded.

"Hey, it's okay, I'm happy to bike," I said. "I'll try to go easy on him. You guys just make sure to get plenty of blueberries, so Frank can get the taste of humble pie out of his mouth later on."

Ann and Frank were Aaron's legal guardians, as well as close friends of mine dating back to college. Their cottage sits three miles north of the center of the town of Wettamesett. It stands back from a narrow gravel road, with a big covered porch on three sides and a large lawn. To the east, a creek meanders out through the salt marsh. Stone-pocked beaches extend up and down the shore. A slender channel runs through the middle of the creek, leading to a quiet cove on Buzzards Bay, on the coast of southeastern Massachusetts.

The house had been handed down in Ann's family, and she'd spent most of her summers as a child there, swimming, fishing, clamming, and sailing. Once Ann and Frank had their own children, Linda and Greg, the cycle started over. Ann showed her kids all the best tidal pools, the places in the creek where the eels hung out, and how to find the largest quahogs.

After a few years, Ann and Frank spent their entire summers at the cottage. Frank commuted to his office at Beth Israel Hospital in Boston, staying at their house in Cambridge during the week. Ann, a biology professor at Tufts University, had the summers off.

We'd stayed good friends, or as good as a single guy and a family can be. I was an honorary uncle, coming over for dinner and taking the kids out to ball games and museums. But Ann and Frank spent most of their social time alone or with other parents and families. I spent mine on basketball courts, in bars, and in front of televisions.

Usually, Ann and Frank invited me to visit the cottage once or twice during the summer. I wasn't much good on their sailboat except as ballast, but I'd take the kids out fishing, beat Frank in golf, and was happy to clean dishes.

Aaron Winters and I first met on one of my visits to the cottage in the summer of 1988, when he was nine years old. He was the son of Ann's cousin, and he came for a visit with his mother and father while I was there.

Aaron had no brothers or sisters. When he was eleven years old, his mother died of breast cancer. Ann and Frank had him visit as often as he could. Two years later his father died of a heart attack, then Aaron came to live with Ann and Frank and their two kids. The summer after his father died, he spent almost all his waking hours alone, clamming on the tidal flats, shooting basketballs, or sailing in a small Laser sailboat out on Buzzards Bay.

But Ann and Frank worked at integrating him into their family. In time, he laughed and joked with his younger cousins. After high school, he'd gone to Southeastern Coastal College outside the city of New Bedford, not far from Wettamesett. He did well his first year, found friends, joined a couple of clubs, and enjoyed himself. Now on the cusp of his sophomore year, he planned to live in the family cottage with a couple of buddies and commute to school. He was a good kid, but one still facing the collegiate gauntlet of newfound freedom, peer pressure, drugs, alcohol, and sex, with the added burden of the loss of his parents.

When I visited the family, I made a point of doing something with Aaron, usually athletic. He'd beat me at whiffle ball, but I could still take him in golf or basketball. We talked about sports, school, and girls, but often he chose not to talk much at all.

Recently Aaron had discovered bicycling, an activity that afforded him plenty of solitude and silence. He rode on back roads throughout the area and joined a club that went on rigorous training rides. So it was that a few hours into my latest weekend visit, we took off. I'd heard about his new passion but had never biked with him before.

As we rode away from Ann and Frank, Aaron took off, but then waited at the first major intersection, about two miles into the ride.

"You okay?" he asked.

"No problem," I said, trying not to pant.

We started up again, and this time he stayed with me. The road was lightly used, so I biked up to ride next to him.

"Looking forward to school?"

"Sort of." If he could have shrugged on the bike, he would have.

"What are you majoring in?"

"Haven't decided." He started to ride ahead of me. I hadn't talked to him in a while and I needed to recover my touch quickly or it would be another long while before we had a chat.

"I hear you're getting pretty good on the bike," I said as I caught up with him.

"Nah, not compared to some of the guys in my club," he said. "They blow me away."

"How'd you get started riding?"

"I used to love biking when I was a kid, real young. I stopped when we moved, after my mom died. At the end of high school, a friend of mine was going to college and didn't want his bike, so he gave it to me, and I started again. It's true, you know."

"What?"

"That you never forget how to ride a bike. Some kind of weird muscle memory, I guess. First time I rode the bike my friend gave me, it felt great."

"Looks new, though," I said. "Is that the one you were given?" Out of the corner of my eye I could see a smile emerge from under the helmet and behind the sunglasses.

"No, it's new. I just got it a few weeks ago. It's got great components, and I had 'em put racing tires on it. It's incredibly light—it's got a neat alloy frame." He went on for another few minutes about the paint job, the welding, the crankshaft, the seat, and a bunch of parts I'd never heard of.

"Whoa, boy, you're getting way ahead of me," I finally said. "All I know is, the bike looks great and you ride it well. Was it a gift from Ann and Frank?"

"No, are you kidding? This thing cost close to a thousand bucks. I worked all spring and summer and bought it myself." He paused. " 'Course, I did use some birthday money from them."

"The club you're in—how long are the rides you take?"

"Depends, but Sundays we usually ride fifty or sixty miles." He flashed me a quick grin. " 'Course I won't make you do anything like that today."

"Yeah, too bad, we've got to get back for dinner." Yeah, really too bad.

Aaron just laughed.

"You ever ride with friends from school?"

"Nope."

"How come?"

He paused for a moment. "They're into other things."

"How about your girlfriend? She bike?"

"Nope," he said. "Race you to the next stop sign." Then he stood on the pedals and took off. I did the same, but he left me behind as if I was standing still. It was a start. Maybe later he'd talk about something besides the bike.

He was off the bike, standing up, when I caught up with him.

"I was just admiring the scenery," I said. "Gotta stop and smell the flowers in life."

"How come," he asked, "when you beat me in basketball, you tell me I should learn from it and it's for my own good, but when I beat you on a bike, you pretend it didn't happen?"

"Just one of the prerogatives of the old and wise."

"Or maybe the old and out of shape."

"Could be."

We started out again, but after a while I could tell I was holding him back, so I told him to go ahead. He led the rest of the way, riding easily yet powerfully, with a steady rhythm. I kept his garish cycling shirt in intermittent view, but only just barely and only by pedaling hard.

He stopped for me at an intersection and we agreed to finish with a sprint to a convenience store on the route. Sprinting well ahead of me, Aaron was forced off the road by an obnoxious group of kids in an old convertible who merely yelled at me and gave me the finger. I slowed down to make sure Aaron was okay. When I saw he was, I rode past him, waved, and beat him to the store.

Aaron grumbled about my treachery, but I pacified him with a couple of sodas and cookies. Then we rode a short distance farther and Aaron showed me his secret place. We walked our bikes down a narrow trail which led off Route 107 through the woods. The trail through thick woods was passable but showed little evidence of use. After leaving the bikes in a clearing, we walked a short distance and then he stopped.

"Start crawling," Aaron said.

"What?"

"You heard me, we gotta crawl to the end so nobody sees us."

"I'm not big on trespassing."

"Don't worry, I've been here lots of times with other people, nobody's caught us. You're not chicken, are you?"

"Give me a break." In my book, you don't cave in to threats or blackmail by youngsters. At least, not often. I followed Aaron, crawling on all fours, until he stopped. I pulled up next to him, breathing hard.

"Pretty awesome," Aaron said.

"Damn straight," I said, "never seen anything like it. Make a few erasers out of all that rubber."

A tire pile in front of us sat in an otherwise pristine evergreen forest with a dirt road surrounding it. A stream ran nearby, running between two low hills. The sky and the tire pile contrasted, the pile black with specks of white against an overcast white sky mottled with dark clouds.

A huge, undulating ridge of black doughnuts rose to fifty feet, and even higher in places, enough to have dwarfed a five-story building; tires once useful but now worn, cut, punctured, or blown up, many of them filled with dirt or water. Somebody had covered a lot of ground with them, at least seven acres, it appeared, now under tens of millions of tires.

Looking more closely, I saw tires that were all black, others that were whitewalls, small ones, bald ones, and some in shreds, all piled randomly, strewn about, like piles of poker chips left behind by kids. I saw tires as big as fifteen feet around, scarred from duty on enormous tractors or heavy construction equipment.

Depending on your philosophical perspective, the pile was either an astonishing monument to

America's enduring passion for cars or an environmental monstrosity displaying our love for technology heedless of consequence. My perspective, from the ground under a bush, was influenced more by intermingled dirt and sweat, summer heat and humidity, pine needles and prickly leaves, than any sociological musings.

The black pile shimmered just as I imagined Mount St. Helens had while its lava fields congealed. The shimmering, I knew, was an optical illusion caused by hot air radiated from the tires. The edges and lines of the pile wavered, giving the pile the aspect of an hallucination. But that knowledge, and the heat of the day, didn't prevent me from shivering as I gazed at the dark contours in front of me.

I lay there with nothing to say for quite a time. "Told you this place was cool," Aaron said.

"Amazing. You won't get complaints from me. One thing I can't figure, though," I said. "I see a bunch of brand new tires over there, with gashes or punctures in their sides. I wonder what happened to them."

"Dealers," Aaron said.

"What do you mean?" I asked, brushing a mosquito away.

"Sometimes, if dealers can't sell the tires, they slash 'em, throw 'em out, and tell the manufacturers the tires were defective so they get their money back." Aaron shrugged. "Pretty scummy, but they do it."

I looked at him. "How do you know about it?"

He grinned back. "One of the older guys I ride with, he works at a car repair place. When I brought him here, I asked him the same question."

The trail led us to the corner of the tire pile. Tires sprawled from the bottom of a glen up the side of a slight hill. The dirt road running around its perimeter went up the hill and ran off into the woods. Where the road entered the clearing, the stream flowed next to it in a big bend. A locked metal gate stood across the road at the point it emerged from the woods. I wondered how many people would try to steal millions of used tires.

I wanted a better look, so we crawled back a bit into the woods and walked away from the gate. A hundred yards or so down the road, a clearing had been cut in the woods adjacent to the tire pile and the road, and a small bulldozer sat in the middle of it. On one side of the clearing stood a slight mound of newly spread dirt, and in the far corner I saw a contraption that resembled a mobile luggage conveyor belt. A ramp with a rubber belt was angled from the ground up, and at the top there was a bin of some kind.

"Any idea what that thing is?" I asked.

"Slices tires into small pieces," Aaron said. "Couple times I've been here, guys have been unloading trucks. It's excellent. They throw the tires on the bottom of the ramp, the tires go up, get sliced, and the rubber gets pumped out onto the ground."

We heard a truck engine then, which quickly

grew louder. I was surprised—I wouldn't have expected anybody at the pile late on Saturday afternoon. Aaron and I glanced at each other and headed back to the woods.

"Let's hit the road," I said.

"Hold on," he replied. "We stay low, they'll never see us."

As the truck approached, we scuttled, hunched over, deeper into the ferns and bushes just off the dirt road. We had a good view of the road on the western side of the pile.

A large, battered green Ford pickup truck jounced into view, kicking up a plume of dust. It moved through the gate slowly, stopping briefly. Then it moved over to the area near the tire chipper. Two men got out. Both wore blue jeans, work shirts, and baseball hats, one plain black and the other a blue Red Sox hat.

The men talked and pointed to various areas as they walked around, examining spots on the periphery of the pile. After a while, they left. I'd had my fill, so Aaron and I left as well.

Back on the bike, my body rebelled. I had not come down to Wettamesett for a lengthy bike tour of environmental atrocities. I'd come for a summer weekend of fun and frolic with Ann and Frank. Usually the biggest excitement of the weekend was choosing between domestic or imported beer and fighting over who had first dibs on the hammock.

Now, the only question was whether I'd have to be discarded along with the blown tires. I'd ridden a bike sporadically for years, but not enough to get my legs and butt in shape. Most weeks, I ran five miles three or four times and dragged myself to the high school gym to hit the weights. I had figured all of that work would suffice for me to keep up with Aaron on the road.

Bad thinking. His wiry, lean legs spun effortlessly. He circled me on his bike like a buzzard circling road kill while I grimaced and squirmed, trying to get back on the bike comfortably.

"Want a pillow for that seat?" he asked. "Or maybe we should mount a lounge chair on the bike?"

I just grunted and started riding. My thigh muscles ached, my rear end burned with every movement, and we still had the entire return ride ahead. I told Aaron to ride straight back to the cottage since we were expected for a barbecue.

"We talked about taking the long way home around the lake," he said.

"Yeah, we did. We're not talking about it now. I beat you once this morning. No need for me to do it again."

"That so? Good luck finding your way back, pal." He took off, his rear tire spitting out dirt and pebbles as he accelerated. I pedaled gingerly at first, wondering what happened to old-fashioned respect for the elderly.

By the time I arrived at the cottage, I had pains in places I'd never heard from before. Happily, nobody I loved or lusted after awaited me. Nothing from my knees to my waist would work for a week. As I staggered off the bike, nasty little men in my knees pulled, twisted, and jumped on my ligaments. Others, with daggers, viciously assaulted the muscles in my hamstrings and my rear. I limped into the kitchen.

"Nice ride?" Ann inquired with exaggerated sweetness. She reached up and mussed Aaron's hair and he just smiled back. "You blow him away?" she asked him.

"Not close," I mumbled after a long pull on a fancy German beer.

Aaron smiled some more and addressed Ann. "He did pretty well, better than Uncle Frank, but I don't think he'll be dancing much tonight."

Frank spoke up. "Walking a bit funny there, friend, sort of like a bronco-busting cowboy."

"You might have mentioned that Aaron's training for the Tour de France."

"We knew you'd been bulking up on Twinkies and beer," Ann said. "We thought you wanted to put that fine, manly physique of yours to work. And Aaron—well, he's just a slip of a boy, can't be more than six-two and 170 pounds of rippling muscle." She shot a teasing glance at Aaron and he blushed.

I grunted, feigning hurt, knowing that once again Ann's warmth and humor would salve my wounded pride far more quickly than the beer would cure the rest of me. Frank just grinned in empathy. Too often Ann had skewered him in the midst of some form of pomposity.

"You win," I said. "I hope you enjoyed yourselves."

"We did." She smiled demurely. "Now don't be a snot. We'd be happier if you found a better way to spend your Saturdays than chasing after a boy on his bike. Bike rides are nice, but how about one with a woman? If you're going to follow somebody's rear end around all day, it should be one you like to look at."

"Or bite," Aaron offered.

Ann's eyes opened wide, followed by her mouth. "Aaron, I don't—"

"Don't think we could have said it better," Frank said, flashing a look at Ann that told her not to reprimand Aaron when he was feeling good. Ann caught the look and herself, took a deep breath, and just shook her head. She'd forgotten just how educated college kids were these days.

For a moment I thought Aaron might have gotten me off the hook, deflected her attention to him. No such luck.

Ann turned back to me. "Next time you come down, bring somebody," she said. "For the last few years there's been nobody. We love to have you, the kids have a great time with you, but it's time for you to get on with your life." She held up her hands before I could reply, adding, "I know, you've told us before. You like your freedom, your grungy weight room and your beer. But wouldn't you enjoy a good woman more?"

"You know no woman wants me. Damn, I can't

even keep up with a college kid on a bike."

"You don't give yourself enough credit—plenty of interests, good job," Ann said.

"Since when does any lawyer have a good job?" Frank interjected. "Unless it's suing other lawyers for malpractice, I guess."

Ann gave him a nasty look and continued, appraising me. "Tall, honest face, strong chin, nice brown eyes . . ."

"Sort of a B movie Tom Selleck," Frank volunteered, "and the hair's just right for a thirty-eight-year-old attorney. The dueling scar's a nice touch, too." The hair reached my collar. The scar on my temple resulted from an attempt, years ago, to teach my younger sister to fish. The only thing she caught was my head.

I waved it off. "Hell," I said, "all the good women I know married Frank." Ann blushed, Frank let out a loud yell of agreement and put a bear hug around Aaron, and we all went to the dining room.

The last few weeks of August passed, and I awoke one morning to a Monday early in September. It dawned with all the miseries of August and none of its rewards. Kids were back in school and urban prisoners had returned from their summer furloughs.

I live in a two-family house on a short, quiet, residential street in Brookline, just outside of Boston, near where the Boston Marathon goes by. I own the house and live on the top floor, renting out the bottom-floor unit. My apartment has two bedrooms, a den, a living room with a bay window and dining room, an old-style kitchen, and hardwood floors. I've never gotten around to putting anything on the walls, and the windows have no drapes, although I do have shades in the bathroom windows. I keep the house, painted a wholly indistinct off-white, in reasonable repair, but the small lawn is no more decorated than the walls inside. The house looks like any other on the street except that, in addition to the front steps, a ramp runs from the front porch to the driveway.

The Steiners live on the first floor. They moved in six years ago. The family includes two children: Jessica, twelve, and Mike, now ten, for whom we built the ramp. Mike's blond, short and stocky, with an engaging grin and an occasional temper, and he has cerebral palsy. He's bright, speaks fairly clearly, and uses a wheelchair to get around. He's also one of the most avid and passionate sports fans in Boston.

Mike and I became fast friends as soon as the Steiners moved in. In the winters, I take him to college hockey and basketball games, with occasional forays to the Bruins and Celtics. In the summers, we catch Little League games and make pilgrimages to the hallowed ground of Fenway Park.

I also had a special carriage built for him so that I can run with him along the paths on the banks of the Charles River. As we run he provides a description of the people and places we pass. He also plays tricks on me, with the help of his father. Sometimes I leave my running shoes on the front porch. Mike hides them, then rings my doorbell and asks me to go for a run. Or I'll put on a running shoe, only to find it full of pebbles and a yellow sticky note on the inside that says "Gotcha." Once, I opened my mailbox and found a toad in it, which also had a yellow sticky note on its back saying "Gotcha."

That morning there were no tricks, so I merely waved to Mike as he went off to school, and then I headed toward work. A dank, gritty bad humor had settled over the city. Boston was vacuum-sealed in heat and humidity. I walked from my house in Brookline to catch the streetcar near Coolidge Corner. By the time I reached the stop, my shirt had soaked through.

I climbed aboard a streetcar in which the air-conditioning had failed and a wave of human odors washed over me. I was also facing my seventh, or perhaps eighth, successive temporary secretary, a prospect no more pleasant than traveling on the streetcar and one that gave me pause. Between the long, sticky ride on the streetcar and the upcoming temp at the office, I spent most of the ride into town wondering just how much more downwardly mobile I could be.

My legal career had started when a friend in the Attorney General's office let me come in at the bottom of the ladder and work my way up a few rungs.

I had some fun, but after three years I became restless.

Then I went up against a senior partner and his team of associates from a large, prestigious firm. We fought over an injunction sought by my client, the Department of Environmental Protection. I trounced them, and the senior partner was impressed. A few months later I was an associate in his firm, with a large salary and a window overlooking Boston Harbor.

During my second year at the firm, a partner I was working with blew a statute of limitations. I'd sent the partner two memos telling him the deadline for filing the complaint on behalf of a computer client. The partner screwed up and filed the complaint a day late because he was on a Caribbean weekend with a woman other than his wife and stayed on two extra days.

Once the partner realized the case was lost because he filed it late, he called the client in and worked out an accommodation. Not surprisingly, the partner fingered me as the culprit.

The senior partner who'd recruited me heard about it. Though loyal to the firm, he was above all an ethical, honest lawyer, and when I went to him, he listened to my side of it. With the documents I'd kept, and a paralegal on the case confirming my story, I was off the hook.

But by then it was too late. Everybody in the firm knew what had happened. Some people thought I was right, but others would never forgive me for turning on a partner. And I would not have forgiven myself if I'd stayed. I left immediately, with a very generous severance package and an apology from the senior partner.

After leaving the big firm, I went to a small firm, which lasted a couple of years. I affiliated with other lawyers twice more. Once, I shared space with a group of lawyers, but that ended when I got into a romantic entanglement with one of them and it blew up. Finally, after having another disagreement with still another lawyer with whom I'd become affiliated, I went to work for the only boss I thought I could stand: myself.

I'd practiced solo for a while with a paralegal and a secretary working for me, but they had both left in the last four months. Indecision about how I wanted to practice, and my reluctance to rebuild yet again, kept me from replacing them.

The train ride ended at the Park Street Station, and I walked up Beacon Street to my office, damning summer in the city, damning secretaries, and damning the Red Sox for once again failing to lift the city from its torpor. For fans of the fourth place Red Sox, only the young football season and the return of the Patriots brought hope.

As I walked in the office door at around eight-thirty, the phone rang. I sat down at the secretarial work station in the front of the office and picked up the phone.

"Good morning, law offices of Dan Kardon," I said.

"Oh, Dan, I . . ." A woman's words trailed off into gasps and sobs.

"Who is this? Can I help you?"

"It's Ann," she gasped, and paused for a moment.

"Ann! What's wrong? Are you hurt?"

"No, it's Aaron. He's dead." She started crying again. "He was shot in Wettamesett. He'd been biking. Somebody found his body on the side of Route 107 this morning. The police just called—" I heard only the sound of my own deep, irregular breathing. I could feel pressure building in my chest and behind my eyes, but I tried to focus on Ann.

"Where are you?" I asked. "Is Frank there?"

"I'm at home. The kids are at school. Frank's performing a short surgery. He doesn't know. I'm going to the hospital to pick him up and we'll have to go down to Wettamesett."

"Jesus, this is awful. I can't believe it. What can I do to help?"

"I want you to talk to the police. They want to search the cottage, they want to talk to Frank and me—"

"Ann, slow down, of course I'll help you, but you don't need me to deal with the police. The police aren't charging you with anything, are they? Tell me what the police said."

"It was such a shock. I don't even remember the name of the officer who called. He only told me a little. Aaron was found shot next to his bike, near the road. They found drugs—they think crack cocaine—on him or on the bike. When I asked what happened, he said it might be a drive-by shooting or some kind of botched drug deal."

"That's ridiculous, it doesn't sound like Aaron."

"I know, that's why I want your help, at least until we understand what's happening. The police might talk to you about things, things they won't talk to us about. I just know Aaron wasn't involved in drugs. It makes no sense. And now the police want to search our house and talk to us. It's excruciating to know that Aaron's dead and that the police are saying these horrible things about him."

"Look, I'll come down there right now and see if I can talk with the police. I'll either call you at the cottage or meet you. You go ahead with Frank, but don't rush. The search will take some time, and you may not want to be there until you actually meet with the investigators."

"Thanks." She paused and sniffled. "Oh, this is just a nightmare. Aaron dead! The last one of my cousin's family. And to have him killed in Wettamesett, such a peaceful, beautiful place."

"I'm sorry. I'll see you soon."

I hung up then, and leaned back in my chair with a throat that could not swallow and eyes that could not see.

CHAPTER ———

TWO

I righted the chair and stared at piles of documents on the desk. The image of a dead teenager, sprawled by the side of a road with a bike's front wheel spinning slowly, would not go away. I was startled when the door to my office opened. A woman with blond hair and a slender figure walked in, dressed in a conservative gray suit and white blouse, and carrying a leather bag. In stark contrast to my drenched, wilted shirt and suit coat, her clothes appeared fresh and clean, giving no hint that the heat had affected her.

"Hi, I'm Jenny Crane," she said, as if I should be expecting her, and gave me an engaging smile. Under other circumstances I might have liked to meet her, but at that moment I didn't have a clue who she was and didn't much care. My face must have shown it.

"I'm the temporary secretary you arranged for today. You may remember that Jack Green recommended me," she continued.

"Oh, damn! Sorry, you're right, I'd forgotten you were coming." I stood up and walked over to a window, not trusting myself to face anyone close up. "Look, I just received an emergency phone call and I need to leave the office immediately." I pressed my hands over my eyes and took a deep breath before I continued. "I can't use you today, I'm just going to leave a phone service on, but I'll pay you for the day. I'd like you here tomorrow, if that's okay. This may not make sense to you, but there's no way around it."

"Are you all right?" she asked.

"Yes," I said, and walked back to the desk.

"I'm sorry about whatever's happened. If I'm not working, I don't want to get paid, but thanks for the offer. And I'll be here tomorrow."

"Thanks," I said, and she walked out the door.

I didn't bother to check for phone messages. I simply turned out the one light I'd turned on and headed back from where I came, into the heat and back on the subway to pick up my car to head south to Wettamesett.

The sky was low and overcast, with rain moving in, as I moved through the traffic on the Southeast Expressway. I looked out over Boston Harbor. Despite the coming bad weather, a number of small sailboats were on the water, out beyond the immense, brightly streaked gas tanks by the side of the road. A couple of tugs guided a freighter in toward a pier. In the distance, large dredges were digging near the airport.

The gray highway miles swept past. Alone in my Chevy Blazer, I cranked up the volume on a Buddy Guy tape to listen to somebody else's blues. I thought about Aaron and my last visit with him in August.

Because of other family obligations, the weekend in August was the last time the whole family had been together before school started. After Aaron and I returned, we all made a serious assault on homemade clam chowder, barbecued chicken, cole slaw, and apple pie, which Ann and Frank had assembled. With Aaron and the kids around, the conversation had careened wildly from clam-digging to the best way to build a sand castle to which courses Aaron intended to take in the fall.

Aaron laughed and kidded the others, though he mentioned a couple of times that I had deserted him when he'd been driven off the road. Thinking back to that last bike ride, I regretted passing him then. I wished I'd remembered how easily college students feel insecure and alone at the best of times.

But no matter how I rehashed our ride, it of course didn't bring Aaron back. And I kept returning to the shock and fear he must have felt, for I knew it had never occurred to him that he would die on a bicycle, doing something he loved.

Thoughts of Aaron soon dissolved into images of my sister Jacqueline, images I kept at bay most of the time. Six years younger than me, with blue eyes, black hair, a narrow face, and a slender frame, she had a solitary nature like Aaron. But where Aaron found bicycling, Jacqueline never found any activity that made her happy for long, not that she didn't try. Clothes, music, art, dance, drama, animal rights, political protests, she tried them all, but nothing grabbed her for long. Gradually, a lively and strong young girl lost her voice and her confidence that anything would make her smile again. After she found drugs, things went downhill quickly.

The memories became too vivid to concentrate on the road. I pulled into a Burger King to wipe my eyes and to bury the pain with a sausage, egg, and cheese biscuit, home fries and a large black coffee.

As I drove up to the cottage, a light mist was falling. There were a number of marked and unmarked police cars around. One uniformed officer stood outside the house, keeping curious onlookers from entering, including me.

I told him I represented the family, but it didn't help. All he would tell me was that there were local police, investigators from the District Attorney's office, and the State Police searching the house. Through the windows, I could see camera flashes going off and people talking with one another. I stood in the rain watching. From what I could tell, they carried out only a few small items in plastic evidence bags. After more than an hour, they left. They told me that they might have to come back, but said the family could use the house.

I walked in. The house was in good order, with few obvious signs of a search. Aaron's roommates hadn't moved in yet so the house didn't show the ravages of having college kids as residents.

I walked back to the kitchen and called the Wettamesett police. A sergeant told me they wanted Ann and Frank there as soon as possible. I told him they were on the way and would check in as soon as they arrived.

By the time the call ended, Frank's car had pulled into the driveway. Ann and Frank walked in. She had dark pits around her red eyes, and Frank, normally calm and confident, appeared gaunt.

Ann gave me a long, hard hug. Frank and I shook hands. He spoke first.

"Thanks for coming. This is just a nightmare. All of a sudden, Aaron's dead, we have no clue why, and the police have searched the house for evidence of drugs." Frank looked out the window. "I just can't believe he won't bike up the driveway and tell us this was all a horrible mistake."

"I'm sorry," I said, again. "I don't need to tell you guys I have a pretty good idea what you're feeling. I'll help if I can."

Ann spoke, her voice soft, her eyes fixed on the floor. "I'm not sure we know what will help, this is so hard. After all the pain he'd endured, Aaron was doing so well. He was doing so well in college. He had a girlfriend, and was having a wonderful time on his bike."

Frank picked up the theme as Ann pressed her face into a tissue. "We've been trying to keep track of him, even though he was on his own more. Something like this happens, you relive every damn thing you should have done and didn't. And now, this drug accusation . . . it makes no sense. . . ." His voice petered out.

I took a soda from the refrigerator and sat down.

"Frank," I said, "the police are just doing their jobs. They have to be thorough. It doesn't seem that they took much with them from here, and they let us in, so I assume they didn't find much that was useful. They'll want to talk to you about Aaron's friends, his activities, that sort of stuff. Usually, in a case like this, the State Police and the D.A.'s office work with the local police. They do good work, they'll figure out what happened."

Frank looked at Ann. She gazed out the window for a moment and finally turned back and looked at me. She spoke quietly. "I hope so," she said.

Frank leaned over and hugged her, and she clung to him, crying softly. He stroked her hair, rocking her gently. Frank's cheeks glistened as well.

After a couple of minutes, Ann came up for air and dried her eyes with a paper napkin. "Sorry I'm such a mess," she said.

"Nothing to apologize for," I replied. "I'll go over, talk to the police and get what information I can. Then I'll come back and get you."

The rain was coming down harder now, and the clouds were low and dark. As I left I thought about putting the hood of my jacket up, but after the misery of the heat, the rain felt cool and clean. I had little confidence the feeling would last.

I drove down the lightly trafficked roads to Route 107, a much shorter trip than the one I took on my bike. After a few miles, I came upon the murder scene. Stakes stood in the ground on the shoulder of the road and yellow police tape surrounded a square about fifty feet long. It surrounded a grassy area between the road and the woods, sloping down toward the forest. Other than the tape, nothing indicated that Aaron had died there. No skid marks were visible, no footprints, no debris. I walked around and through the area for a few minutes, and satisfied myself that there was nothing out of the ordinary. Then I got back in the car and headed for the police station near the center of Wettamesett.

CHAPTER ——

THREE

T he police station was a small, two-story brick building next to the town hall. It needed some paint on the trim and a couple of new gutters. Off to the side, a bike stood locked to a bike rack under the cover of a small open shed. A greenish racing bike: Aaron's.

I walked in, shook off the rain, and introduced myself to a cop sitting at a desk behind a counter at the front of the office. I told him I wanted to talk to somebody about Aaron's murder. He told me the chief was on the telephone.

I was left to pace, inspect the bulletin board, and read a two-day-old *Boston Globe* sports section. I checked out police department memos and read about the schedule of paid holidays, an upcoming touch football game against the fire department, faxed flyers concerning missing children and various ne'er-do-wells whose pictures adorned the walls.

Chief Richards came out about five minutes later. He stood five-ten, trim, with light brown hair and a great tan, white teeth, cleft chin, clear blue eyes, and a firm handshake. More than you expected from a small-town police chief.

"Hello. I'm Chief Bruce Richards. I understand you're here about the murder of the Winters boy."

"Dan Kardon. I'm an attorney representing the family. I just wanted to talk to you before they come in."

"It's not my practice to talk to attorneys before I talk to the families of victims, unless they're suspects. Any reason you didn't just bring them?" Richards asked.

"Look, they're hurting badly, the drugs you found shocked them, their house has just been searched, and I just wanted to get some information before they walk in."

"Okay, didn't mean to jump on you. This is a tough day for all of us. We need to talk to them as soon as possible. The more information we have, the faster we can move."

"I'll go back and get them as soon as I leave here. Is there anything you can tell me about the investigation?"

Richards looked at me for a moment. "Anybody I can call to check on you?"

"Call Lieutenant Colonel Randall Blocker with the State Police. He heads up their investigation unit. You probably know him, come to think of it."

Richards looked at me coolly, not showing a thing. "Just like to know who I'm dealing with. Give me a few minutes." He stood up and walked into his office.

Richards came back in about ten minutes, no more relaxed. He offered me a soft drink and brought me back to his office.

An old wooden desk, two battered gray-metal file cabinets, and piles of paper on each side of the desk gave the office a purposeful, utilitarian air. Whatever else was true about Richards, you could not accuse him of wasting taxpayer money on elaborate office decorations.

Two five-by-seven black and white photos sat on a filing cabinet. One showed a middle-aged couple standing stiffly with tentative smiles in front of a small house behind two kids, a girl and a taller boy. In the other, a crew-cut teenager in a football uniform caught a football in the end zone. Richards, presumably, in his athletic hero days.

As I sat down in an ancient wooden chair in front of Richards's desk, I pointed to the pictures. "You and your parents?"

He looked over at them and smiled. "Yeah. Sometimes when things aren't going well, those pictures help me remember how I grew up and how I'd like it to be for kids here now." He sounded smooth and sincere, laying it on a bit thick perhaps, but still a man concerned about his town.

"Blocker tells me you're smart, hard-headed, and don't care much what other people think. And that you're a much better lawyer than a basketball player."

I smiled. "He's right. But I'm still a better ball

player than he is." Randy and I had played high school basketball together. We were like mismatched six-foot-three-inch bookends on the team. He was black and could shoot. I was white and could rebound. He had become one of only a few lieutenant colonels in the State Police, in charge of the criminal investigation unit.

I wanted to take advantage of whatever goodwill I had from Richards's conversation. "I'm not here to interfere, just to help the family figure out what's going on."

Richards leaned back in his chair, seemingly considering what to tell me. After a moment his chair came down and he picked up an envelope and fiddled with it. "I'm pretty new to this job," he said. "This is the first homicide I've had here, maybe the first the town has ever had. I'm going to make damn sure we handle it right. Nobody wants this thing screwed up, not the D.A., not the state troopers, and most of all, not me. I know your clients are concerned and upset, but they're not suspects. No need for you to be involved."

I shrugged. "This has knocked the hell out of them. They don't believe Aaron was involved in drugs. They want his name cleared and they want to know why he died."

Richards sighed. "I'll tell you a little, in hopes the family can begin to come to terms with this thing. We had three shootings last night."

"Three? That's awful," I said. "Anybody else hurt?"

"Nope. Probably somebody went on a drive-by shooting spree. The other two sets of shots were fired at a house and a car. Maybe some punks had a few beers, got their courage, and took a shot at the kid as a lark, to scare him. But we also found crack cocaine in a small bag on the kid's bike.

"Didn't find much at the scene. Body lay face-down in the grass just about midway between the road and the woods. Shot in the chest. Autopsy hasn't been completed. We'll know more about the weapon at that point."

"What about the bike?" I asked.

"Found it on the ground, couple of feet from the body. Nothing unusual about it."

"Any damage to it?"

Richards gave me a questioning look. "Don't know. Here, these are some instant photos we took this morning. We'll have more later."

The bike was lying on its left side. Aaron lay adjacent, only half of his pale and empty face visible in the photos. His hair was wet and matted, no hel-met on his head. He wore a yellow bicycling jacket and black cycling shorts. Nothing distinctive about the outfit, other than the hole and the blood in the center of his chest. My hand was trembling when I returned the photo to Richards, and I had to take a long drink of the soda before I could talk. Richards just waited, not saying anything.

"These show how you found him?" I finally asked.

"Yup."

"No helmet?"

"Wasn't wearing one," he said.

"Not much else here. What about the other shootings last night?"

"One truck, parked by the side of a road in a fairly isolated area about three miles away, was shot twice sometime after ten P.M. Then, around midnight, shots were fired into a small bank about four miles from here. Like I said, no harm to anybody else. We've retrieved a couple bullets, all nine millimeters, not inconsistent with what we could tell from the kid's wound. Didn't find any cartridges, and right now we have no suspects.

"From what we've got, the kid was the victim of stupid punks or he got into a drug deal over his head. As we make progress, we'll let the family know. But this kind of case, we need to talk to the parents right away. We want to know who the kid hung around with, what he spent money on, was he blowing his nose a lot, stuff like that."

Richards didn't know that Ann and Frank were not Aaron's parents, but I let it go. Everything he said made sense, but still it grated to hear him refer to Aaron as the "kid" over and over again. And it seemed Richards had already pigeon-holed the case, classified it either as a random, drive-by shooting of an unlucky teenager or as a drug killing. He was probably right, but I knew Ann and Frank would want more.

"You have any idea what he was doing, riding his bike late at night on that stretch of road?" he asked. "Damn stupid thing to be doing, without a light and a helmet."

"No idea, and it doesn't make sense. Aaron was a good bike rider, safe, not stupid," I said. "He loved to ride. He often took long rides and came home at night."

"The light was in the bike bag with the cocaine," Richards said. "It still worked. He should have clipped it to the bike or his clothing." I didn't understand. The Aaron I knew took his riding seriously, including his safety precautions. But then, the Aaron I knew would not have carried crack. I wondered what I'd ever really known about Aaron.

"Something's out of kilter," I said.

Richards didn't argue, but he didn't look interested in my comment either. "Hey, you never get 'em tied up with pretty bows and ribbons, you always have loose ends. And like it or not, the drugs were there, so we have to follow up."

"Isn't it unusual that he was shot in the chest?" I asked.

"What do you mean?"

"Well, to shoot him in the chest, somebody had to drive past in the opposite direction while he biked. Not an easy shot. A shot in the back or the side I could understand."

"We discussed that. It's one reason we think it might be drug-related. Maybe he stopped to exchange the drugs and got shot close up. Which you don't want to hear." Richards paused and shifted in his chair. "He may have been dealing or buying, but whatever, if it wasn't a drive-by, it was a drug deal gone wrong."

I tried to keep my voice under control. "The drug connection is particularly crazy. Have you ever had him under suspicion for drug use? I can't see Aaron as a crackhead."

"You wouldn't be the first adult fooled by a teenager," he said. "Nobody here had any suspicions about him. But we're like any other town. We have dealers and users, and we do what we can to stop them."

"Aaron's dead now. Why say anything?" I asked. "Particularly if the autopsy doesn't show any cocaine? Why destroy how people think of him, when he's not around to defend himself?" Even as I spoke, I knew it sounded lame, but I couldn't quell the impulse to defend Aaron, even in death.

"I know you don't want your friends hurt," he said, "but this is a criminal investigation. Can't worry about people's feelings. Besides, this is a small town. No matter what I tell my people, information will leak out in a few days. Also, if we get the word out quickly, maybe somebody involved in the deal who didn't want it to go this far will give us information. I'm sorry, but you know I have no choice. When we have something new, I'll let you know. In the meantime, I'd like to talk to the family."

He stood up suddenly and looked out his door. My dismissal was not hard to miss. I gave him my card and stood up. "You mind if I look at the bike on the way out?"

"No, go ahead. We'll keep it for a while, and then give it back to his family."

On the way to my car I stopped at the bike. It looked too slender, stiff, and sleek for me. But it had suited Aaron perfectly, and he had ridden it well.

Since it was a racing bike, unlike its heftier mountain bike cousins, the components were lightweight and not built for banging around. The bike appeared fine except for some nicks in the paint on the right front fork and damage to the rear derailleur. The chain was supposed to run easily through the metal derailleur, which was designed to make shifting gears easier. It hung down near the rear axle on the right side and was visibly bent. I lifted the bike and rotated the pedals. The chain and derailleur gave a grinding sound and the chain wouldn't move smoothly. The bike could not have been ridden more than a few feet with the damaged derailleur.

Under the saddle, on the back, Aaron had suspended a small black nylon bag. The cocaine discovered by the police must have been in that bag. I opened it up and found what I expected. No wallet, but some change, and tools. I also found a small but powerful blinking light powered by batteries and built to attach to the back of his shorts or bike. It would have made him highly visible at night. I turned it on and the amber light beat out a steady rhythm.

I put the light back, not wanting to be accused of tampering with evidence. Which I had. I was only surprised that the contents of the bag hadn't been set aside. A small mistake, signifying nothing. Richards knew about the light and had a firm grasp on how the investigation would be conducted. As well as a strong notion that Aaron had been buying—or selling—drugs when he died.

CHAPTER ──────────
FOUR

I brought Ann and Frank back for an interview with the police. Richards sat in, but the State Police and D.A.'s investigator did most of the questioning in a straightforward and professional manner. A lot of questions about Aaron, his habits, his friends, places he hung out and spent money. More stressful questions for Ann and Frank about Aaron's past difficulties and any recent problems he'd had. I didn't say much, and the interview ended when it became clear that Ann and Frank had nothing further to assist the investigation.

During the ride back to the cottage, the rain lifted as high pressure moved in from the west. The front passed on and moved the storm offshore. City dwellers and suburbanites would celebrate, while fishermen out on the Atlantic would suffer for a while longer. The clearing front, though, did not clear my mind. For me, questions still loomed as large as the clouds had.

Back at the house, Ann tried to restore a touch of normalcy by turning on the radio. Wynton Marsalis played a long, quiet piece. Frank got on the phone and immediately discovered an emergency at the hospital. He gave Ann a hug, asked me if I'd get her back to their home in Cambridge, and took off when I said yes.

Ann and I sat at the old wooden kitchen table, fiddling with mugs of coffee.

"How could it possibly be a random shooting?" she asked.

"There've been similar situations in the last few years. Couple of guys in a town near here took a shot at a high school bus carrying a girls' basketball team. One girl was killed. In Rhode Island there was a spate of shootings. Bullets fired through living room windows at night. Nobody was hurt."

"Did they catch the shooters?" Ann asked.

"The cops found the guys who shot the girl in the bus. In Rhode Island they discovered the snipers were three kids who had gotten hold of a World War Two rifle from one of their fathers."

Ann shook her head. "I don't understand. You've done some criminal work, maybe this makes sense. Why do people do this, knowing they might kill someone like Aaron? And how do you find these people, if all they leave behind is a bullet?"

"Usually the people who do these kinds of shootings are plastered or high," I said. "Maybe they're out with buddies thinking they're having fun. They're not pros. They do something like this, then get scared or excited. They've got to tell somebody. They brag, tell a girlfriend. Or get drunk and tell a friend, who's also drunk, and he tells somebody else. Finally, somebody with brains or a conscience finds out and tells the police."

Ann got up and put a sweater on. "And what about the drugs? How will we ever understand that? What will the police do?"

"They'll check out every drug dealer in the area, all the kids they know who use drugs, push everyone to figure out if there's a link. They'll talk to Aaron's friends, see if he spent money in any funny ways. They'll test the stuff, see if it has any characteristics like other drugs they're finding."

Ann started to cry, softly, and I put my arm around her shoulders.

"Why don't you lie down for a bit, before we go back to Boston, and I'll just walk around?" I suggested. She didn't say anything, but she let me lead her to a couch, where she lay down and I put a blanket over her.

I sighed at the threshold of Aaron's bedroom, then waded in through layers of discarded clothing, athletic shoes, and comic books. Dozens of posters festooned the walls, each wall with a different theme. Aerosmith and other rock groups peered at me from one wall. Larry Bird, Michael Jordan, Greg Lemond, and other athletes adorned the wall directly over the head of the bed. A couple of posters of females in athletic poses, albeit in skimpy uniforms, were also up. Pinned to a corkboard near the door was a series of undistinguished photos of windsurfers sailing near a lighthouse.

A small stereo with a pile of tapes sat on the top of an old, marred and nicked clothing chest. Aaron had placed a small, old Zenith color television on a clothing bureau. The small nightstand next to his bed had tissues on top along with two science fiction books and three biking magazines. There was a box for a dozen condoms in the drawer. Only seven were in the box. I wondered if Ann knew about them.

The desk had a few papers on it and a small and mostly empty address book. A picture frame on the desk held a five-by-seven snapshot of an attractive teenage girl, the only female with all of her clothes on pictured in the room.

I opened a closet door and found what looked like a cemetery for used athletic gear. Besides a mountain of dirty socks, it held a baseball glove, a basketball, swim fins, a mask and snorkel, a football, and all sorts of other sports paraphernalia. Aaron had a floor pump for a bicycle in there and an old-style red bicycle helmet. The only thing I didn't see was the new iridescent-blue racing helmet he'd worn when we rode together. I rooted through the dirty socks on the floor but didn't find the missing helmet.

I walked down the stairs and saw that Ann was still asleep. I went out onto the porch and then down to the beach. The wind now came out of the southwest, blowing steadily and starting to kick up whitecaps on the bay. The rain clouds had moved on and the sky showed large holes of blue. Two windsurfers shot back and forth along the shore, while a couple on a large sailboat raised the mainsail and left the mooring.

I changed into a pair of Frank's bathing suits and went for a long, brisk swim. Focused on stroking through the small waves, I forgot, for a time, why I'd come down to the cottage.

Ann awoke around six-thirty P.M. The air had cooled with the passage of the sun. We heard the ocean, but could only see a dark pool below a horizon in the evening light.

We went outside and sat on a pine double rocker on the porch. I asked Ann about Aaron's recent behavior.

She said she hadn't seen anything peculiar. She talked a little about Sarah Burnham, whose picture, Ann confirmed, was on Aaron's desk. Sarah was also starting her sophomore year at Southeastern Coastal. Ann said that earlier in the summer, Sarah had been around more. She had a car and came to visit Aaron—particularly, Ann suspected, when she and Frank were away. The mystery of the condoms stood revealed.

"Ann," I said, "I know what you told the police, but did you have any idea that Aaron might use drugs, maybe with his roommates? And did you notice any changes in his life recently?"

"No, no, not a clue about drugs, and we saw nothing different," she said. "He and I were pretty close. He'd get down sometimes, would go off by himself, but he had nothing to do with kids in school who drank a lot or used drugs. And with the biking, he had to stay in shape. Sure, he could have fooled us, but I won't believe it unless I see something more."

"How about the people he biked with, any problems there?"

"Not that I know of. I don't really know them, and it's an older crowd, most of them out of college, but they seemed to like Aaron and help him with his biking."

"Did he ever ride to places he shouldn't have? Any particular places you told him not to go to?" I asked.

"No. We told him not to trespass on private property, but there's nowhere around here we thought was dangerous."

"Do you know anything about the tire pile near the Houghton place?"

"What a peculiar question," she said. "Aaron told us he biked there occasionally with others in the biking club. Why do you ask?"

"Mostly just curious, trying to make connections. Aaron took me there when we went biking. Bit of a spooky place, and it occurred to me it's only a few miles from where he was found. You know anything about the Houghton family?"

"I've only heard about Jean Houghton. She's

got a good reputation, sort of a local legend. And Aaron never talked about any difficulties at the tire pile."

The questions just seemed to stop coming. I could feel Ann become still and sad. We both looked up as a large cloud drifted by, uncovering an almost-full moon beginning its ascent. Ann took my hand and put her head on my shoulder.

"This killing is so perverse," she said, in a voice I had to strain to hear. "And my cousin, it's as if there was a curse on her family. Aaron was so young, so innocent. It's hard to have faith. I know it's stupid and naive, but I've never felt so vulnerable, scared, weak. Somebody's out there with a gun, and any of us could be his target. Maybe Frank driving home one night, or our kids picking blueberries in the bushes by the road."

Then she searched my face. "Oh, Dan, I can't believe I'm saying these things. Your sister, then Elaine. You must think I'm cruel and spoiled."

"People deal with this stuff differently," I said. "It was horrible to bury my sister, and just as bad, maybe worse, to bury Elaine. Still tears me up when I think about it." I stopped for a moment, feeling a familiar ache in my gut and a tightness in my throat that threatened to choke off any words. "Doesn't matter who you are, this stuff knocks the crap out of you. There'll be holes you can't fill, days that don't feel right. I still have feelings, memories triggered by scenes in the corner of my eye or smells in the kitchen. Don't want it otherwise. Painful as it is, in time you'll integrate it, as you did with your cousin, and hold on to your kids a bit tighter."

Ann looked at me with an anguished face awash in watery moonlight. "Dan, why didn't you ever talk to me about this before? Why couldn't you tell me? I can't believe the hurt you must have felt, and yet you never said a word. Why?"

Any answer lay buried deeper inside me than I could retrieve. "Can't answer that. Hell, if I could, I'd be a shrink, not a lawyer."

We both sat quietly for a minute. The moon on the ocean was exquisite, sparkling silver lines dancing in the darkness.

"I remember in college you fell in love with Shakespeare. Junior year, you walked around quoting him all the time," Ann said.

"Yup. The one literary period in life. I still love the old guy. My favorite line is, 'Wise words from mouths of fools do oft' themselves belie.' Reminds me to shut up most of the time."

"How about, 'To thine own self be true.' Isn't that from one of his plays?"

"Yeah. Polonius lecturing Hamlet. Still good advice," I said.

"But how can you say that and not practice it?" she asked. "I mean, if you don't know what's inside you or let it out to the people closest to you, how can you be true to yourself?"

I let the question go unanswered. Wise words from mouths of fools and all that.

My silence didn't stop her. "Frank and I worry

about you. We love to see you, but recently we've felt you slipping away. No girlfriend for a long time, you don't say anything good about your work. You're the only one left in your office, all the other lawyers and secretaries have left. We've been afraid you might be picking up and moving again."

For a moment I didn't speak. "I've had some thoughts about that," I said. "I don't know what to tell you, except that my practice has the flavor of cardboard and the promise of a broken balloon right now. It's been a long time since a client has told me I've done something that really makes a difference."

"Everybody goes through tough stretches at work," she said.

"I know, but the difference is, I don't have much to keep me here. Been thinking about Bali or Thailand. Maybe Queenstown in New Zealand, where I could ski, hike, and do some rafting. Beautiful places where I could live a more relaxed life. Wouldn't be hard for me to manage a living. Lots of people I met in my travels had left most of their problems behind."

"I wonder," she said. "Did they leave their problems behind or just carry them to a place where they avoided them more easily? If you left here tomorrow, whatever hurts you carry inside now, you'd still have in Bali. Probably with sun and beer and surf, it's easier to ignore the problems, but maybe people just take their loneliness and alienation with them and find ways to fool themselves." She stopped and sighed, peering straight ahead at something I couldn't see. "I'm sorry. I think we're all wounded souls on earth, and the differences between us are in how we salve the wounds."

It became even harder to speak, and I had to take a deep breath. "I don't know what to say. Maybe you're right. I've moved around a bit. Sometimes moving is just easier than staying. But even so, I haven't done badly. Most people would say I'm pretty successful."

She looked away from me, out toward the sea. "Are you one of those people?" she asked.

Then she wrapped her arms around her shoulders and shivered. "Dan, I'm sorry. I don't mean to be so hard on you. I'm just frightened and hurt. You know we care about you. Aaron's death is so hard, there's so much we wanted for him. And now I feel awful because we haven't been there to help you, and we want you to be happy, too." She turned back to me. "There's no way you can understand. Maybe you think we're a bit silly, wanting all the answers. But you and me, we're not alike. We react differently to things.

"Like when my cousin died," she went on. "I lay awake at night, wondering why, what happened. Now this time, it's scarier, closer, and it'll eat at me even more. I'm afraid we'll never get closure. Somehow, though, you can have terrible things happen, but you don't dwell on them, you move on."

"I'm sorry, " I said. "I didn't mean—"

"Dan, this is important, please listen. I don't

care about abstract principles, ideas like revenge, justice. I only want to know if we did something terribly wrong with Aaron, if we misjudged him, failed him, or never knew him, or if this is just a terrible, random thing which happened to him. For me, finding out the whys and hows will help heal the awful pain and emptiness I feel."

It took a minute before I could respond, and then all I could say was, "You'll find them."

Ann smiled sadly and her eyes teared at the same time. She looked at me for a moment, then reached over and gave me a big hug. "Thanks for listening. Now, I'm going to pack up some of Aaron's things. Coming in?"

"No, I think I'll go for a bit of a walk. I want to check out the beach."

I wandered down to the beach. Gentle waves lapped on the shore and the dusky scent of the mudflats was in the air. It felt like days had passed since I'd first heard Ann's voice that morning, since I'd thought about Aaron and my sister on the drive down. And now, in the wake of my talk with Ann, I had visions of Elaine.

I met Elaine Freedman on the first day of our third year of law school. She wore a burgundy cable-knit sweater and black jeans and had brown hair, brown eyes, and a breathtaking smile. Four months later we were engaged, with the wedding planned for June, after graduation. In May a drunken carpenter drove the wrong way down a one-way street, hitting Elaine's car head-on. He walked away unscathed. Elaine died. All I had left were memories and a loss I still felt.

For a while after Elaine died, I took to driving past the house of the guy who killed her. Then I began following him at night if he went out.

One humid, sticky night, I followed him to a small pizza place then waited across the street for an hour. As I walked behind him back to his home, blood rushed to my head and time slowed down. I moved up in front of him as he came down an empty street with flickering yellow streetlights. He was taller and heavier than me, but my legs bounced and my fists clenched and unclenched, and I saw only his face.

"I'm Dan Kardon," I said, "Elaine Freedman's fiancé." And I hit him with my right hand, hard in the gut, then gave him an uppercut with my left which bounced off the side of his mouth. When I pulled back, my hands elevated and braced for his return blows, he remained doubled over, his hands over his eyes, sobbing. "God, I didn't mean to," he cried.

"Stand up," I said. "You deserve a hell of a lot more."

He straightened. "Go ahead," he said.

When I saw the tears and blood from his lip stream down his face as his chest heaved with sobs, my limbs went from electric to leaden and the energy I'd felt leaked away. After staring at him for a moment, I walked away, nauseous, sweating, and shaking. I never saw the carpenter again, never attended the trial.

Then I took off and traveled the world for about three years. I worked and lived in all sorts of settings, some of them fairly unpleasant. Finally, I returned to Boston and lawyering. But I hadn't managed to stay with one job, or one woman, for long. I'd told Ann the truth—I had been thinking about leaving Boston and the law. Ann, though, forced me to recognize that leaving might not change anything.

Staring out at the lights flickering over the water from the far shores of Buzzards Bay brought no resolution to my personal quandary. My nocturnal musings only led back to Aaron and how he died. Nothing made sense. No helmet, an unused light, a bike that wouldn't ride, and cocaine. I couldn't conceive of a set of events to explain those facts and be consistent with the Aaron we all knew. I looked upward, but the answers weren't in the stars. Shakespeare said as much in *Julius Caesar*. We'd all have to find them elsewhere.

CHAPTER ————

FIVE

On Tuesday morning the new temp, Jenny Crane, arrived shortly after I opened the office. I had more of a chance to think about her this time.

She was blond, five-seven, with a firm handshake. She wore a charcoal suit, white blouse, black heels, and kept her shoulder-length hair swept back from her face with some kind of pull or tie. She had high cheekbones, a slender nose, and hazel eyes set wide apart, which appraised me more closely than I did her.

"Do you want me to start today? Of course, if you want to give me a paid vacation, today I'll take it," she said, in a voice with an accent out of the hills of Appalachia.

"Yeah, come on in. I'm sorry about yesterday. Bad day all around. Glad to have you. I talked with Jack Green about you last week and he speaks highly of you, a rare tribute." All true. Jack, a friend, and a client as well, ran a chain of sporting goods stores. He was a great employer, but only for competent, hardworking employees.

"I like Jack. He runs a good business. The job wasn't interesting, though."

I gave her a quick tour of the office, imparted the little knowledge I had of the phone system, and proved to her I knew how to make coffee. Before the phones started going, I sat down with her to go over what I wanted done. In twenty minutes she'd figured my systems out.

"So how do you know how to handle all the paperwork?" I asked. "You have a background as a legal secretary?"

She looked at me with an opaque expression. "No, a lawyer."

I sat up in my so-called executive chair. "So why are you temping instead of practicing law?"

"If your question is, was I fired by a law firm for absconding with a client's money, or even worse, a partner's money, the answer is no. I did work for a firm. I didn't like it, they didn't like me, so here I am. I've been looking for a good situation where I might have the chance, over time, to do some lawyering. Most important, though, I want to work with an honest lawyer. In the meantime, I'm temping because I need to pay the rent—it's not too demanding, and lets me look for work as well. I'm not a whiz on the keyboard, but I've done a good job at the offices I've worked at this summer."

I looked at her for a moment without saying anything. She looked back, at ease. Most people, when they've opened up about themselves, need to fill any silence that follows, to explain, cajole, persuade, or plead. Jenny sat calmly, waiting for me to react.

"Sounds like you've been burned by a law firm. You wouldn't be the first. Where did you work last?" I asked.

She shook her head slightly. "I'd rather not say. I have good references from other places. And I'll start just doing the secretarial stuff. If I prove to you I'm good, I'm hoping you'll let me do some of the legal work. I don't think it matters where I was last."

"Maybe to some people it doesn't," I said. "To me, it does, if you're more than a secretary. If you have the background, know what you're doing, I have small stuff I can give you, starting today. This is my livelihood, though. My name's on the door and the bank account. You want me to rely on you for case work, there are things I want to know." I shrugged. "Sorry if it won't work out. I'll pay you for the day."

I started to turn away in my chair, figuring our chat was over.

"Wayne Sharman," she said.

"Is that a reference?" I asked.

"No, I worked in his office."

"For how long?"

"Just about nine months. Before that, I worked for a few years doing litigation in-house for a bank. Then I went to Sharman's. I was bored with the bank work."

I stood up, walked to the window and looked out. As I turned back, I gave her a half smile. "I know Sharman," I said, "but don't tell me, let me guess." She sat up sharply, a frown on her face. "He does mostly personal injury, workers' compensation cases. His phone has the buttons set so he can speed-dial a handful of doctors and chiropractors who churn out whatever reports he wants. He has a bunch of witnesses and even a few plaintiffs who he uses over and over again.

"You had a large number of cases with a quota you had to settle each month. Didn't matter whether you thought you could do better at trial, you were told to settle them as soon as possible. 'Move 'em or lose 'em,' Sharman would say. Squeeze the insurance company for what you could get quickly, then move on."

By now Jenny gripped both arms of her chair fiercely and looked at me with a mixture of fear and fascination. I continued: "After about six months, you were flattered to discover that Sharman spent more time talking with you about your cases. He asked you to assist him in preparing one of his cases, supposedly a big one that would require a lot of work. Told you how great your work was, how smart you were, how he enjoyed working with you. He said you had all it took to be his partner, in every sense. You'd have wonderful opportunities in the firm, so long as you played your cards right. Finally he looked deep in your eyes and kissed you."

"What the hell's going on here? How do you

know anything about it?" she asked, standing up.

"Let me see if I know the ending. Two weeks later, a month, whatever, you woke up one morning and realized he was nothing more than a drunken, pretentious slob. You threatened to tell people about his scams. He laughed, leered, and threatened to blackball you in this town. You walked out and haven't had much luck with law firms since. Did I get the story right?"

She looked at me, letting the silence turn frigid. "Most of it, except that when he went to kiss me the first time, I pushed him away and told him I quit," she said. "I told him his paychecks bought the use of my brain, nothing else. He said, and I'll never forget it, 'I'd love to make you a deal for the whole package.'"

"Ouch," I said.

"When I asked for my pay, he told me that if I ever told anybody, he'd ruin me as an attorney. I think he's done that anyway, doesn't want me to stay in Boston. I had no idea what a sleazeball he was when I took the job, I really thought I was getting a good job. Now I'm not sure I'll ever find a place at a firm in this town."

Her eyes had turned to lasers. "So how do you know all this stuff? I haven't told anybody, apart from my parents, and as far as I know, you don't talk to them. You one of his drinking buddies?" She picked up her bag, walked over and opened the door. "Actually, though, it doesn't matter, given the assumptions you've just made about me. Thank you, but I think I'll be leaving, Mr. Kardon."

I laughed and held up my hands. "Please, take it easy, come back. I'm sorry. Two other women have come to me with complaints about Wayne Sharman. Both were smart, good-looking women, like you. They knew each other, actually overlapped in his office about three years ago. When they each had figured out they were victims, they compared stories.

"They came to me after a number of other lawyers refused to take him on. We almost sued the son of a bitch, although I still don't know how it would have come out. Both women got cold feet at the last minute, and we agreed to settle for good jobs for them in the suburbs, with his assistance."

"If they didn't get damages, what did you get— fees from him?" Jenny asked.

"Nope, just a couple of free dinners after they got jobs. I'd known about Sharman for a while— not about his thing for women, but about the way he practices. Once he tried to nail Jack Green on a phony workers' comp claim. The women came to me, needed help, and I was happy to provide it."

Anger and defiance flashed across her face. "Well, I don't want anything from the bastard, whether it's money or a job. But I'll be damned if I'm going to let him run me out of town. He's thrown one at my chin. Next time I face him, I want to take him to the bleachers."

A baseball metaphor from an attractive, blond attorney. She left all the other temporary help I'd had in the dust, along with most of the women I'd met in the last few years. "I'll be happy to give you the chance. Things work out here, I'll give you the next case we get against him. Any adversary of Wayne Sharman is a friend of mine. You want to start here, you're on. I'll call your reference at the bank. If it checks out and you can handle some cases along with the office stuff, we'll see how it goes. In the meantime, though, let's see what you can do with the piles of paper lying around here."

We spent the next hour going over some of my most neglected files and correspondence. She grasped things quickly and took on menial tasks along with the more interesting ones without complaint. I had an extensive but idiosyncratic computer setup which I showed her, and which did not seem to faze her. After meeting with Jenny, I spent the next two hours returning phone calls and revising a memorandum for an afternoon hearing in court.

CHAPTER ———

SIX

For the next two days, I plowed through piles of paper to pay the bills. Jenny went through her work quickly, doing a little legal work on top of the secretarial. We managed to move a few cases along and turned out some comments on contracts and agreements.

Two new clients came in, a woman with a case against a stockbroker for placing her in disastrous investments, and the other a small business owner with a garden variety dispute over a big bill. Jenny and I met with them together.

The client with the case against the stockbroker was a widow and close to eighty years old, smart and angry. Her broker had sold her a big slug of risky limited partnerships in airplanes, though he knew she was not wealthy and was entrusting her entire fortune to him. The partnerships did very badly and had been an outrageous investment for the woman. Jenny was instantly a crusader on her behalf, and we discussed how to investigate the case and obtain the expert opinion we'd need on how badly the woman had been treated. By the end of the meeting she was treating Jenny as a long-lost daughter and me as a knowledgeable but slightly suspect functionary who lacked the necessary zeal for the job.

Indeed, when they left, both clients seemed as happy with Jenny as with me. The clients left happy— happier, I thought, than clients usually looked after meeting with me alone.

Late on Wednesday afternoon I spoke to Ann, who told me the plans for Aaron's funeral, scheduled for late the next morning. She also said that the police had reported no progress on the case.

The morning of the funeral dawned clear and became prettier with each hour. Bright sunshine, scant humidity, and occasional high wispy clouds moving slowly across a brilliant blue sky. A day for windsurfing, biking, or walking the beach with a girl, not for grieving and burying.

The funeral was held in a small wooden church in Wettamesett. The crowd was small, since Aaron had only spent summers here until last year. But his college friends and biking buddies could attend. Most important, he had loved the town, so it was more his home than any other place.

The service was short. Ann spoke last. Her voice, soft but with an intensity I'd never heard before, reached every corner of the silent room. She looked out to the mourners and spoke of Aaron's struggles and his accomplishments, with an occasional smile amidst the tears.

"Finally, I know how much Aaron loved biking. In the last few days, I thought I'd speak about that, about how excited he became when he climbed on his bike. But today something else became clear to me.

"As I walked on the beach this morning," she said, "I looked out on our small cove, a tiny corner of Buzzards Bay. The wind was still, the water like glass. It was dead low tide. The sea had fled the shore. Boulders, sand, and grass stood revealed. The cove seemed absent of any activity, of any purpose, of any life. For a moment, I thought it fitting, for that was how I felt, too.

"But then I felt something, a breeze, a bird overhead, or maybe Aaron's spirit, and suddenly I saw our cove through Aaron's eyes. He loved it when the tide went out. He went clamming, found crabs and mussels, looked for minnows and scallops, and watched birds dive into the water for fish. He'd watch cormorants preening on their chosen boulders, drying their wings in the wind. He knew that even at low tide, life is close to the surface, not absent. And when his parents died, when he reached his own spiritual ebb, nonetheless he managed to replenish the emptiness within him with purpose, joy, and laughter. That's how I will remember him, and that's what he would urge us to do now. The next time you find a beach at dead low tide, go to the water and think of Aaron."

When she finished, nobody, not even the minister, moved for a minute or two. Only the sounds of grief and sadness filled the church. I watched Ann as she hugged her children, touched their faces, and then embraced Frank. Overcome by an aching sense of loss, I watched the affection and bonds so palpable among them.

At the cemetery, most in attendance were Aaron's younger friends, from college or biking. The teenagers fidgeted, cried, held each other, and clumped in groups, completely unprepared for the death of a friend. They turned away from the adults, except for Ann. She knew them and reached out to the bewildered, the hurt, and the frightened.

While Ann talked with some of the kids, Frank pointed out various people to me. Aaron's girlfriend Sarah was particularly anguished, dabbing her red eyes with a handkerchief and clutching a tall, thin girl as if she'd fall down without her.

"Never have gotten used to putting the youngsters under." One of the few other adults at the service, a man standing next to me, spoke quietly, whether to me or the burial plot in front of us was hard to tell. Everything about him was neat and trim. He had short gray hair and was about five-eight, wiry and slender. He looked well over sixty, but neither age nor retirement had gone to his stomach. His eyes were clear, an unusual gray color, and they seemed to scan like radar as we talked.

"Al Thompson," he said, turning to me and thrusting out his hand.

"Dan Kardon," I said. "A friend of the family's. I've spent a lot of time with Aaron over the years. How do you know the family?"

"Used to be the police chief in Wettamesett. I've known the family casually for a long time." He nodded at the group of teenagers climbing into four or five cars. "I know some of 'em. Good kids, even the ones who raise a little hell once in a while. Couple have parents I'd like to put away, but I think the kids will turn out all right. I always wanted to keep them safe here. I knew they'd leave town, but I figured at that point, we'd have given them whatever strength we could, and then they were on their own. Now we can't even protect them at home."

"Ever have anything like this on your watch?"

"No. We had gunshots fired once in a while," he said. "Guys got drunk and stupid, kids took potshots at sea gulls. We're not perfect. We had some nasty domestic violence, guys beating their girlfriends or wives. Nothing like this, though." He took another look around the crowd before he turned to look me straight in the eye.

"I was chief in Wettamesett for twenty years, and on the force for nearly twenty before that, and we didn't have a single murder. Probably luck as much as anything, but it's just as well people stop thinking this kind of thing can't happen in their towns. This might wake 'em up, force 'em to pay attention to what's happening."

"You sound like you suspect something here, that this was part of something bigger. Not just a random shooting," I said.

His eyes grew a little harder. "Son, in my view, there's no such thing. The killing's there for a reason, whether it's obvious or not."

Someone called his name, and it seemed to break his concentration. "Sorry, got carried away," he said. "Sometimes I forget it's not my job anymore. I'm out to pasture and there's no need to pass my old-fashioned whimsies on."

Ann and Frank waved to Thompson and motioned me over to their car. "Sorry, I've got to go," I said. "Nice to meet you. I'm sure the people in town appreciated your whimsies."

"Some did, some didn't," he said, and walked away.

CHAPTER

SEVEN

"It's been two weeks since he was killed, and the police tell us they still have no suspects," Ann said. She, Frank, and I were sitting at their dining room table in Cambridge, finishing off pizzas and fielding the homework-inspired "Dad, what does 'industrial development' mean?" and "Mom, I need you" calls from Linda, twelve, and Greg, nine.

"I've heard from a few of our friends down there that stories are going around about Aaron being a drug dealer," Ann continued. "We just can't stand it."

"We want you to investigate," Frank said to me.

"Me? I'm not a private investigator."

"You do some criminal defense work, right?"

"Yeah, but—"

"And when you worked in the Attorney General's office, you did some criminal investigations."

"There are people who do that stuff for a living who'll do it better."

"We've already talked to a couple of investigators," Ann said, "and we didn't like them. We know the police are understaffed, other crimes are happening every day, and we just don't trust them to care about this the way you will. We have confidence you can help."

"We know that moving quickly is important," Frank said, "and the police don't seem to be doing that. We'll pay you. If you want to hire an investigator to help, that's fine."

"It's our family, our loss," Ann said. "The violence was done to us. We have to know why. You understand how important it is for us to find out the truth, Dan."

I remembered too well what Ann had said about her need to know what happened in order to come to terms with Aaron's death. I sat for a moment, saying nothing. I figured it would be a wild goose chase, but Ann and Frank had been good friends for a long time and they'd been there for me when I needed help. "I'll do whatever I can," I said.

"Thank you," Ann said. "And if you look into things and tell us that the police investigation is all that should be done, we'll accept that." I got a hug from Ann and a gruff thanks from Frank.

After most of the pressing tasks were done the next morning, I put a call in to Lt. Colonel Randy Blocker of the State Police, my longtime basketball buddy.

"Hey, Colonel, caught any bad guys today?"

"Well, the good Mr. Kardon. Been missing you on the basketball court lately. I hear tell you've been cavorting with the yachtie types down in Wettamesett. When you can hang with the elite, no need to mess with us blue-collar guys, that it?"

"Well, you know how it goes, even when you can afford steak every day, you still have an occasional hankering for a hamburger. Think of yourself as the hamburger in the buffet of my life." He gave an enormous snort and laugh all at once and I laughed as well. Our conversations usually started with good-natured abuse, except for the times on the basketball court when the abuse was not quite so good-natured.

"So tell me what's happening, my man," he said.

"I gather you had a brief chat with Chief Richards. I'd appreciate your help. What do you know about him?" We were good friends, but Randy was still a smart, straight-arrow cop. He had a sensitive nose for the out-of-the-ordinary. I could almost see it start twitching.

"Tell me, what's this about?" It was more a statement than a question from Randy.

"I'll fess up. Just give me the lowdown on Richards."

"Don't know him well. I've talked to him a few times at meetings where we coordinate statewide drug efforts and the like," Randy said.

"You worked with him at all?"

"Nope, just talked business."

"Know anything about his background, personality? Is he going to give me a hard time if I do some sleuthing around a homicide in his town?" I asked.

"I hope to hell he does," he said. "Kardon, where's this going? I told Richards you're okay when he called ten days, two weeks ago. What are you getting into here?"

"I'll get there, just give me what you can."

Randy sighed. "Not much to give. Only had a few conversations with the man. He was a high school football and basketball star in Wettamesett, then went south to play college ball. After that he went to the Atlanta police force. Did well there but ended up back in Wettamesett when his folks died and left him their house. Seems bright and ambitious, so it's kind of an unusual step, but he says he's glad to be back, loves the job and the area. He fishes, sails, windsurfs, stuff like that. Guy seems to be doing a good job and it's nice to have young, sharp guys signing up. Too many of the small-town chiefs we have are tired, bored, or just waiting for their pensions. We need help in that area, too. Too many drug shipments coming in down there."

"Why there? They come in from the water?" I asked. "Makes no sense. The shipping channel in Buzzards Bay is so busy and narrow, I can't believe anybody would send a mother ship in there."

"You're right. We think some large yachts or cruise ships drop off shipments to cigarette boats. Some old freighters and tankers and fishing boats also come through. The stuff could also have come up from New York on the interstate, I–95. Richards is looking around, but nothing solid yet. The economy is still in tough shape down there, so plenty of people are willing to earn a buck selling crap." With that, an edge came into Randy's voice. "Enough from me. What kind of no good you up to?"

I told him what I'd been asked to do, and about the observations and discrepancies I'd discussed with Richards, the apparent lack of progress by the investigators, and, above all, the conviction among those who knew him that Aaron would have stayed away from drugs.

Blocker was skeptical, to say the least, of any notion that Aaron had been killed in anything other than a drug deal or a drive-by shooting. "Dan, goddamn it," he said. "You know these random shootings have occurred everywhere. No place is immune. And Richards is a good cop. There's no reason for you to go off on a wild goose chase. He'll work with us and the D.A.'s office. We'll find the guys who did it. They'll be punks who went drinking, decided to have some fun, and one of them took a shot out of a speeding car. Or else, whether you like it or not, the kid was involved in a drug deal and got nailed for it. Your clients got to be prepared to live with the truth."

"They are, but mostly they're desperate to find out why Aaron died. I won't get in the way of the police, but something's wrong here and I want to help sort it out, if I can."

Randy gave a loud, martyred sigh. "Don't say I

didn't warn you. You're wasting your time, and you damn well better not get in anybody's way."

"I'll be a good boy, I promise. By the way, what do you know about Al Thompson, the police chief in Wettamesett before Richards? I just met him."

"He's a good cop and a good guy. Knows the area and the people cold, he's honest and just as ornery as you."

"I'm thinking I might go talk to him."

"You want to talk to anybody down there without pissing off the investigators, he's probably the guy. 'Course, you'll piss somebody off, somehow."

I thanked Randy for his confidence in me, told him I owed him a six-pack of Harpoon Ale, and promised to return to the basketball court.

When I called Chief Thompson, he remembered our brief meeting at the funeral.

"Damned sad event," he said. Thompson would have seen his share of funerals. His voice resonated with anger and sadness as we talked again about Aaron's death. Not the kind of man you'd like to cross, but one you'd like to have worrying about your town and your children.

"Well," he said, "whatever happened, it didn't happen on my watch, so I'll let it go."

"Do you mind meeting with me to talk about Aaron's death?" I asked him. "Randy Blocker said you're a good guy to talk to."

"Sure. Blocker's a good man. Happy to talk. How about some fishing?"

"Great. When do you want me to come down?"

"How about this afternoon? At my age, I can't let many opportunities slip away. I've got a small fishing boat down in Wettamesett harbor. We can go out for bluefish and talk there."

An afternoon on Buzzards Bay sounded better than the paperwork I had at the office, and I'd be starting the search I promised Ann and Frank. I told Jenny where I was going and headed out. I went back to the house to get the car and then drove to meet Chief Thompson.

Thompson had an eighteen-foot open, fiberglass, V-bottom boat with a center cockpit and an eighty-horsepower outboard—exactly the trim boat I expected him to have. Clean, well-maintained and seaworthy, she sat gracefully on her mooring in the harbor, the name *Serenity* on her stern.

The harbor opens out to Buzzards Bay, which lies between Cape Cod and the southeastern shore of Massachusetts. It's shallow, rarely more than forty feet deep. In the north it funnels down to the Cape Cod Canal, which slices across the base of Cape Cod.

Most people don't think about the bay except when a ship runs aground going into or out of the canal. A few people think about the bay a lot. Throughout the summer heat, when so many areas don't have wind, Buzzards Bay always delivers for sailors and windsurfers. Thermal winds develop when the shores around the bay warm up more quickly than the sea. The air above the land rises and the cooler air over the water rushes landward. On Buzzards Bay these thermals usually kick in around noon, and a steady fifteen-knot wind blows out of the southwest for a few hours.

For fishermen, scup and tautog hang around throughout the summer. In the spring, and then again in the late summer and fall, striped bass and bluefish show up. Fishermen line up on the rocky shores of the canal, fish off town piers, or anchor boats in the bay. In the shallows among the marshes, occasional osprey make air attacks from above for fish, while cormorants dive below the surface, looking for food. Heron walk in the shallows. Sea gulls pick up mussels and clams and repeatedly drop them on rocks until the shells break and dinner is ready.

Thompson rowed us out to his boat's mooring with a simple, practiced stroke. He moved agilely on board and handled the boat comfortably as we maneuvered through the nearby boats at anchor. The wind had started to drop and the tops of the white-capped waves were gradually turning a blue-green, losing their bleached frothing. The boat sliced through the water cleanly, giving off a small wake.

We spent the first few minutes setting up the essentials. First the beer, and then the two trolling rigs. The boat moved slowly, taking the small chop easily on the bow quarter. We rolled, but not uncomfortably. We were going after bluefish, which have sharp teeth. We put steel leaders on the lines, and fastened plugs, which we'd pull across the surface. Bluefish will go after anything if they're in a feeding frenzy.

Thompson questioned me a bit about my background and then asked straight out about Aaron's murder. What did I know? Why was I involved? What did the police know?

I gave him a brief summary of what had happened and then talked about the stalled investigation. "Ann and Frank are frustrated and want to see if I can dig anything up. From what I know, Richards has all the right people involved, and I'm sure they'll do a good job, but the pace of things is just real slow. You and Richards get along okay?"

"Didn't have much contact. He moved in, I moved out, and that was that. He thanked me for turning over a department in good shape and we shook hands. He kidded me about how I'd let him go once after I'd found him parking with a girl when he'd been a kid." Thompson emitted a grunt as he steered the boat around a bright red lobster-pot buoy with numbers on it. "I've got no right to complain and he's done nothing wrong. But I guess I expected him to ask me more about the town, people in it, and some of the problems. I know he needed to make a clean break, establish himself, but I could've helped him."

Conversation stopped for a moment as we hit a couple of smaller waves. Spray flew from the bow onto my face, giving me a quick cool slap.

Thompson changed the course of the boat and turned toward me, wind in his face and giving a full laugh this time. " 'Course, I'm just an old fart, not happy to give it up. But I still want to know why you're getting involved in this thing. Richards is a good, smart cop with a first-rate investigative background."

"I told Ann and Frank much the same," I said. "They want me to look around anyway, and I do know Aaron better than the investigators. Don't know how far I'll go with it, but there are some discrepancies I want to check out. Richards didn't think much of them, but they bug me. Can I run them by you?"

"Shoot." Thompson barely nodded, but he stopped looking back at the trolling rigs and focused on me.

"First, none of us believe Aaron would have anything to do with drugs. I assume you've heard about the crack found on him."

"Sure, Aaron's an unlikely user or dealer. But these days, I wouldn't be surprised at anybody using the damn stuff."

"The light for Aaron's bike," I said. "He used it for riding at night. It was in the bag on the back of his bike, with a full battery."

"So what?" he asked.

"I've ridden with him. He was a careful, experienced cyclist. The light clips onto a bike or a piece of clothing. It's an important safety device and Aaron would have used it. Why wasn't it on his bike or jacket when he was found?"

"Yeah, but there was a full moon," Thompson said. "I remember because I went out in the boat that night and heard about the murder the next morning."

"Did you operate the bow lights on your boat?"

"Of course, I'd be foolish not to."

"Aaron felt the same way about biking at night. The light's not to help the rider see but to make sure drivers see him. Anybody who rides a lot knows that car drivers have a big blind spot for bike riders, even during the day."

"Not much to show a murder. What else do you have?"

"None of this is a smoking gun, but there are a couple of other things. First, in the pictures of the site where they found Aaron, the bike was lying on its left side. When I inspected the bike, there was damage to the derailleur—the gizmo that changes gears, which is on the right side. There was enough damage to make riding the bike difficult, and it was bent in a way that couldn't have happened when the bike fell on its left side. Aaron couldn't have ridden with the derailleur as it was. Second, there was no helmet at the scene. I've searched his house and didn't find his helmet, though I found other bike equipment. Finally, he was shot in the chest—tough shot if he was on a bike and it was a drive-by shooting."

"The police banged up the bike when they brought it in, and maybe Aaron never wore the helmet that night," Thompson said.

"You're right, I've thought about those things. But I'm certain Aaron wouldn't ride without a helmet, even more certain than I am about the light. I know these things may all have explanations, but I can't believe that Aaron rode around on Route 107 without a light and a helmet late after dark."

"Might have been if he was buying drugs." He stopped talking for a moment as he steered across the path of a gleaming old wooden sailboat, then turned back to look at me. "What do you think happened?"

Until that moment, I hadn't been conscious that I had a theory. I came up with one, but it sounded meager to me and I knew it would sound skimpy to Thompson.

"Perhaps Aaron rode somewhere in the early evening, before he needed to put the light on. He got involved in something, or saw somebody. The bike was damaged, he was discovered and shot. Then he and the bike were moved and dumped on Route 107. Whoever shot him didn't find the helmet."

"You've got a lot of ifs and maybes there, son," he said. "In my experience, whatever it looked like happened, usually happened. Here, it looks like a random, drive-by shooting or a drug deal gone bad. Two pretty strong possibilities. Spend some time on it, one of those are likely what it'll turn out to be. And besides, if it wasn't drugs, who in hell would have a reason to shoot Aaron?"

That question had stumped me for the past few days. I checked out the few puffy clouds overhead and a Coast Guard helicopter flying by overhead. "I don't know and I don't have anything to go on."

Thompson seemed to mull it over for a bit. He fiddled with the trolling rigs, which still had yielded nothing but seaweed. "So what happens now?" he asked.

"Don't know, except I'll poke around a bit. One possibility is that I'm wrong and there are good explanations for all this. The other is I'm right and the police are doing a sloppy job. If so, I want to give them something more substantive so they can't, or won't, screw up the investigation. You know better than I that the police are right a hell of a lot more than they're wrong. But Ann and Frank want me to look. If there's nothing there in the next few days, I'll pack it in."

"Probably a waste of time," he said.

"Yeah, I figured you might tell me that," I replied.

"But I also know it's hell on the family," he said. "Aaron deserved a whole lot better."

"What would you look for in a situation like this?" I asked.

"If it were me, I'd look for something tangible to give you a lead. Sometimes you look for motive first. This case, you've got a dead college student. Tough enough to figure out the life and motives of a live kid that age. It might be a whole lot easier to begin sorting things out by finding a witness, the gun, the helmet, the reason the bike's broke, something like that."

"So you think there's something there for me to find?"

"I doubt it. But as much as I love this part of the world and the people in it, I'd be the first to tell you that there are a lot of strange goings on out there."

A bluefish hit Thompson's line. We had come upon a school, and by the time we finished, we—mostly Al—had caught six good-sized fish and lost another three.

Thompson handled them carefully as he brought them in and then packed the fish on ice. We avoided getting bitten. You don't want bluefish to have you for dinner, rather than the other way around. As soon as the frenzy passed, we headed into the harbor. Bluefish spoil quickly, so we wanted to get back to put them to good use.

On the way in I handled the boat as Thompson quickly filleted the fish. Sea gulls flew behind the boat, squawking and diving into the water as he threw the heads and insides overboard. Thompson put the fillets into two plastic bags, and after mooring the boat, we rowed back to the pier.

I thanked Thompson for the fishing. He insisted I keep some of the fillets and told me to call him as soon as I had anything else on Aaron's murder. More important, he told me to keep the fish on ice and cook it that evening—preferably on a grill, the fish smeared with mayonnaise to keep it moist.

I stopped in a convenience store to pick up

some ice, and called Jenny to check on the office. She sounded chipper. Both of the clients she'd met with the day before had decided to hire "us," she said, and they were sending small retainers to get started. She also asked me to be in the office at ten A.M. the next morning to meet with a prospective new and important client, Mickey Rawlings, a baseball player whose name I recognized.

"We caught some fish, and I'm thinking about having them for dinner. You ever had fresh-grilled bluefish?" I asked. For some reason, my throat got dry and scratchy all of a sudden. The thought of inviting her for dinner hadn't come to me until I heard her voice on the phone, and then the invitation popped out of my mouth before I had a chance to quash it.

"No."

"You can tell me about what you're getting me into with this Rawlings guy over dinner."

She laughed. "I'm not getting you into anything you can't handle easily. Tell me where and when I should show up."

I gave her directions and told her to come late enough so that I'd have time to make a quick pass at cleaning the house.

CHAPTER

EIGHT

I managed to dig the dining room table out from under domestic debris and to throw the dirty laundry into the washing machine. Just before the doorbell rang, I cranked up a Lucinda Williams CD.

Jenny walked upstairs into my home and took off a tan canvas coat. She was wearing close-fitting blue jeans and a royal-blue blouse, nothing like the suits she'd worn in the office. Her hair was down and danced above her shoulders, and she had on a simple silver choker. She smiled when I opened the door for her, and I felt a slight tension in my gut.

For an instant I thought about shaking her hand, but it didn't feel right. I brought her in, much less sure of what to say and do than I had been in the office. Following her around as she checked the place out, I tried not to focus on her long legs and slender waist.

Back in the living room, she laughed softly and

shook her head. "I like the stuff on the walls," she said.

"There's nothing on the walls."

"I know. But it's more attractive than your furniture."

"You're showing remarkable courage in front of someone who signs your paycheck, not to mention someone who's about to serve you dinner."

"I've seen enough of your office to know you can do better when you put your mind to it. You take some kind of perverse pride in a spartan home?"

I couldn't help but laugh. "What can I say, I hate shopping. Let's go out on the porch while I cook the fish on the grill." We talked about the office while the fish cooked. Finally, I got everything on the table and we ate.

"Great fish," she said.

"You sound surprised."

"Well, I thought your cooking skills might match your interior decorating. But I'm happy to find a distinguished male lawyer who has some household skills as well."

"Kind of a backhanded compliment, but I'll take it. Truth is, I don't care what I look at on the walls, but I do care what I eat."

With office chat behind us, I took an internal deep breath and shifted ground. "So how did an Appalachian mountain girl who loves baseball end up in Boston?" I asked.

"You want to know why I'm here or why I love baseball?"

"Let's start with both."

She explained that her father was a professor and her family had moved among a number of university towns, finally settling at Eastern Tennessee State University in Johnson City. Jenny had lived there for most of her school years, and her parents still did.

"My dad is one of those English professors who love baseball. You know the type—Bart Giamatti, John Updike, Roger Kahn. He loves to watch the game, keep score, and write stories. Johnson City has a minor-league team and Dad used to take me. And I played baseball and basketball with my three brothers, used to shoot at bottles and squirrels with them."

"Classic tomboy stuff."

"Yup. Then I went to ETSU, played on basketball and softball teams and also did a little writing for a literary magazine. After graduation I married Tom Roberts, a third baseman with the minor-league team. Couldn't field much, but he hit with power, ran well." More of her beer disappeared.

"I remember him. He's an announcer now, right?"

"Yes. Two years after we married, he was in the major leagues. The marriage lasted a few more years."

Jenny stared into her translucent brown beer bottle for a moment, then looked back up at me. "After the divorce, I was heading toward thirty with not much to go on, besides knowing about sports and athletes and how to do well in school. Finally, it came to me—I'd go to law school, maybe become an agent. Sounds bizarre, but I do know players and people in the game, and I know both basketball and baseball.

"So then it was easy. I always loved Fenway Park and the old Boston Garden, Boston has great schools. I went to Boston College Law School. After graduating, I found a job with the bank. The rest you know. And I still think I can become an agent."

"Tell me a bit about this guy coming in tomorrow, Rawlings. All I know is, he used to hit the ball pretty well."

She sat up sharply at the table and leaned toward me.

"Still does. He can play first base but he'd be best for an American League team with a designated hitter. His agent has picked up a couple of young, rising stars, and Mickey's been thinking about someone new. He plays for the Angels now, but used to play in Johnson City. I met him there. Good guy. I called him, knowing the Angels were coming to town, just to see him. So he's coming in tomorrow to talk."

I shook my head and smiled. "I'll be happy to sit in and pretend I know something about the business. But I've got to tell you, there may be easier things for you to think about than becoming an agent—you need to know about taxes, finances, and you end up babysitting prima donnas. Not to mention that there aren't many women in that world, and I suspect the good ol' boys won't welcome you with open arms."

She rolled her eyes at me.

"Oh, damn, I didn't mean—"

"Don't worry," she said, "a lot of boys in baseball made it clear they'd open their arms for me, not to mention other things, but none were as obnoxious as Sharman. Anyway, you're right. We've talked about that. High risk, maybe, but I'll fight for him harder than anybody else. I can hire financial consultants, if we need to. And I figured your reputation couldn't hurt."

"What reputation is that?"

She sat back and gave me a cool, small smile. "Prickly, independent, but willing to take on difficult cases. People say you do your best work when you're on your own—not much of a team player."

"I guess you got the sanitized version of my character, probably from Jack Green. Most people just say I'm stubborn, some say worse than that. Why do you want to hook up with somebody who's not a team player?"

"You're honest and you don't discriminate. No easier on men then on women, as far as I can tell. You don't put up with a lot of bullshit. Those things are important to me. As long as you're straight with me, and I'm straight with you, I'm betting we'll get along. I've known plenty of athletes. Some of them aren't team players until you find the right team for them." That got a laugh out of me.

Then she shifted back to the question of how

she might develop some work as a sports agent. The idea had little appeal for me. But she knew the business and I had little doubt she'd be good if given the chance.

As she continued telling me her plans, I found myself thinking that if it worked, she'd be moving on to a more suitable office—maybe with tax attorneys, accountants, people to handle money, all those things. I would have to start looking for a new secretary soon. And I realized I didn't want that to happen. I enjoyed working with her, having dinner with her—but I had no interest in following Wayne Sharman's lead. I could still hear the vitriol in her voice as she described her last conversation with Sharman. She was an employee, not somebody I met at a bar. The paycheck I signed entitled me to nothing more of her than Sharman's had.

Jenny must have caught me not paying attention, and quickly changed subjects, asking me about Aaron's murder. Initially she was as skeptical as Al Thompson about my theories. But she suggested she could talk with Aaron's girlfriend, pointing out that I might not have much in common with a grieving teenage girl. I had the good sense not to tell her my reaction, which was that I'd interviewed a hell of a lot more witnesses than she had.

After dinner I cleared the table. She immediately got up and turned on the television in time to see Rawlings hit a double and knock in two runs. She wandered in as I did the dishes, animated and excited.

"Mickey will be in a good mood tomorrow. He's got two hits and three RBIs tonight. I'd better get going. I want to put some ideas together on paper for our meeting."

"I'll see you in the morning. After the meeting, I'll be heading out to talk with people."

"Thanks for dinner. You did a nice job on both the fish and the dishes. Obviously I'll have to enhance your reputation." Her eyes flashed as brightly as the silver choker around her neck as she walked out the door.

The house felt lonelier than it had in a long time, and I kept thinking about her smile. But I didn't like those reactions and I knew damn well I had to watch myself. The admonition of my old friend Bill Shakespeare in *Measure for Measure* came to mind: " 'Tis one thing to be tempted, Escalus, another thing to fall."

It was ten-thirty P.M. Talking with Thompson about the murder and having Jenny for dinner left me on edge, so I went for a run. I went through Coolidge Corner, past the high school, and uphill to the Brookline Reservoir. Trees lined the southern rim of the reservoir, while from the east the John Hancock Building glowed brightly in the background. The sky was warm and clear. Ten or twelve couples strolled on the path around the reservoir and a few more necked on benches. I couldn't remember the last time I'd sat on a bench and necked with a woman. I ran harder to forget what I couldn't remember.

CHAPTER

NINE

The meeting with Rawlings went about as expected. He seemed to like us, but wanted time to think about his situation. He and Jenny left afterward for coffee and a chat. I left for Wettamesett.

Before heading south, I stopped to talk with Ann. Her eyes were lined and heavy. People tried to be supportive, she said, but she could hear notes of curiosity or disapproval in their voices, with the faint echo of the drug allegations always in the background. Part of her did not want to let go of Aaron and the images she had of him. Another part of her wanted desperately to restore order, normalcy, and happiness to her family. There wasn't much I could add on either count. I just told her I'd be in touch.

I stopped first at Southeastern Coastal College. It was small enough to walk around and check out the clumps of students planted around the campus.

I asked around and finally located Sarah,

Aaron's girlfriend, sitting outside in a courtyard at lunchtime in a group of five girls, all of whom, except for hair color, were indistinguishable in over-sized, dark sweaters or sweatshirts, baggy pants and colored shoes. The girls each chewed gum and they coalesced into a tighter group as I approached them.

None of them spoke a word as I introduced myself, told them that I was working with the Hastingses and wanted to ask a few questions about Aaron. One of the girls, a bit braver but voicing the suspicions for all of them, or perhaps having seen more police shows on television, asked me for some identification. After showing them my license and bar card demonstrating I was a lawyer, I told them I'd be happy to talk with Sarah with her parents present.

"No. My friends are enough," she said. "I'll talk to you for a few minutes but we're going to class. What do you want?" Her voice quavered. She took the gum out of her mouth.

"Did you notice anything unusual about Aaron's behavior in the last week or two before he was shot? Did he mention anything strange that he'd seen or done, or any new people he'd met?"

She'd never make a good poker player. An anxious look flitted across her face. She bit her lip and one of her friends took her hand. "I didn't see anything different. He'd been biking more, going longer distances, and we didn't see each other as much. I've heard the police found drugs on the bike, but none of us believe it. Aaron would never have used crack." They all shook their heads in agreement.

"I know. That's why I'm trying to follow up. Did he say anything to you about seeing drug dealers while he was out on a bike ride?"

She shook her head.

"How about his biking? Did he have places he biked to regularly? Was he just riding for fun or did he have specific training loops worked out?"

"He did both. Sometimes he and some other guys biked to an industrial park and raced there, did circuit races on the weekends. Other times he trained on his own. Aaron wanted to go up to some races in Boston this fall."

"Where did he go when he rode alone? I went to the Houghton tire pile with him. Do you know it?"

"He went there sometimes. Other rides, he went along the coast, riding from Tern Point in Wettamesett on to the harbor in Marion and then around the point beyond the harbor, where the golf course is."

As she spoke, tears began welling up in her eyes. Her brave friend popped up and said they had to get to class. I thanked her and they stood up and walked off, talking furiously together. They stopped and gave me a last look before they entered a building.

Then Sarah broke away from the group and ran back to me.

"Mr. Kardon," she asked, "did you know Aaron well?"

"Yes. He was a great kid. I miss him, and I'm sorry you've had to go through this."

"I— This is hard for me," she said. She looked at the ground. "I loved him, I wanted us to get married after college. You probably think I'm silly, but you can't imagine how much this hurts."

I didn't have to imagine, but I didn't tell her that.

She stopped for a minute to gather her breath. "I wasn't completely honest before. Something happened this summer, I don't know what, Aaron became more remote and didn't want to see me as much. He wouldn't tell me why. I don't believe he was into drugs, and he never said anything about another girl, so I don't know what was going on. Please, Mr. Kardon, find out what happened. I just don't understand."

"Thanks for telling me," I said. "He was lucky to have you care for him. I'll do what I can."

She put her hands over her face and started toward her friends. They scurried over and gave her a hug.

Another call for help from a woman with a grieving heart and a disbelieving mind. Aaron, in a short and tortured life, had appeared a loner, but he left behind people he'd touched powerfully.

Sarah, though, indicated that Aaron might have had something to hide. I only hoped it would not visit more pain on his loved ones. Ann had said Sarah hadn't visited as much over the summer, but Ann had no inkling of the growing distance between them. Perhaps figuring out what Aaron might have been hiding would lead us to who killed him.

Left with a pleasant afternoon and nobody to talk to, the only thing I could think of doing was to follow Thompson's advice and look for any kind of evidence of what happened. I decided to start with the places Sarah had mentioned, but with the passage of time since the murder, finding something would be a long shot.

I left the college and drove to Wettamesett. I spent about forty minutes walking over the small park at Tern Point, including checking the rocky embankment at the park's edge. Tern Point consists of a small, well-kept grassy expanse surrounding a lighthouse sitting at the edge of Wettamesett harbor. The lighthouse, about fifty feet high and built in the early 1800s, no longer operates, but it looks over a serene picnic and fishing spot and a favored site for windsurfers. I found nothing.

I dropped by the Wettamesett police headquarters on the way to the Marion harbor. Richards spoke to me only briefly.

"Anything new?" I asked.

"Nope."

"How about the autopsy—are the results back?"

"Yeah, I know what you want to know. No drugs in his system."

"That's good news."

"Kardon, it only tells us he hadn't been using it for a short period before the murder. It doesn't tell us whether he was buying or selling, or what the hell he planned to do with the stuff in the saddle-bag. Right?"

I sighed. "Right."

Richards pumped me a bit, but when he was satisfied that I had nothing more, he let me go. He didn't say so but I could tell from his questions and tone that the police investigation was losing steam. There had been other murders in the county, so the D.A.'s office and the State Police were moving on. And investigators generally hold that the best evidence in a homicide case shows up in the first three days. That time had come and gone with nothing of consequence showing up.

I moved on to the pier at Marion. The boats bobbing in the harbor framed large, wooden mansions with perfectly manicured lawns running down to the water. Nothing looked out of place.

Then I drove out on to the point, where the golf course met the ocean. I drove slowly along the road, checking the obvious places to stop and gaze at the waves breaking on the shore or out to Bird Island lighthouse. No bike clothing, stuff from his bike, or any other traces of Aaron.

The places Sarah had identified had yielded nothing, but I had time for one more stop. With a couple hours of daylight remaining, I headed back to the tire pile. I drove there by way of Route 107, as Aaron and I had biked. It took me a couple of trips back and forth before I spotted the small trail Aaron and I had used. To avoid having my car spotted there, I parked it about a half mile north at a turnout on the other side of the road. I walked back and went down the trail quite slowly.

The trail revealed little. I found boot treads here and there, along with some discarded soda and beer cans, but my only training in tracking came from *The Last of the Mohicans*. I couldn't pretend to learn anything useful from the impressions. There were no obvious bike tire treads, trash, clothing, or bike accessories.

As I approached the tire pile I heard voices and the sounds of equipment operating. I stayed within the woods and watched as three men worked at the tire shredder. Two fed tires onto the escalator belt. The tires were carried upward and another worker watched the shredded rubber as it emerged from the whirling, cutting blades. That guy used a shovel to move the shredded rubber around. The men were absorbed in their activities until a truck drove through the open chain-link fence and blew its horn.

The men loading the shredder stopped throwing tires on the escalator. When the last tire had been fed in and diced, they shut down the machine and all three went over to the truck. One of the men directed the truck to a spot on the western edge of the tire pile and it began dumping tires on the pile. Now and then a tire rolled off the pile. One of the men would grab the errant tire and throw it back. After the truck had dumped all of the tires, the truck driver stepped down and the men began talking.

I was too far away to hear or see much, and the light was beginning to fade, so I headed back.

On the way out I stepped off the trail into the small clearing where Aaron and I left our bikes when we'd been there. A scan of the ground showed nothing but grass, dirt, and embedded rocks. Higher up, ten feet over my head, a squirrel sat on a branch and looked back at me. I was just turning to go when something flashed. I looked more closely and saw a deep blue bicycle helmet hanging on a branch at shoulder level, right on the tree that Aaron had used to support his bike. I stood there for a moment, suddenly short of breath and trembling.

CHAPTER

TEN

Without looking hard for it, nobody would have seen it. I had a hard time believing it myself and I felt simultaneous surges of anger and vindication. Before I approached it, I took a look around for other evidence that Aaron had been there, but I found nothing.

The iridescent blue helmet top faced the trail, blending in with the forest. I'd seen the last beams of sunlight reflected off it. The helmet had to be Aaron's—it looked like his, and I hadn't found his at the cottage. He'd been to this site often enough to select a regular place to leave his bike and his helmet. In a public place, he would have locked the bike and the helmet together to a bike stand or sign post. In the middle of the woods, Aaron wouldn't have cared. He'd simply put his bike and helmet in a secluded and convenient place.

He must have biked down the trail, walked to the clearing, and then left the bike on the ground or against the tree. He put the helmet on the branch, then walked farther along to check out the tire pile. I figured someone who wanted no witnesses saw him, brought him and his bike out of the woods, shot him, and dumped him with the bike along the road. They missed the helmet, though, leaving the only clue that the killing hadn't been random.

I had few facts and no motive, but it was the only pattern that fit. The bike's derailleur was banged up from being tossed around in a car or truck. The bike light had never left the seat bag because Aaron never had the chance to bike home in the dark. And the gunshot in the chest was not a tough shot after all.

The cocaine was still a mystery; finding the helmet did nothing to explain it. If a drug deal was planned, why pick such an obscure place? Plenty of easier places existed for safely exchanging drugs.

More important, inside I couldn't accept the notion that Aaron had been buying crack. He might well have fooled me, but there was no way he could have duped both Ann and Sarah. Perhaps the crack was planted to confuse the investigation or to give the police the notion that they shouldn't be too zealous since the kid was a druggie.

I thought about leaving the helmet there and coming back with the police later, but I worried that somebody might see me and figure out what I'd discovered. Richards might be pissed off at me, but I didn't want the only hard evidence we had to disappear, so I pulled the helmet down.

Whatever happened to Aaron in the clearing, it was no longer a drive-by killing. I finally had somewhere to start.

Where to start posed a problem, though. To keep from going directly to jail myself, I needed to tell Richards what I'd found. As soon as I did, whoever owned the tire pile, presumably the Houghtons, would come under scrutiny. If it was the Houghtons, as soon as the police started following up on the helmet, the family members would become suspects and avoid me. I had only a small window of time in which to talk to them.

After taking the trail back out of the tire pile, I followed Route 107 south to nearby side roads until I found the one leading to the front entrance of the tire pile. At the intersection, a number of small wooden homes clustered on either side. There were only eight or ten homes on the road to the pile before undeveloped forest began anew. Finally I saw a faded wooden sign painted green and white, HOUGHTON ENTERPRISES, INC., with an arrow pointing up a fairly wide gravel drive.

I drove a couple of hundred yards and came upon three old, brown mobile trailers on the left, sitting in a clearing. Just past the trailers was a dirt parking area with a half-dozen cars parked in it. And beyond that, a chain-link fence stretched east and west, appearing to circle part of the tire pile.

The gate of the chain-link fence stood open and

men were at work on the pile. Much of what I saw was new to me. From where I'd seen the pile previously, I'd not had a view of the entrance area.

A couple of trailers had lights on, and I walked into the first one. Two young women sat at battered gray metal desks working by hand on bills or invoices. A radio played country music in the background. Inside, the walls were dirty and covered with letters, invoices, and orders either taped or tacked to a number of bulletin boards.

As the door banged shut behind me, both women looked up. They looked interested in me for a moment.

"Hi, I'm looking for whoever manages this place," I said.

Their faces went slack. One of them said, "Talk to George or Bob, next door." They both went back to their papers, their eyes dismissing me.

Next door was a slightly older, more dilapidated trailer. Instead of invoices and papers on the walls, car, truck, and tool posters and calendars replaced work papers. Most of them featured women in bathing suits or less. There were four men inside, two on a couple of phones and two sitting at desks talking to one another. The talking stopped when I walked in.

Two of the men looked familiar. I'd seen them from a distance, the day Aaron and I had surreptitiously visited the site. The older-looking one stood up and walked over to me. He stood about five-nine, with only a fringe of gray hair. He was dressed like the others, in blue jeans and a checked flannel shirt with the sleeves rolled up. His hands and forearms were streaked with dirt, oil, and grime.

"Can I help you?" he asked.

"Yeah, name is Sam Watson. I'm from Worcester, looking for some help." I offered my hand. His callused hand felt firm and rough in mine.

"Pleased to meet you. I'm Bob Houghton. This here's my brother George. We run this place. What can we do for you?" The brothers shared faces, although George's was harder and flatter, like his body. George just looked at me from a desk behind his brother, offering neither a handshake nor a smile. He was a shade taller, with a full head of brown hair.

"I've heard your company is in the disposal business. I've got some stuff to get rid of."

"We do tires here. You probably saw the pile out there," Bob said, waving his hand toward the tires.

"Yeah, I heard that. I have a bunch of 'em."

"What kind of business you run?" Bob asked. George just stared at me, playing with a paper clip.

"I'm not really in business. My dad ran a furniture repair and refinishing business near Worcester for forty years. Used to be a much bigger operation than it is now, but it's still going. He died and I'm trying to sort things out. I'm a school teacher. Going to sell the place, but there's work to do to get it in shape. Dad let some things go in the last few years. Heard about you folks, was in the area and decided to check things out."

"Meaning you've got a pile of tires in the back from company pickups and vans, I guess," Bob said. I saw him look away to an invoice posted on the wall. Maybe my project didn't sound big enough to interest him.

"You got it," I said. "A big shed in the back of the property has a huge mess of tires. I don't have a clue where they came from or how old they are, but I'd like to get rid of them."

"I'm sure we'd take 'em. We charge by the truckload, so we'd have to look at what you got before we could give you an estimate. I can give you some written stuff about our services and fees," Bob said, reaching into an envelope on a shelf.

"Thanks, that'd be great. Say, what you do with the tires? Your pile is amazing—seems an incredible waste to have them all just sit there." I didn't have to fake curiosity. I really did wonder if there were any uses for the tires.

"Yeah, about thirty-five million tires out there," Bob said.

"People paid you to take them all?"

"Yeah, between a quarter and fifty cents a tire."

"Wow, that's a bunch of quarters. They just sit there, or can you do anything with them?"

"George works on places to sell them. Wasn't much we could do for years. Occasionally we'd sell some to towns or developers for artificial reefs. Last few years, some new things have shown up. A few companies are starting to burn tires for energy— that's coming fast, probably be a big thing in five years or so." Bob sat on the edge of the desk his brother sat behind and looked at George. "Probably wipe out new business for places like us." George's face didn't change, but he started tapping the paper clip on the desk.

"I've seen some ads for products using recycled rubber—doesn't that help you?" I asked.

"Oh yeah, for now, old tires are going into crazy things, things you'd never think of," Bob replied.

"Like what?"

Bob turned to George. George scratched his ear with the paper clip and looked right at me. "Shit, companies use 'em for cushioning in road beds and playgrounds, for tugboat bumpers, hoses, mud flaps, ballpoint pens, garbage pails, car mats, speed bumps, you name it. One place makes snowshoes using strips from tires. But, hell, once they get those new incinerators in place to burn the damn things for energy, won't be any need for recycling."

"Any chance I could go out on the site, see the pile? You know, as a prospective customer?" I asked.

"No," a hasty chorus of Bob and George came back. "Liability problems," George added.

That response, combined with their dim view of the tire pile's future and my memory of the two brothers surveying the tire pile periphery when I'd visited with Aaron, sparked a hunch. Maybe the boys were diversifying, burying more than just tires.

"Too bad, but I understand," I said. "Just looks like a great business. People pay you to take them in and then pay you again to take them out. Any decent market develops, you're sitting on a gold mine. Wish my dad had thought of this one instead of furniture."

Bob gave a little grin. "You may not be a businessman, but you catch on quick. My mom, Jean Houghton, started this place. It's not a gold mine, but we're not complaining."

"You ever dispose of other stuff here?" I asked.

That got George's attention. His eyes narrowed and he leaned forward at the desk and dropped the paper clip. "Not real often. What do you have in mind?" he asked.

"Well, there's a lot of junk, old tools and paint cans, woodworking equipment, car parts, things like that." George's eyes started to wander. "And I've got about a dozen fifty-five-gallon drums. I'd pay a lot to get rid of them, along with the tires."

George's eyes whipped around and settled on Bob, who looked back at him for a moment.

"Drums," Bob said, frowning and rubbing the back of his neck.

"Yeah, looks to me like they're in good shape. No leaking."

"Any idea what's in them?" George asked.

"Nope. I teach history, not science."

"How'd the drums get there?" George again, staring directly at me.

"Don't know. As I said, my dad ran the place. Except for when I ran around there as a kid, I never had much to do with it. Probably stuff they used to strip furniture. All I know is the drums are just sitting out back with the tires and other crap." George looked at Bob, but I could decipher nothing of what passed between them.

"You have anybody else look at the drums?" George asked.

"No, we're just starting to clean things up."

"What are the drums made of?" Bob this time.

"Regular metal drums, no markings on them."

"How'd you hear about us?" Back to George.

"Friend of mine runs an auto repair place, told me about you."

"What's his name?" George asked.

"Dave Charlton."

Bob looked to George. George stood up and walked toward the back of the trailer. Bob shoved his hand out at me again. "Sorry, can't help you with anything but the tires. Happy to send somebody out to look at your place if you'd like."

"Thanks, but I'm hoping to hire a single contractor to get rid of everything. I'll keep looking, get back to you if I can't find somebody for the whole kit and caboodle. Thanks for your time, though."

Dave Charlton hadn't worked as a reference. Since I'd made the name up on the spot, that came as no surprise.

Back in the car, I headed toward a convenience store I'd seen near the small center of Glassbury, the town next to Wettamesett and the town where the tire pile was located. At a pay phone inside the store, I located a phone book and wrote down Jean

Houghton's phone number and address. After asking at the counter for directions to the street where she lived, I bought a hot dog, chips, and a large soda and drove off, thinking about my chat with the Houghton boys and what I should do next.

The boys said they operated the tire pile. I couldn't tell whether they would consider dumping something other than tires there, but they hadn't given a definitive no. And while Bob talked about the tire pile, George had a definite interest in drums.

Fortified by the junk I'd scarfed down, I decided on one more interview before checking in with Richards. I wanted to talk with Jean Houghton while I had the chance.

Visiting her at her home, I couldn't pretend I was there on business, so I knew I'd have to play it fairly straight. Most of the time, when I interview a witness, I have pretty good information about the person. This time I'd be flying blind, without even background material on her. I didn't like it, but I didn't have a choice.

I stopped at another pay phone and called Jean Houghton to ask if she'd see me. Happily for me, if not for her, she was home.

"Ms. Houghton? My name is Dan Kardon. I'm a lawyer from Boston."

A moment of silence followed. "Yes?"

"I represent the guardians of Aaron Winters, the college student from Wettamesett who was killed recently. In the course of my work I've learned that he occasionally biked to your tire pile, along with a bunch of other places."

"So he trespassed on my property. It's nothing to do with me."

"I'd like to talk with you briefly, if I could."

"No, I don't think so."

"Chief Richards and former police chief Al Thompson both know what I'm doing and I've talked with them. I'm just gathering information."

The mention of Al Thompson's name got me an audible noise. More important, she didn't hang up. When she spoke, her voice was gruff but not angry. "Cops never asked me about any of this. This is the first I've heard about the kid ever coming to our place. Why should I talk to you?"

"Well, I can't speak for the police, all I can do is tell you that I'm following up on some information I have. Along with a couple of other places, the tire pile has come up. Maybe it'll be a dead end for me. But the police have other things to worry about and I have the time to chase things down."

"You said you're a lawyer—you planning to sue me?"

"No, Ms. Houghton, I'm not looking for lawsuits, I'm just trying to help out some people who are hurting and want answers."

"Still don't see much reason for me to get involved."

"As far as I know, Ms. Houghton, you're an honest citizen who cares about her neighbors. I assume you'd want to ease some of the fear in town, if you could." I decided to play my ace. If it didn't work, I'd be driving to see Richards in a minute. "But more important, Aaron was still a teenager. He'd just finished his first year of college. You're a mother—if anything happened to one of your boys, wouldn't you want to know what happened and why? I've got clients who're pretty broken up about Aaron's death, asking just those questions."

There was silence for a moment. "First thing I thought when I heard about it was burying my oldest boy. He was killed in Vietnam."

"I'm sorry," I said.

"Shit," she said, "talking about a good kid who died young is about the last thing I want to do, but I've lived here a long time and I care a lot about the people who live here. They're good, quiet folks. There's been an awful lot of worry and speculation since the killing happened, so what the hell, come on over."

"Now?" I asked.

"May as well get this over as soon as possible. I'm going out later on, but I can talk for half an hour if you head over right away." I took directions and headed to her house.

Jean Houghton's house in Glassbury was a well-maintained, old colonial set back from the road. A high screen of bushes shielded the house and a large lawn from the road. A long driveway led to the house through a break in the bushes. The house was painted white with green shutters. Empty flower boxes perched at the edge of each window in the front. The only vehicle in the driveway was a late-model Chevy pickup.

She met me at the door, showed me into the kitchen, and offered me coffee. If I hadn't known the tire pile had made plenty of money, I'd never have guessed it from the house and the kitchen. Nothing was new or fancy. The kitchen was large, clean, and in good condition, but it was all well-used. We sat at a large pine table on wooden, high-backed chairs.

Up close, Jean Houghton radiated intensity. Her face was tanned and deeply lined. Crow's-feet crinkled at the corners of her eyes, eyes that gave me a long, searching scrutiny. Wearing black pants and a green sweater, she looked heavy, but solid and strong. Looking past the lines and the extra flesh of her face, I could see the core of a younger, prettier face. Her hands resembled no female hands I'd ever seen—callused, dirty, gashed and scarred, hands that might have handled thousands of tires.

She started the conversation. "Al says you're okay. So you answer some of my questions, then maybe I'll talk."

I gave her a small smile. "That's not what I bargained on, but under the circumstances—"

"I'd say you don't have a choice. I don't care much about what you think, it's my way or not at all." She looked at me with no hint of anything other than indifference.

I sat back in my chair and gave a gesture of

acquiescence with my hand. "I bet you're a hell of a businesswoman. Go ahead."

"You're a lawyer. What kind of practice do you have?"

"I'm a sole practitioner. I do both criminal and civil court work, some business cases, environmental work, personal injury, you name it. Mostly individuals and small companies as clients. Probably I'm a lot like the lawyers you use for your business."

"Not hardly." It was still her play, so I let the comment pass. She followed up with another series of questions. "How'd you get involved in this investigation?"

"I know Aaron's guardians, they're old friends. They want to find out what happened. You may have heard there's a possibility of drugs in the case. My friends don't believe Aaron had anything to do with drugs. They asked me to check things out. Not my normal work, but I want to help them and I cared about Aaron."

"Where do you live?" she asked. This new tangent threw me off immediately.

"Why is that important?"

"Getting a bit defensive? You want to ask questions, I want to know who's doing the asking. I told you the rules." The face across from me never wavered. She looked at me calmly. Her face was creased and tired, but the eyes were bright and alert.

"Brookline," I said.

"Fancy big-city lawyer with lots of rich clients and a big mansion, huh?"

"Not even close."

"You have family?" she asked.

"My parents."

"See 'em much?"

It was my turn to sigh. "On occasion."

"What about a wife and kids?"

"Never married and none I know about."

There was silence for a minute before Jean Houghton spoke again. "Must be lonely."

I shrugged. "I'm used to it."

"Not too talkative, are you?" She gave me a small, malevolent grin. "Rare thing in a lawyer. All right, I've grilled you enough," she said, and walked over, turned on the faucet, poured a glass of water and gave it to me without asking.

"Thanks," I said.

"I'll talk to you, but don't expect much."

"Fair enough. Mostly, I'd like to know how the tire pile operates. I know you have two boys who run it."

"Not exactly. They'll run it soon enough, but it's still my place." She sat back from the table.

"I still control the business," she continued. "I stay fairly active in the operations, except for a couple of months in the winter when I go down to Florida. We have a few trucks for picking up tires. People pay us by the truckload to pick up the tires and deposit them at the pile. Once in a while we sell some of the tires to other companies. That's all we do." She stood up. "More water?" When I said no, she got some for herself.

"Nothing else dumped at the site?" I asked. "No trash, construction debris, anything like that?"

"Nope, never wanted to expand. Made plenty of money with tires. No need to dispose of anything else, though I've had offers. If you're wondering whether I ever buried chemicals and crap out there, answer's no."

"Glad to hear it. Ever had fires or environmental problems at the site?"

"Nothing significant. Had a small fire in a trailer out at the site years ago, but nothing in the tire pile. We try to keep fire lanes cut in the pile, otherwise the fire chief gets on our ass."

"How many employees do you have?"

"Varies some by the season. Full-time, year-round, besides my boys, there's only ten or twelve, including a couple of girls in the office." Presumably the ones I'd seen working on invoices. "We use ten to twenty others at various times to work at the site, drive trucks, special projects and the like."

"Where's the business come from?"

"Mostly Massachusetts, Rhode Island, Connecticut, some from New York. Up north, they don't have much volume and they've got plenty of spaces for dumping."

"What do your boys do at the site?"

She frowned and clasped her hands in front of her, but she answered the question. "One's in charge of the trucking operation and making nice with customers, other's in charge of the tire pile. I watch over both of them."

"In my business, I see plenty of family businesses run into problems as the founding parent gets older, kids move in. That happening here?"

I sensed a change in her, as if I'd hit a vulnerable point. She took a long drink and then looked right at me. "I do my best. They'll have the business soon enough, when I retire in a few years. I haven't made my kids rich, though I may when I die. It's a strong, profitable business. They'll get it. Wanted them to learn hard work first. I've talked to people about how to pass things on and everybody's got different ideas. Only thing I've learned is, there can be problems no matter what you do."

"I know the way it works," I said. "The parents who start the company, who have the money, have to decide how much to give the kids. Some don't give them much money or responsibility at first, figuring the kids should learn on their own. Others give them a lot of money and responsibility early, hoping they'll learn from the parents—"

"Which they almost never do, because most of what the parents learn has to do with busting your ass and having a goal which drives you. With kids, if you don't give them money, and they know you have it, they resent you or maybe one gets pissed off because the other one gets something different." She got up and put her glass in the sink.

"Sounds like you've been down this road."

"Hell, I talked with consultants." She gave a short, joyless laugh. "Mostly they want big slugs of money. So in the end I'm just doing what I figure is best."

"Any major problems so far?" I asked.

She looked back at me and gave me a firm head shake for a no, but didn't volunteer any more information. I knew I was trespassing on private turf, but my last trespass had yielded a helmet. I kept intruding.

"What about the boys, they do well in the business?"

"You're getting out of bounds here," she said, shaking a finger at me. "All I'll tell you is, they probably make more money than any lawyers I've ever hired. 'Course, far as I'm concerned, everybody should make more than lawyers."

Jean Houghton was a tough lady and probably a tough client. Under other circumstances, I'd have enjoyed representing her.

"And the boys figure it's enough to make more than lawyers?" I asked.

"You represent family businesses, Mr. Kardon, you know that sometimes there's never enough. And that's all I'll say, except I know damn well my boys had nothing to do with the killing of that Winters boy. They may not be saints, but they're not criminals, not killers."

She looked at her watch and I could see my time with her was coming to an end. Only time for a few questions.

"You've talked about your boys in the business. Do you have other children?"

"One daughter." Her voice rose a notch.

"She in the business?"

Her eyes blinked and then she pursed her lips, and for the first time in the conversation she looked away from me and out the window. "She's not in the business, never has been," she said, speaking much more quickly than before. "She and my sons have occasionally done some projects involving the trucking operation, but that's it. This is no business for a woman. She's smart, can do a lot better for herself. I never wanted her involved in the tire pile."

"What does she do?"

"There's no reason to talk about my daughter," she said. "I'll tell you only what you'd find out anyway. Used to work up here at a big computer company, Dynacomp. Now she lives in New York City, works as a consultant. She's not involved with the tire pile, that's all you need to know. I'm afraid that will have to end our conversation."

"Sorry if I upset you, and I appreciate your cooperation."

"You're right, I wouldn't call this pleasant. But I understand what you're doing and I hope to hell you find out what happened. I may not like your questions, but that doesn't mean I don't want the killer caught."

With that, she stood up and showed me to the door. She didn't wear expensive clothes or live in an exquisite home, but she had more integrity, strength, and class than most of those I'd met who did.

I had learned something, though. She said she was in charge; the boys said they were. She believed she was passing on a valuable business to the boys; they had a less sanguine view of the company's future. And she said she'd dump only tires there. The boys, thinking the best days of the tire pile were behind it, might well want to expand their product line.

I stopped back at police headquarters in Wettamesett before returning to Boston. Though it was after six P.M, Chief Richards was still there. He didn't want to see me at first, but I told the patrolman at the desk that it was important. When Richards brought me in to his office, he said he had only a few minutes to talk before heading out to a meeting. That suited me. I pulled the helmet out of the small backpack I had placed it in and put it on his desk.

"That's Aaron's. I found it a long way from where he was left on the road. You might want to take a long, hard look at the Houghton tire pile. He must have been shot at the tire pile and moved." I gave him a more detailed description of where I found the helmet.

Richards walked around the desk, looking at the helmet. His nostrils flared and he seemed to start breathing more deeply as he focused on it. He used a pencil through an air hole to turn it over and check out the inside for a minute. Then he turned to me and gave me a flat stare.

"What are you talking about? You'd better be careful if you're screwing up our investigation."

"Look, I'm not trying to screw anything up."

"What the hell were you doing at the tire pile?"

"One day last summer, Aaron and I went for a long bike ride. He took me down the trail to surprise me. The trail ended at the tire pile. Aaron said he went there sometimes to watch. I thought I might find something there."

"Why didn't you talk to me or somebody else about this?"

"First, nobody asked me what I thought. Second, I told you at the start I was bothered by the missing helmet and some other things. When you guys weren't making progress, Ann and Frank asked me to check things out. I looked at a few other places for anything to help explain what happened. Found the helmet at the last place I looked, this afternoon, and brought it here." Not directly, but I didn't tell him that.

"Maybe he left the helmet there another time."

"Maybe, but I don't think so—and I don't think the family will either."

The lines of his jaw tightened and he moved within a foot of me. "You're making some big assumptions here."

"I think I'm right about what happened. And as far as I know, you've got nothing but the helmet near the pile as evidence. I'm not trying to mess you up, I'm giving you some hard evidence."

His face turned red, his efforts to control himself visible as he breathed hard. "Damnit, Kardon, you get any more bright ideas, you'd better tell me in nanoseconds. I don't want you mucking up this investigation, giving the sons of bitches that did this any advantage."

"You've got it all backward. Finding that helmet isn't screwing up your work."

"Once you found the helmet, you should have told us and we would have picked it up. You ever think you might have messed up the scene, blown some other evidence?"

"No, I didn't think—"

"That's the problem, Kardon, you didn't think and you were way out of line."

"No, Richards, you're out of line. Maybe you're right, maybe I should have left it there, but I was shocked as hell and didn't want the thing to disappear again. Anybody else, including your people, could have found the helmet." I saw him look away. "I don't want to fight with you," I continued, "and I'm not trying to interfere. But since I've turned up something and nobody else has, I don't think I'm the one causing problems here. I'll stay out of the way and cooperate, but I have clients and a job to do."

He looked at me and shook his head. I braced myself, but instead he stood up and walked over to the window. Dusk had passed and lights were on outside in the parking lot. Richards raised his hand to his face, rubbed his chin and pinched the bridge of his nose.

He turned back toward me, sat back at his desk, and gave me a more resigned look, the redness in his face seeping away. "Shit, I'm sorry. You're right, I shouldn't be jumping on you. I'm angry at myself and my men for missing something important. We screwed up, I guess, we didn't find it, and it doesn't make any of us look good. But I'm pleased that we have this lead and I appreciate your efforts.

"Now, though, Houghton's land is in another town, so the investigation is going to get more complicated. And I guess a part of me is sorry that this murder might be tied to a local family. It makes it hit home harder. But we'll take it from here. I'll be in touch with the D.A.'s office about the helmet, and we'll start to look at what connection the Houghtons might have to this. I'll let you know what kind of progress we make." He called in another officer to deal with the helmet.

He stood up and held out his hand. "Again, sorry for blowing up at you."

I gave a shrug and told him it was no big deal. We'd locked antlers but in the end he backed off and was gracious. Since others in the law enforcement community would soon know about my discovery and would gauge Richards accordingly, I gave him credit for the apology.

I told him I'd be in touch and would let him know if anything new came up. The bright light had faded in his eyes. Now he looked only grim and tired. He probably saw the same things in me.

CHAPTER ———————

ELEVEN

T he next morning, I placed my first call to Ellen Brown, an environmental engineer who'd worked in the State Department of Environmental Protection for years. I'd teamed up with her during my tenure at the Attorney General's office.

Brown was at her desk when I called, and happy to talk. Until I brought up the Houghton tire pile.

"Hell, yes, I know something about the pile," she said. "There's nothing I want to talk about, though."

"Why not? I'm just looking for background stuff here. It won't go anywhere."

"Oh, it's nothing confidential—just embarrassing."

"Ellen, you remember plenty of stupid things I did working with you guys, I'm sure. I'm not interested in you, just the tire pile."

She sighed. "All right, I'll tell you the story. One day in April 1986, another engineer in the depart-

ment, Jim Barton, called to say he'd heard from a
Glassbury resident that trucks had gone into Jean
Houghton's tire pile late the night before. The
neighbor reported drums lying by the side of the
road near the tire pile. The caller was convinced
that there had been some midnight dumping.

"Jim got excited. He'd heard about the tire pile,
had suspicions about the place. When he heard
about the drums, he decided this was the time to go
after the operator. Jim called up a couple of our private consultants, some other department people,
and our lawyers, to make sure we did things right.
He asked me to come along as well.

"When we got there, the lawyers hadn't arrived,
but that didn't stop Jim. He wouldn't wait for a
lawyer or a court order. He said he had plenty to
talk to Houghton about and he wanted to make
sure there was no further dumping. He took off, I
followed, and next thing you know, we're banging
on the door to a trailer just by the gate at the tire
pile."

"What happened? She throw you off the property?" I asked.

"No. Jean Houghton came out. Jim told her
about the drums, asked for permission to go on
the property to see if there had been any dumping. Houghton said that nobody had been on the
property the night before, the gate had been
locked.

"Jim insisted that he had to do an inspection.
She told us we had no authority to go on her prop-

erty, but that she always liked to cooperate with government officials."

"I'll be damned. She let you on," I said.

"Hold it," Ellen said. "You going to let me tell the story or not?"

"Sorry."

"Jean Houghton looked at us—I'll never forget her smile. She said, 'Wait a minute, I'll unlock the gate,' and she went back into the trailer. Jim turned to me and said something about how Houghton knew we'd nailed her.

"Then Houghton came out with a rifle. Scared me shitless. Walked slowly over until she was about fifteen feet from the gate, and fired at the lock. Blew it open, walked over and opened the gate. Told us we were welcome to check out the tire pile. She went back into the trailer without saying a word."

"Wow, great move. She gives you what you want and scares the crap out of everybody so nobody wants to go back."

"You got it," she said. "No surprise, Jim and I were the only ones willing to go on the site. The others mumbled, stood around like sheep and said they'd wait for us. He looked around the site for all of ten minutes and pronounced everything okay. End of story. Found some rusty drums but no evidence of recent dumping."

"Did Jean Houghton have a permit for the gun?"

"Nah, didn't need one for a rifle back then, but the police knew about the gun. We checked it. That was a wild and crazy day. Happened a while ago, but I won't forget it."

"What did the local police tell you about her?"

"Said she's real tough, but everybody insisted she was honest and wouldn't dump chemicals at the site. She pumped a lot of money into the town, contributed to local charities, paid for renovation of the Little League field, stuff like that. Apparently, business people and town officials asked about dumping solid waste, construction debris, all sorts of crap at her place. She always turned them down, said it would be more trouble than it was worth."

"You ever follow up on the tire pile?"

"Yeah, we went back and tried to see if we could exercise jurisdiction over the pile as hazardous waste, but she came up with another angle. Turns out she sold some of the tires to towns or developers for artificial reefs, so the tires couldn't be classified as waste. Sometimes she contracted to build the reefs. We couldn't do anything, no jurisdiction. Whole thing was a mess."

"I've heard about these reefs. What are they for?"

"Some coastal towns, particularly in the southeast, put artificial reefs offshore. Brings in fishermen, scuba divers. Sometimes they scuttle ships, other times they create reefs."

"Yeah, but how do they use tires?"

"They ship the tires to the coast, then tie 'em together with steel cabling and cement blocks to weigh them down. Haul 'em offshore with barges and dump it all overboard."

"Why use tires?"

"Supposed to increase marine life. Vegetation grows on the tires, attracts small sea life, fish hang out in the holes. Small fish attract big fish, which attract people. And money."

"Sounds like a great system," I said.

"Yeah, except for when the cables snap, the concrete blocks break, and the tires scatter. That happens, the area is just trashed."

But I saw the beauty of it for Houghton. As Ellen Brown had discovered, for the regulatory agencies, the sale of the tires meant that the tire pile became something more than just a disposal site. Houghton did not have to sell tires for many reefs to claim that her tires were not just discarded, but resold as goods. Then, since the tire pile did not contaminate anything, the state and federal governments had a much tougher time regulating the business.

The artificial reef business was clever from another angle. Jean Houghton had already been paid by people wanting to get rid of their tires. A single tire wasn't worth much, but she'd accumulated millions of them. As a result, most of her expenses for a reef were in the transportation of the tires and the cabling. And she got paid a second time for used tires. Pure marketing genius.

I talked a little longer with Ellen about things in the department and promised to buy her dinner. She laughed and told me she was still waiting on about a dozen others I had promised over the years.

After the call, I had to appear in Middlesex Superior Court in Cambridge. Happily, the judge moved things quickly and I was finished before eleven A.M. Before leaving the courthouse, I called to check in with Jenny. She was engrossed in finishing a memorandum and didn't need me around. She told me about a couple of calls that needed answering, which I did from the pay phone, tying it up and earning me unpleasant stares from a couple of other attorneys who wanted to use the phone to do exactly what I was doing.

My last call was to Al Thompson to ask if I could come by. He told me he was going fishing again in the afternoon and I was welcome. I declined, requesting a rain check because I had too much to do, but we settled on lunch. I volunteered to bring sandwiches and a six-pack, which cheered him.

The only hard lead I had was a connection with the tire pile. I knew very little about the Houghton family, and before I could do much else I needed more background information. Richards, the D.A., and the state troopers would be all over the family. The Houghtons wouldn't want to talk to me, particularly if they'd discovered that I found the helmet. I had to start learning about them the hard way, from the outside. I wanted Thompson as my tutor.

CHAPTER ———

TWELVE

L unch started with Thompson opening a beer and asking a host of questions about my discovery of the helmet and my discussion with Richards. It was a half hour before I was able to steer the conversation around to the Houghton family.

Thompson, a natural storyteller, settled into a rhythm, sipping from his Harpoon Ale and taking bites from a sandwich. He clearly enjoyed talking about his past. He was good at it, and the story helped. It was a twist on an American classic—Jean Houghton, a female Horatio Alger. I relaxed and let him have his head.

Thompson and Jean Houghton, born Jean Bernay, had been in high school together in New Bedford, Massachusetts, graduating in 1942. Thompson went into the Navy as soon as he could and served in the Pacific on a submarine in World War II. He came back to the area immediately afterward.

In New Bedford, in the mid–1800s, families that owned whaling ships became rich. The Houghtons were one such family. They managed to hang on to their money and then made even more of it by investing in textile mills in the early twentieth century. By 1930 the textile industry had fled. Happily for the Houghtons, the money they made stayed behind.

"Randall Houghton was a businessman who shunned publicity and was active in the Episcopal Church," Thompson said. "Son of a bitch kept going to his office until the week he died at the age of eighty-seven." Al's story was taking him back to a place I couldn't see, but it was all there, in his head. "Jack Houghton was Randall's only child. Right from the start, he was the opposite of his dad. Favored flashy clothes, loud parties, and pretty girls. Avoided church like the plague and stayed out of his father's businesses."

"What did Jack do for a living?" I asked.

"Enlisted in the Army after high school, served at the end of World War Two. Never made it above private. Returned to New Bedford right after the war. Six months later, his father died, leaving a small fortune to Jack."

"Who spent it wisely?"

"Nope, not even close. Spent it on liquor, gambling, and ladies. He went off to Boston, Newport, New York. He gave extravagant parties, wildest in New Bedford. And married Jean."

"How'd he hook up with her?"

"Don't know. Maybe a party, maybe he knew her in school. She came from the other side of the tracks, my side actually. Daughter of a French-Canadian father and a Portuguese mother, both worked in the mills. She worked as a kid and stayed close to her family. But she had a wild streak of her own. Loved dancing and parties."

"Sounds like you had a soft spot for her back then. Maybe still do."

"Son, a lot of years ago I'd have denied that and popped you in the jaw, 'cause you'd have been right. Now," he said, and laughed, "I'm too old, seen too much to have any soft spots at all. But you pick things up, boy, I see that."

Thompson said that Jack and Jean both moved comfortably outside their own social strata; each was gregarious, charming, and easily able to attract a crowd of followers.

The Jean Bernay of Al Thompson's memory was a shade under five-six, a brunette with high cheeks, a turned-up nose, and long legs. Her smile was a small one; Thompson said her eyes told you whether she was happy or sad, angry or joyful. And she shocked the town when she married Jack in 1951. Thompson's eyes told me that the marriage hadn't made him happy.

"I don't know much about what went on between them in the 1950s, but Jack never changed much, far as I could tell," Al said. By this time, well into the story, Thompson had graduated to a second beer and was having fun.

"The Houghton family still had some money, so Jack and Jean bought a place here in Wettamesett on the water with a large stone pier where Jack kept a couple of boats. They also bought a couple of the larger, more prosperous gas stations in New Bedford. Jack was supposed to manage them since he liked working on cars.

"I don't know whether Jean actually believed he would work, but she was pretty sharp with finances and management. I always wondered whether she bought the businesses as protection for the future. Anyway, once the kids came along and the high times with Jean stopped, Jack partied less but gambled more. He pissed away a lot of the family's assets."

"You ever hear that Jean was involved in the gambling?" I asked.

"Nope. Never heard a bad word about her, except her judgment in marrying him was pretty crappy."

"What happened to him? I gather he's not around."

"In June 1969 he was on his cabin cruiser at the family's pier here in Wettamesett, about to head out on the bay. He started the engine and it blew, killing him and two of his gambling buddies, low-level scumbags from Fall River.

"I heard about it, went right over. Jean was there, standing nearby on the pier. She'd gone on board and hauled Sandy—their daughter—off the boat just before it went up. I guess Jack had left the house with Sandy and was planning to take her out on the water with his buddies. Jean and Sandy were watching when the boat went up."

"Sounds pretty awful all the way around," I said.

"When I talked with Jean afterward, she was shocked, but I could tell she wasn't wholly surprised. She'd been upset with Jack about taking Sandy on the boat with his gambling buddies, so the whole thing left her with loss, anger, guilt, you name it."

"Jean have any idea what happened on the boat?" I asked.

"I asked her. Said she didn't. But I always thought she suspected, as I did, that Jack cheated one too many gorillas in a poker game, or went into debt way over his head and got whacked.

"The girl, Sandy, I always wondered how the explosion and her father's death affected her. When I saw her that day, on the pier, she was white, holding herself, and rocking back and forth, crying."

"What happened with the two other guys?" I asked. "Ever find out why the boat exploded?"

"Nobody much cared about the other guys. The explosion and fire destroyed the boat and we never did find out what happened. Back then, boat explosions were more common. Either it was an accident or it was maggots killing cockroaches."

"You ever think Jean might have set it up? Given what he put her through, she'd have reason."

"Yeah, we all wondered. And even though I was

a friend, I put the question directly to her. She's the kind you could talk to straight. She denied it. She told me that if she'd wanted to kill him, she could have done it much more easily than that, without killing other people as well. Made sense to all of us, and we never found any evidence involving her."

"What happened to Jean after he died?"

"She still had the house in New Bedford, the Wettamesett property, and the gas stations. Jean sold the Wettamesett property immediately. For a while the gas stations were all she had. She ended up buying a couple more and never remarried."

"Where does the tire pile in Glassbury fit in?"

"Jean was always bright. Once she and the boys were running the gas stations, she realized people might pay her a little bit to take auto parts, tires, stuff like that off their hands. So she bought the land in Glassbury and a truck and they started carting stuff out there.

"After a few years, the business began to grow, particularly as dumps became more regulated and some closed down in the 1970s. Then she sold the gas stations and she and the boys just ran the tire pile. Turned into a mint, too. She moved from New Bedford to Glassbury and stayed there."

"Ever hear anything about the family being involved in drugs or any other organized crime?"

"Nope, and I don't believe Jean Houghton would have anything to do with it. She's a tough businesswoman, runs a rough business, but I've never heard of any funny stuff. She went through too much agony with Jack and worked damned hard to protect her family. There's no way she'd sell drugs, particularly to kids. Besides, she's sitting on more money than she'll ever need. Why take the risks involved in running drugs?

"Worst you can say about her, she was tight with a dollar. Grew up poor, and then Jack went through most of what they had. When she finally put her hands on cash, she didn't want to let go. I heard she didn't pay her boys or her employees much for a long time, could be tough on them. But I don't see her in the middle of either a drug deal or a hazardous waste disposal scheme."

"What do you know about her kids?"

"Hasn't been a picnic for her. Oldest boy was killed in Vietnam. The other two boys, George and Bob, each started local colleges and left pretty quick. Both ended up in the service for a while, though after Vietnam. George, the younger one, was booted out real quick, graduated to a motorcycle gang for a period. The boys both like their liquor and their cars. They each worked at other places, but ended up back in the family business. Still there, far as I know. They're not the brightest lights, and they like to gamble now and again, but they've worked harder than their father ever did, I'll give them that."

"How about the girl?" I asked.

"Sandy? Smartest of the bunch. Took after her mother, bright and stubborn. Also good-looking and a hellion in high school. I found her at plenty of the parties I broke up back then. Went down south to college. I heard a rumor that she almost got bounced out at the last moment due to some sort of scandal, but nobody in town knew anything about it and I never had the heart to ask Jean about it. Anyway, she graduated and then got some kind of joint degree, business and law, I think. Hasn't had much to do with the family, according to Jean.

"But if you're wondering if the kids are involved in this, seems unlikely. The boys probably don't like working for their mom, but hell, she's not going to live forever and the business will be theirs. And from the little I've heard, the girl's doing well. Doesn't make sense that any of them would be involved in running drugs or killing people. And I will say I'm pleased to call Jean Houghton a friend. She's done a lot for the town. I just don't see her involved in this killing."

Thompson's opinion counted for a lot. Nothing I knew linked Jean Houghton to the murder. But somebody had killed Aaron near her tire pile and, I was convinced, put the cocaine in the bike bag. Thompson and I talked a bit more, giving us time enough for another beer.

"So what are you in this for?" Thompson said, breaking a short lull in the conversation.

"Like I told you, the Hastingses asked me. I knew Aaron, and they figured I could help out, maybe get some information to help the police."

"Yeah, I buy that they asked, but seems to me you're pushing this pretty hard. What's in this for you? Why not stay home, let the pros do what they're supposed to do?"

"You worried I might find out something about Jean Houghton?" I asked.

He gave a little laugh. "Damn, son, you do like direct questions, don't you? Sure, I'd just as soon nothing bad happened to Jean, but I'm certain she's not involved in anything. The police are investigating the killing anyway, and if I'm wrong about Jean, so be it. No, I just listen to your questions, see all you're doing, and get a little curious about what kind of itch you're scratching. And maybe I'm a little nervous that if you rush in too fast, not careful enough, you may get your head handed to you."

I fiddled with an empty beer bottle as I thought about his question. "Maybe you're right, maybe I should drop it. I know I'm not a cop making my living doing this stuff. But I cared about Aaron and it hurt like hell when he was killed, more than I ever expected." I raised my head and faced Thompson. "You've been good to talk with me, and I appreciate the warning. All I can tell you is I've had a couple people close to me die, and I didn't do much for the ones left behind grieving. This time, I want to do what I can for Ann and Frank, for Aaron's girlfriend, his reputation. No more regrets later on about stuff I should have done."

Thompson held my gaze and then reached out, put his arm on my shoulder just for a moment before speaking. "You've lived through some pain, I see that. However you want to handle this thing, you're entitled. But be careful, and I'll only say one more thing about it. I've seen parents who lost kids, kids who lost their parents, husbands who lost their wives, you name it. Sometimes when one person dies, others die with them, even though they're still breathing. Maybe you lost somebody and you were like that, a zombie for a while. I understand, you got to honor the dead. But pay attention to the living, too."

"Yeah," I said. "Thanks."

We talked awhile longer, but in a few minutes his words stopped flowing and his eyes started wandering. I could tell the look. The fish were out there. Too many times before, he'd passed them up on beautiful afternoons to pull over speeding drivers, give lectures to elementary school kids on bicycle safety, or battle with town officials over whether the town could afford to buy a new cruiser. The least I could do was let him enjoy the afternoon.

I left Thompson not quite knowing where I was going. I needed time to think about what to do next—look into the Houghton family and the tire pile, go back over Aaron's actions and contacts, or learn more about the local drug trade. Probably I needed to do all three.

Before heading back to Boston, I took a quick detour to Tern Point to get a glimpse of Buzzards Bay. The last time I'd been there, I'd been looking for the helmet. This time I could just sit back and enjoy the view.

The entrance road to the park led me past a string of large, wooden homes on both sides. Those on the right had immaculate, large lawns sloping down to the water. Halfway down the road sat a boatyard with storage and launching facilities. Boats on iron stanchions and wooden supports were tucked into every available crevice of the boat-yard, in disorderly contrast to the neat, lovely and large properties all around it.

Not quite a peninsula, the park juts out on the northeastern shore of the harbor just before a string of sandy beaches to the east. To the right, the harbor still held a few boats on their moorings. To the left, the beaches were empty. Looking straight out, Buzzards Bay sparkled and I could see Cape Cod as well as the shadowy outline of Martha's Vineyard.

With Ann and Frank and their kids, I once saw a magnificent lunar eclipse from the park. The ocean was dead calm that night, like glass. As the eclipse progressed, the moon's reflection glittered clearly in the water. Everybody, even the kids, became quiet when the last silver sliver of the moon went dark. That quiet beauty had been a long time ago.

This afternoon, the wind blew briskly out of the southwest, kicking up small chop on the water. Two large sloops raised their sails to head out, and a number of open fishing boats motored out into Buzzards Bay. Al Thompson would follow shortly.

Most striking, half a dozen windsurfers zipped back and forth right in front of the park. Some sailed along at twenty to thirty miles per hour. The battened sails looked like neon leaves skittering across the water. The sailors all wore wet suits. A few, the really good ones, jumped off some of the bigger waves. Others practiced their jibes, turning quickly back and forth with the wind at their backs. A few more windsurfers had their rigs in the grassy interior of the park, getting ready to put their boards in the water.

I'd never been at Tern Point when the windsurfing community descended upon it. It looked like a group of aliens had arrived, bedecked in black and colored neoprene. The aliens walked down the ramp into the water with their boards and sails. Like magic, the wind picked them up out of the water, onto their boards, and they jitterbugged across the ocean surface. I thought of it as the kind of scene Aaron had loved to watch.

Though I'd never seen windsurfers there, the scene looked familiar. It took me a while to recall, but I realized that I'd seen some pictures of windsurfers at Tern Point on a wall in Aaron's room, maybe taken by Aaron on one of his bike rides. I wondered if I could recreate any other visions Aaron had, anything he might have seen that led to his death.

CHAPTER

THIRTEEN

M y first call at the office the next day came from Randy Blocker, my buddy in the Massachusetts State Police. He'd heard about my discovery of the helmet. He'd also heard that the police and the D.A.'s investigators, while working on the new leads, were embarrassed. He asked me to explain how I'd concluded that Aaron had been shot elsewhere and then moved. I gave him everything and waited for the lecture.

"Well, shit, I hate to say it, but you did a nice job tracking down that helmet. I just wish you went through the D.A. or police channels first."

"Come on, Randy, those guys weren't going to listen to me. Nobody wanted me around."

"Yeah, well, maybe you're right, but just be careful. You've opened up the whole investigation, and enough people know what you did so the bad guys might find out. And Richards and some others aren't too keen on you right now either."

"Randy, I appreciate it and I'll keep a low profile. I have to stay healthy. I plan to be beating your ass on the basketball court for a long time. Enough sentimental stuff. What's going on? You guys hearing about drug shipments in the area? Anything on the cocaine found on Aaron?"

"No, nothing new. Just the usual rumors about upcoming shipments. Nobody has come up with a motive for the murder, and most of the sleazeballs we know in the area wouldn't go this far."

"Anybody looking hard at the Houghtons?"

"You think we're all morons here? Sure, they've got people looking up every Houghton orifice, but I gather the mother was away the weekend of the murder and the boys have clammed up."

"What about the daughter?"

"Nobody's talked about her, and I didn't even know there was one, so I expect she's been cleared."

We talked awhile longer. I promised we'd play basketball again. I promised him I'd be in touch. I promised him I'd stay out of trouble. He knew from years on the basketball court that my shooting percentage was about one out of three.

As a start, I wanted more information about the Houghtons than the police might give me. Thompson had helped me but there were gaps he could not fill.

I'm not a fan of dusty records and microfiche or the meticulous, painstaking search for lessons about today in the printed entrails and numerical leavings of history. But maybe there were shards of the Houghtons' lives that, unearthed and refracted in the light of the present, would lead me closer to the killer. And my computer made the looking a lot easier.

Or it should have. First, the computer froze on me twice just after I got it started, and neither Jenny nor I could figure out why. It was an aging model to which I'd added memory, a larger internal hard drive, a modem, a scanner, and an external hard drive for backing up, along with software. I'd done the installations myself, which meant that I'd probably screwed some things up, so the computer occasionally went haywire for reasons I could never discover.

Finally Jenny and I got it going, but when I tried to go on-line to the legal and financial information service I subscribe to, the message on the screen kept telling me there was a delay in the signal so I couldn't get a hook-up. Live by technology, die by technology. I was about ready to offer the computer to Thompson for an anchor.

After fiddling for an hour with all the parts I could and using every trick I knew, I connected with the on-line service. That enabled me to track down data on Bob and George Houghton—social security numbers, phone numbers, vehicles they owned, and their addresses. Not only the addresses actually, but what they paid for the houses. I also obtained a commercial credit report on the business and a little about them individually. Checking through real estate records made clear that the boys owned expensive homes. In addition, Bob owned a couple of fancy cars, while George owned an expensive car and two expensive motorcycles. Nothing like a keyboard and a modem to intrude on an unsuspecting citizen's privacy.

Then I called a probation officer I'd dealt with on a number of cases. I'd given him tickets to a few Celtics games, so I called in the favor. He checked the state's criminal records for me. Nothing showed up for Bob. George had a couple of arrests and one conviction for disorderly conduct, but had done no jail time. All of the incidents were more than ten years old and were minor.

There was more to do to check up on the Houghton family, but the information I'd obtained gave me a start. I would have liked the personal credit reports on the two boys. Given their homes and vehicles, I wanted to see if they were over-extended and in need of a little cash, but legally I didn't have grounds for obtaining that information, so I let it go for the moment.

I also wanted to know more about Aaron and his life. The computer wouldn't help there. His professors and his friends were the only immediate sources I could come up with.

Before heading back down to Wettamesett and its environs, I made a few phone calls for clients. I worked out a settlement in one contract case and got into a heated argument with an insurance adjuster on another one.

At that point, Jenny walked into my office. For

the first time since she'd started with me, her eyes were listless.

"Mickey Rawlings decided to go with someone else as his agent. And the court denied the motion we filed in Cheryl Smith's case. Mickey was good about it, but I could tell that my being a woman made him nervous, as well as the fact that I don't have much business experience."

Wisely, I refrained from saying that I'd have had the same concerns if I'd been in Rawlings's spikes.

Instead I said, "Hey, Rawlings was just your first time at bat. Getting that first signed up is always the toughest. You knew it was a long shot, but you came close. And the motion, hell, it could have gone either way. It's still a strong case, it just means we'll need to put a little more work into it."

"I know you're right, it just feels bad."

"Just so you know, as far as I'm concerned, you're doing real good work. You've done well with the stuff I've given you. Just keep it up. And if you do, it'll be a problem for me, because I'll have to start looking for a secretary again."

"Thanks. I'll be okay once I've had a chance to mope." She looked at me a bit maliciously. "But I can't mope for long. With the billable hours you're putting in, you'll have trouble even paying me." Just what I needed, my employee telling me to work harder.

"You're probably right. But for now, what the hell, I'll buy you a good meal to cheer you up." That got a grin out of her.

We went up the street to the Black Goose Cafe, a slightly more upscale place than my usual lunchtime deli. I thought about ordering a beer, but looked at Jenny and decided against it. We talked some about the office, what we needed to do on certain cases, how to attract more business, some new software Jenny thought we could use. When she saw my concentration faltering, she switched the subject.

"You're still putting in a lot of time trying to find out what happened to Aaron Winters—didn't the police jump on the case when you gave them the helmet?"

"Well, they're active, as far as I can tell, but we've still heard nothing from their investigation, so I've just been doing research and background work, checking on some people and on some things near where the helmet was found."

"What will you do next?"

"Talk to more people, I guess. Maybe go back and meet further with Aaron's girlfriend, then get hold of some of his biking buddies, and his college friends and professors. I want to know if he mentioned seeing anything unusual, or talked about the area where I found the helmet."

"I'd be happy to help you." She'd volunteered before, and I'd just let it pass.

"I appreciate that, but I'm not sure what's going on, so it's easier for me to do things for myself."

"I understand, but there are some things that I could do quickly and maybe even better."

"Thanks, but—"

"For example, how much experience do you have chatting with teenage girls?"

"What do you mean?"

"From what you've told me, you didn't get much out of Aaron's girlfriend or her friends the first time. I can't imagine you'd have a lot more to talk about now."

"Yeah, well, I'll use my famous boyish charm."

"Tell you what. You stick with the professors. Let me have his girlfriend and his other friends. I guarantee better results than you'll get."

"Let me guess. You'll talk baseball and basketball, maybe discuss the salary structure for high draft picks in the NBA."

"Hey, pal, in case you haven't noticed, I'm a girl, too," Jenny said. I had noticed, I just hadn't let on. "I won't have trouble coming up with things to talk about. I listen to hip-hop, rap, you name it. I can talk clothes and makeup and guys. And I'm not far enough from adolescence to have forgotten just how miserable it can be." She smiled a bit too sweetly at me, and leaned forward, putting her hand on the table close to mine. "What would you talk about?"

I looked at her for a moment. Her smile invited me to involve her in the case, bringing her closer to me. Her hand would fit nicely in mine. And she was probably right about my prospects with Aaron's girlfriend. But I was still her boss, not her boyfriend, and I had no interest in using her in a murder investigation when I didn't know what I was doing myself. I moved my hand away and took a deep breath.

"This isn't your average civil case, where people are pissing on each other over money. Somebody killed Aaron, and whoever it is may not be enthusiastic about people tracking him down. I don't want you to get involved, maybe get hurt."

She pulled back from the table and the smile vanished. "I know what I'm doing. If I can help, I want to, that's all. Are you telling me this is too tough for a woman?"

One mark of a good trial lawyer is knowing when to end your cross-examination. "No, no, I just want to make sure you're, well . . ."

"Safe and protected," she finished my sentence.

"I guess."

"I've handled my ex-husband, as well as Wayne Sharman and plenty of other jerks, without your help. I appreciate you're looking out for me, but I'm pretty good at it myself."

"Yeah, you're right. Sorry."

"So I'll talk to Aaron's girlfriend next week."

"But you won't do anything else without talking to me," I said.

"That's fair," she replied, and the smile came back. "You know," she said, "I was only half joking before when I mentioned that you're not putting in a lot of hours in the office. It's your law firm, not mine, but you sure seem to like working on this investigation more than the straight legal stuff."

"What do you mean?"

"Well, you're more excited about it. You work harder at it than anything else."

Have to watch myself, I thought. I liked the fact that she'd figured out the office systems quickly. But it didn't make me happy that she was figuring me out just as fast. "It's only because I've got to move quickly to find anything useful. You wait too long on something like this, you lose evidence, connections. Don't worry, in a few days I'll be back full-time, telling you what to do, and you'll be looking back at these as the good old days."

She gave me a skeptical look. "Maybe," she said, "but I doubt it."

On Friday, I worked for a while then headed out to catch some of Aaron's college professors. Using records Ann had given me and a course catalogue, I tracked down most of his professors from the previous year.

The interviews got me nowhere. Aaron's biology professor liked him, since Aaron had an interest in marine biology, but knew nothing about his private life. Aaron's math and English professors thought of him as a good, quiet kid, undistinguished academically but also a solid-citizen type.

Professors and students spilled out of the campus buildings quickly as most classes finished at three P.M. The end of the school week charged everybody with an energy they'd probably not had since the weekend before.

The looks directed my way told me adults weren't welcome, and I had trouble deciphering the language anyway. Feeling like a stranger in a strange land, I left.

I spoke with Ann later that night. She'd spoken with Chief Richards. "He told me that Jean Houghton was out of town the weekend of the killing, with friends in the Berkshires," she said, "and the boys say they had nothing to do with it but don't have any alibis, other than that they were at home."

"Did he say anything about what they would do next?"

"He said they've got a search warrant, but the tire pile is so big, they haven't searched much of it. Basically, he said they have nothing on the Houghton family at this point."

"Ann, I know the uncertainty feels awful. Hang in there—we'll find out what happened."

"God, I want to believe you," she said.

CHAPTER ────────

FOURTEEN

Monday, I had to go to a meeting and then to court on a couple of long arguments on motions before I headed south. Afterward I called Jenny to tell her I probably would not get to the office. She was on another line, long-distance, and couldn't talk long, which suited my plans just fine.

Before heading out, I stopped at my house and changed out of my lawyer's uniform of dark suit, white shirt, black shoes, and conservative tie and into dark blue sweat pants, a blue canvas shirt over a T-shirt, running shoes, and a dark fleece jacket. My bike went on the back of the car, and a thermos with coffee, a flashlight, and a sandwich went into a small backpack.

By four-thirty in the afternoon I was on the road, and something over an hour later I was driving slowly along Route 107, looking for the path Aaron and I had taken to get to the tire pile. I passed it going south and then turned around. I parked the car in the rear of a convenience store parking lot about two miles north of the trail. After buying a large package of peanut M&Ms in the store, to top off the sandwich I'd eaten in the car, I unloaded the bike and shrugged on the backpack. I felt a bit naked biking without a helmet, but I was going only a short distance and the helmet was white—too visible later.

When I reached the path on my bike, I slowed down until I saw no cars in either direction and plunged into the woods. I walked the bike down the path until I reached the same clearing where I'd found Aaron's helmet, and left the bike there.

Before the tire pile became visible through the trees, I could hear machinery and voices. I stayed low and tried to walk quietly on the trail. At the end, I crawled under the same bushes where Aaron and I had lain and watched the activity at the tire pile. I settled in under the bushes to stake out the pile, see what was going on and who showed up.

Nobody did. Work stopped, people left, and nothing happened. At around ten P.M., tired, stiff, dirty, cold, and cranky, I reversed my trail, using a small flashlight, rode the bike to the convenience store lot where I'd left the car, and went straight home. I crashed on the living room sofa.

On Tuesday and Wednesday, I followed the same routine, only I was even more exhausted and cold by the end of each night. My surveillance was premised on the theory that there might be some illegal dumping going on, which Aaron had stumbled upon. Three nights of lying in the cold bushes left me no closer to proving the theory, but farther from good spirits.

Jenny could tell I was tired and frustrated. Wednesday afternoon, she came into my office.

"You okay?" she asked, sitting down in a chair across from my desk.

"Yeah," I said. "I'm fine. Why?"

"Other than that you're grumpy as a hungry bear, you missed about three places shaving, you've come in late every morning this week, and you've got bags that could hold groceries under your eyes, nothing. I'll repeat the question. Are you okay? That's all I want to know—if you're sick or something. I'm not trying to pry into your private life."

"I'm okay. I've just got some things I'm doing that are keeping me out late. I'm not sick, and I'll try to be a little pleasanter around here."

"It's okay, so long as there's nothing wrong. Just remember this when I'm a bear to you sometime down the road." She got up and walked to the door, turning back at the threshold. "But take care of yourself a little better, huh?"

I knew Jenny was right. My productivity at work had dropped even further. The only consolation was that the weather held, and I didn't have to put up with rain or really cold nights.

Thursday, I got to the pile at around five-thirty P.M. after parking behind the convenience store and biking to the trail. Another familiar walk, and I settled in for a long night.

Three dump trucks, battered and dusty, and a grimy black pickup sat around the perimeter. One dump truck was empty, one was full, and one truck had its bed elevated with tires pouring out of it. Three men worked with the tires as they came off the truck. The men threw tires back onto the pile when they bounded off or rolled away.

At another corner, near the tire chipper at the northeast border of the pile, an operator in a small bulldozer was pushing tires around. It looked like he was clearing tires from a rectangular area of dirt.

The tire chipper was not operating, but there were a couple of people working on it, perhaps trying to oil or repair it. After fiddling with it for a while, they hooked it up to the black pickup truck and moved it. The repositioned chipper, when it became operational, would slice and dice tires, spewing them out in small pieces onto the rectangular area being cleared by the bulldozer.

Activity continued at the site for about an hour. As the light faded, the black pickup and the larger, empty dump truck were driven over to where the bulldozer worked and their headlights were turned on over the area. From behind the tire pile to the east, one of the workers drove up with a medium-size digger with an arm and began digging out a pit. A couple of the workmen left the pile through the gate to the south, and the few men left gathered around the pit.

I circled around the pile in the woods and brush to get closer to the activity. I didn't recognize any of the workers, nor did I hear anything distinctly enough to figure out what was going on.

By seven P.M. the September sun was gone, taking with it the day's warmth. After another half an hour, two men came back with a case of beer and packages of snacks. A little cool outside for drinking, but something was keeping them there, so I stuck around. The men got louder as time passed, and two of them started to push each other around. The others jumped up and separated them before anybody did real damage.

I stayed under the bushes, rolling a bit now and again, but doing what I could to stay quiet. I stifled a couple of sneezes, and finally, despite my attempts to stay awake, I dozed off a bit after eight P.M., lying on my stomach with my head on my arms.

Sometime later the sound of a new, deep-rumbling engine startled me awake. For a moment nothing looked familiar. It was clear and cool, and there was a big, beautiful, full moon in the sky, but it was dark enough so I could move closer among the bushes and trees without being seen. The engine noises came from a dump truck driving through the unlocked south gate. It traveled slowly along the road on the tire pile perimeter, passed within ten feet of me and stopped near the pit and the chipper.

Two men got out. The taller one, in blue jeans, a dark jacket, and a baseball hat, emerged from the passenger side of the truck and immediately started ordering people around. I couldn't see facial features, but the men emerging from the truck had the height and builds of the Houghton brothers. They might not be killers, but I'd lay odds that they were about to illegally bury hazardous waste that they'd been paid to take.

In the moonlight, I counted seven men at the site. They stood around the pit area for about ten minutes, talking and gesticulating. Then one of them jumped into the pit, which looked about five feet deep, to shovel it out more. Another workman stepped up into the cab of the newly arrived truck and turned it around so it could dump into the pit. Metal clanged as he turned the truck and raised the truck bed for dumping, then I heard something going into the pit, though I saw nothing clearly. The volume of the dumping didn't sound great. After the noise stopped, the men shone flashlights into it and then checked out the truck. When they completed the inspection, they began covering the pit with dirt.

By then my illuminated watch face said it was after ten P.M. I knew all I had to know. Time to leave, while all the boys concentrated on the pit and the dump truck. Once they filled the pit with dirt, the tire chipper would cover the area with small pieces of rubber.

I shuffled back to the woods, found the trail and then the clearing where I'd stashed the bike. I couldn't see much along the trail, and after a few hundred feet I turned on a small flashlight I had brought along.

My legs had gone stiff from being cold and still

for so long, but I didn't much care. The tire pile had produced for me again. I didn't know who I'd seen, but I knew they weren't putting in a new swimming pool. Almost certainly, the pit now contained drums of waste chemicals that weren't supposed to be there. That pit I'd seen would hold only a small number of drums, but the boys could hide a bunch of similar pits on the periphery of the pile and still bury them easily.

It took me a good half hour to negotiate the trail back to the road, pushing my bike and lighting the way with the flashlight. I finally emerged onto an empty road. Clouds had moved in, covering the moon, so I rode back slowly and carefully.

At the convenience store, as usual, the lights were out. No need for twenty-four-hour stores out here. Curiously, parked near my Chevy Blazer on the far side of the parking lot in the back was a large truck that had a walled bed in back but no top. I was seeing trucks all over this part of the world, but I didn't see anybody in the vicinity or hear anything.

I wheeled the bike around to the back of my car and lifted it to place it on the bike rack. I heard the sound of running feet then, and turned to see two men come out of the darkness at my left, from the far side of the truck. I tried to pick the bike off the rack and throw it at them, but the bike caught on the arms of the rack.

I turned to face them. In the dark, I couldn't distinguish their faces, though I had no trouble recognizing their intentions. One came in close, and I threw a right hand that landed in his soft stomach. He gave out a whoosh, but something crashed over my left ear. Pain and streaks of light filled my head and I fell to the pavement.

I tried to get up, scrambling onto my knees and hands. The effort earned me kicks to my temple and chest. I scrabbled at the leg of one of my attackers and tried to punch another near the groin. But the one I punched stepped back, and the other one hit me with something hard and heavy. I fell back, hitting my head again. Last thing I thought was, should have worn the helmet.

CHAPTER ——————

FIFTEEN

A cold wind swirled around me, metal rattled as we bounced, and it was still dark when I awoke. It took me a few minutes to figure out where I was and find all of my limbs. No hangover I'd ever had compared with the pounding in my head; and my ribs, shoulder, and right knee didn't feel quite right.

Warm, sticky stuff ran down the left side of my face. The right side was dry, but when I brushed it, I could feel dirt. With some difficulty and considerable pain, I moved my arms and legs. I lay amidst dirt and rocks on the steel floor of a truck container bed going somewhere I didn't expect to enjoy.

I struggled up until I could move on all fours. I crabbed to my left to find the wall and tripped over something—my bicycle. The men had thrown me in with the bike, presumably planning to dispose of it with me and making no mistakes, as they had when they left Aaron's helmet in the woods. I guessed my car was still at the parking lot, but they could dump me and go back and move the car before the store reopened.

I had no idea how long the truck had been on the road, although it was moving relatively slowly. It wouldn't take long to get back to the tire pile, but I didn't want it as my tomb, if that was where we were headed. The truck slowed, lurched, and came to a stop, apparently at an intersection.

I stood up to see if I had any chance of jumping over the side. The top of the wall was beyond my reach and I couldn't jump high enough to grasp it, though it didn't look much more than eight feet high. Given the condition I was in, if I'd had a trampoline or a ladder, I might have made it over the top.

The truck rumbled off again, turning right and causing me to slide left. Sometime soon it would stop and not restart. Men would come around the back and lower the gate, looking to take me out. I didn't want to be there when they arrived.

Unfortunately, they hadn't left me either a ladder or a trampoline. I felt around more and still came up with only the bicycle. The front wheel had a quick release axle, so with a flip I freed the wheel, removed it from the front fork and put it aside. Next I found a rock on the floor of the truck and used it to bend slightly some of the spokes of the back wheel, creating a space just big enough to get my foot in.

I then stood up, leaning against the side of the wall as the truck moved again. Bracing myself against the wall, I pushed the bike up and placed the front fork, where the front wheel had been, over the top of the truck wall. The bike hung down, held by the fork, with the rear wheel on the inside and falling to a point somewhere between my shoulder and my waist.

The bike had become an expensive temporary ladder. My chances of escaping zoomed from none to ridiculous.

The next moves required the strength and skills of a rock climber and the suppleness of a dancer, neither of which I had at the best of times. Fear, adrenaline, and desperation provided some of what I lacked.

The truck slowed to another stop. I leaned back, braced on a strut on the side of the truck and swung the bike back toward me. Standing behind the rear wheel of the bike, I raised my left leg and placed it on the left side pedal, which hung down below the bike. I stood up a bit straighter and pulled on a strut closer to the bike, pulling myself up and jeopardizing a screaming hamstring.

Before the next move, I paused, trying to conserve my energy. My legs trembled and my arms hurt. With luck, I'd have one shot at the top.

I pushed myself up from the strut with my arm and used my left leg to pull myself up on the bike. As I bent my leg and pulled up, I lunged for the metal tube holding the seat. I grabbed it with my right hand, then my left, and pulled myself up.

I fumbled around until I was able to place my

right foot in the space I'd made in the spokes in the back wheel. From there, I balanced for a moment, then threw my right leg over the seat just as the truck started moving again, this time turning slowly to the left onto an empty, rural road.

As the truck turned, the bike started to swing. I'd never been on a bull. This felt pretty close, except I was going to slam into the side of a truck. With my left hand I grabbed the wall to keep the bike from whipping around toward the back. I held onto the wall as the truck went through the turn.

I leaned forward and grabbed the middle of the handlebars. With a kick, I pulled my left leg over the top of the truck wall. Then I moved my right leg on the left of the bike frame. To pull that off, I lowered my chest onto the handlebars to maintain balance. My rib cage joined the rest of me in bitter complaint, particularly when the truck hit a large pothole or bump and bounced.

And bounced again, causing the bike to swing wildly. My chances on the professional rodeo circuit plummeted; I lost my balance and couldn't hold on. As the bike swung away from the wall, I jumped back down, crashed my shoulder against the truck wall, and caught my breath. My shoulder hurt, and while I didn't detect any more damage to flesh, I didn't have the strength to climb back up.

Before it banged more, I pulled the bike down and sat with it on the floor, catching my breath. The truck moved on, and still I saw few lights overhead and heard only infrequent sounds.

After a few moments of rest I felt around and found the front wheel. Using feel instead of sight, I reattached it to the front fork. I also found a decent-size rock.

In a few more minutes the gears ground down and the truck slowed. I stood up and prepared.

The truck groaned to a stop. Two doors slammed and I heard footsteps. Rattling sounds came from the rear gate. The gate fell open, revealing only more darkness. I took a deep breath.

As I let it out, I mounted the left pedal of the bike and swung up onto the seat. I pedaled hard toward the left rear corner. Two or three strokes had me at the end of the truck.

I threw the rock in my right hand downward at the white face at the right corner and heard an "Ouch, goddamn it, shit" ring out. And I kicked another head on my left as I passed, striking as hard as I could.

Then I was in midair, sitting astride the bike. I stood up on the pedals as I landed and bounced wildly to my left. I didn't have a lot of speed, so I was able to spread out my left leg to keep from falling over. The back wheel felt funny, probably damaged because the spokes had already been weakened when I landed hard on the wheel.

The truck had parked on a dirt road in a forest, adjacent to a pond or lake which twinkled merrily at me. Fear, not merriment, drove my legs hard while I rapidly lost breath.

When I'd pedaled down the road a couple hundred yards, past a bend, I heard the truck engine start up. I immediately headed into the woods, away from the water and the road. I watched the truck rumble by from the trees, then I left the bike and kept going into the forest, in fear that the men would double back or that one of the men was walking behind the truck, waiting.

In the dark, I blundered into trees and tripped over roots. Finally, I stumbled over a large branch, fell to the ground, and lay there panting.

Gradually, the adrenaline dissipated. I curled into a ball on my left side, holding my chest. The shakes and dry heaves started almost immediately. The pain kept me from opening my eyes. For a time I saw and thought of nothing. My breath came in short bursts as I listened for voices or footsteps. I had pain from places on my body I hadn't heard from in years. The cold and black settled around me. Within a few minutes I passed out, or slept, or both, lying on the ground in a ball.

I awoke briefly two or three times in the dark, heard and saw nothing, and went back to sleep. When I finally awoke for good, the sun streaked through holes in the leafy canopy overhead. It was warmer than it had been the day before. For a while all I could do was open my eyes and stare at the leafy canopy and occasional holes to the sky.

Apart from a bird chirping, it was quiet. I was too confused and sore to do or think much at first, so right on cue, as I lay on the forest floor in the silence, I heard my sister's voice and the last conversation I'd had with her.

When I started college, Jacqueline came to visit on some weekends, and in my later years she came more often. In February of my senior year she called me on a Thursday night, just after her fifteenth birthday.

"Dan," she said, "it's Jacqueline."

"Hi, Jac, how's it going?"

"Okay," she said, code word, I knew, for life sucks. "I wondered if I could come to visit this weekend."

"Well, um, uh, this weekend's not so good, I've got some studying to do, gonna be in the library a lot—"

"You mean you've got a hot date and you don't want your little sister around in case you get lucky."

I laughed. "Where did a fifteen-year-old learn stuff like that?"

"Hanging around with you and your buddies."

"Yeah, I guess so. You pretty much nailed it. I'm sorry, I've got a couple of things planned with somebody. How about next weekend? I won't plan too much."

"Unless things go real well this weekend. But that's cool," she said. "If I'm around next weekend, I'll come."

"Okay, well, you have a good weekend."

"I wish. Love ya, Dan. I . . . ." There was silence for a moment.

"You okay, Jac?" I asked.

"Yeah, I'll talk to you soon."

On Sunday morning, long after my hot date had turned into a lukewarm short night, I called home. My mother answered.

"Hi, Mom. Can I please talk to Jacqueline?"

"Dan, we were just about to call," she said, in a hoarse voice I almost didn't recognize. "I'm afraid you can't talk to your sister. She's . . . Dan, Jacqueline's dead." And my mother started crying.

I gasped for breath and sat down. Nausea filled my stomach and I tasted bile rising in my throat.

"What? What do you mean? What happened?"

I heard only sobs from my mother, and my father took over the phone.

"She took an overdose of pills early this morning. She left Mom and I a note, and it looks like she left you a letter, too. Please come home as soon as you can."

I hung up the phone. I thought, if I'd just listened to her and gave her the one thing she asked for, if I'd just said yes when she asked to come for the weekend, this would never have happened. I lay on my bed crying for half an hour before I could move.

I'd kept the letter, the only thing I still had from my college years. The letter talked about life as a teenager, about the chasm between her and my parents, about friends lost, the lure of drugs, physical defects perceived, and thoughts she found unspeakable; about seeing me do things she never believed she could do, and about isolation, despair, and distance from others. There was no unusual event in her past to explain what happened—no sexual abuse, no traumatic event. But looking back, I now understood why Jacqueline, as a young teenager, took to going to the bathroom after meals, sometimes after snacks. Her eating disorder, which she hid from us and which we failed to recognize, didn't kill her, but was another symptom of her underlying distress. Like thousands of teenagers every year, she just couldn't find a way to accommodate herself to the world, whether because of biochemistry, neural wiring, surging and conflicting hormones, or the simple delicacy of her soul. And a part of me could never accommodate how I'd failed her.

Now the facts, the place, the time, and the people were different. But the result was the same, and another teenager had died needlessly. Lying on the ground, still confused, my thoughts intermingled the two, Jacqueline and Aaron, as if they were one. At one level I knew they weren't, but at another, there were no boundaries between the holes inside me where each had once lived.

Memory cells and powers of deduction kicked in gradually. I recognized a New England hardwood forest—oaks, maples, and birches. While I sorted things out, I stayed quiet to avoid anybody in the area who might be looking for me.

Birds sang and twittered over my head. A woodpecker hunted for his insect breakfast in a nearby tall tree stump. Crows squawked. A couple of chipmunks came out from behind a large rock, took one look, and went right back to their hiding place. The birds and chipmunks seemed fairly happy, so I figured nobody was rummaging around nearby.

I heard a brook running nearby and an occasional car or truck pass in the distance, though I could not see a road. While I needed to find civilization, I also needed to make myself more presentable. I had no idea where the bike was, and didn't want to take the time to find it. I still had my wallet in my pants. My clothes were dirty and torn in a couple of places. With some brushing, they might look no worse than awful.

Though I couldn't see it, I knew my face was dirty and bloody. Probably looked worse than the clothes.

I walked, or lurched, to the brook and took off my jacket and two shirts. After soaking the T-shirt in the brook, I rinsed my face and torso off as best I could. I wouldn't be allowed into court as a lawyer, but I'd had clients who hadn't looked much better.

Standing by a sparkling stream in the woods on a crystalline fall day in New England, bloodied and bruised, it was easy to reflect on the beauty of nature and the brutality of man. There were committed, hardworking murderers afoot in southeastern Massachusetts. The glorious fall morning unveiled eternal verities, not all of which involved love and the brotherhood of man.

I found my way to a paved road and walked

east, for no particular reason. I never saw the lake I'd seen the night before. For a while, each time I heard a car, I went into the woods. Within a half mile, houses and stores appeared and I stayed on the road, looking for some indication of where I was as well as a public phone. Moving slowly, I passed a series of modest wooden homes, mostly Cape style, with toys, lawn furniture, or small flower gardens on their front lawns. On a couple of houses the paint peeled badly, but the yards were all well-tended.

After I'd walked for more than a half hour without reaching a store or pay phone, I stopped and sat down to rest under the shade of a large maple tree. I was sweating heavily and I was thirsty.

The maple, bedecked with brilliant orange and red leaves, stood at the edge of a yard in front of a small, white cottage. As I sat back against the tree, pain radiated equally from all over. I closed my eyes, hoping to find something in the darkness to anesthetize the hurt.

I awoke with a start.

"Young man, are you all right?"

A short, stout, white-haired woman in a black woolen skirt, green cardigan, and heavy black walking shoes clutched her mail to her chest. She called to me from a distance of about thirty feet, near her mailbox.

"Yes, ma'am, I'm fine, I didn't mean to scare you. You have a beautiful tree here, and I needed a bit of a rest. I'll just head on toward town."

As I pushed myself upright, using the tree as a support, she took a few steps closer.

"Young man, I'm no nurse, but I'm not a fool, either. You're in terrible shape. I'm going to call the police and get you some water this instant."

"Ma'am, if you want to call the police, go ahead. I would appreciate it if you'd call a couple of people for me, though, to see if one of them would come down and pick me up." She approached slowly, cautious but showing quite a bit of spunk under the circumstances.

I eased myself back down against the tree. While she stood at a distance, I told her my name and asked her to call Frank Hastings at his hospital office and Jenny at my office. I also told her that the local police should check with Randy Blocker. She took it all in with equanimity.

"Young man, from what I see, nobody is going to pick you up unless it's in an ambulance. I'll call the police and make the calls you suggest, then I'll be right back."

I looked upward through bright orange and fire-engine-red leaves to a brilliant blue sky. It was pure, almost achingly bright, just how a movie would depict a perfect fall day in New England. Everything hurt, but I welcomed the pain. Last night I'd thought that my days of feeling anything were behind me.

I closed my eyes. Almost immediately I saw a bicycle race. I was somewhere in the pack, on Aaron's team, laboring to catch him. Aaron and a faceless rider were at the front. As they sprinted to the finishing tape, Aaron surged ahead of the rider without a face. Just before reaching the finish line, I saw him turn and look back, raising his arms in triumph. Then, two men wearing the same kind of shirt as the faceless rider jumped out of the crowd, knocked Aaron off the bike before he could reach the finish line, and carried him, screaming, into the crowd, which swallowed them all. As the faceless rider crossed the finish line, a horn went off announcing him as the winner. I jumped off my bike and frantically searched for Aaron in the middle of a crowd of other cyclists and spectators. All I found was his bike lying useless on the ground.

CHAPTER————

SIXTEEN

The horn, it turned out, was actually a monitor sounding from a hospital bed across the hall from where I lay. The other bed in my room was empty. The room was clean but spare, not even a small television or flowers.

Two women hurried into the room together, almost running. Each one called out for a nurse. Ann and Jenny looked at one another. Without a word, Jenny moved back and Ann stepped forward and put a hand on my forehead.

"Dan, we're so glad you're awake. You've been hurt pretty badly."

"This is where I'm supposed to say, 'You should see the other guy.' Instead, could one of you Florence Nightingales give me a glass of water while the other one tells me where I am?"

Ann turned to Jenny. "We should have known. He's okay if he can give orders and be sarcastic." She turned back to me. "Nothing from us until the nurse and doctor have checked you out."

I was saved from further discussion by a doctor who marched in and brusquely asked Ann and Jenny to leave. He looked over my charts, pointed a flashlight in my eyes, asked me a few questions, and poked, pulled, and prodded.

"Looks like a partially separated shoulder, a bruised rib, a sprained knee, some minor scalp cuts, and you probably had a mild concussion. No apparent internal injuries or permanent damage, but you need time to recover, and we need more time to monitor you, perhaps take further tests. I'll be in later." He proceeded to give a set of rapid-fire instructions to the nurse. She had a small smile as she listened. At the end of his speech he added a flat "So you'll be staying" and headed out without another word.

"Have a nice day," I called after him. Then I asked the nurse: "Do you mind telling me where I am and how I got here?"

Tobey Hospital is located in Wareham, a town next to Glassbury. All she could tell me was that the police had brought me in with sirens blaring and lights flashing, with only the information given to them by Mrs. Reid, the elderly resident of another adjacent town, Carver, who found me on her lawn.

When the ambulance had arrived at the hospital, I was unconscious. They examined me, put me on an intravenous, bandaged me, gave me some drugs, and left me in the emergency room until they could figure out what to do with me.

The nurse reported that Ann and Jenny had then each shown up separately. They made sure I was admitted to the hospital. The nurse left after adjusting the bandages on my chest and the sling on my shoulder.

Ann and Jenny resumed their places next to my bed, filling me in on the details of my rescue. Roberta Reid, an elderly widow, had wrapped a blanket around me and notified the police. Police EMTs picked me up and delivered me to the hospital. Reportedly, the police had checked with Randy as well, on Mrs. Reid's insistence.

Mrs. Reid had also done as I asked and called Frank's office. He was in surgery, but his secretary had taken the information from Mrs. Reid and called Ann. Mrs. Reid also called Jenny. Meanwhile, Ann and Jenny told me that the police had standing orders to be alerted so they could interview me when I was able. To their questions about how I ended up so battered, I responded that I'd been taken for an involuntary ride in the course of my investigation and that I'd give them details later. Both looked a bit ashen, and Jenny started to ask more. Ann, though, knew me better and reassured her that they'd get more from me in time.

Ann had also figured that if the there were no serious internal injuries, I would insist on going home. When I reported the doctor's findings and said that I wanted out, she acquiesced, probably knowing Frank would check me out anyway.

"After you talk to the police, I'll take you

home," she said. "Frank and Jenny will join us. If you can stay awake, we'll talk, if not, we'll load you up with painkillers and have a merry old time without you."

Before leaving, I had a brief visit with Carver's finest. Two of them came to get a statement from me. Happily, they had talked with Randy. When I could truthfully say that I didn't recognize the men who attacked me and had no idea why it had happened or where I'd been taken in Carver, they deduced there was no way for them to investigate. They left within half an hour.

The nurse walked in as I sat up from my bed.

"Thanks for the hospitality," I said. "I appreciate the help. Time to head home, so could you please take me off the IV?"

"You're not serious. You're badly hurt, and moving you could make things worse."

"Yeah, maybe you're right, but I'll be better off at home. Most of the damage just requires time to heal. Now, either you can remove the IV your way or I can do it mine."

She did it her way.

Ann promised the nurse that Frank would look at me later that night. After we weathered further remonstrations from the nurse and her supervisor, they finally gave me some more high-powered painkillers and washed their hands of me.

Ann and Jenny wheeled me to Ann's car. Buttressed by a crutch, a knee brace, and a sling, I shuffled out of the wheelchair into the front passenger seat. Ann released the seat so I could lie back. She and I talked for a few minutes as she drove. I suddenly remembered my own car, but she told me we'd take care of it later. Then I conked out. Only when the car stopped in my darkened driveway in Brookline did I awaken.

After another shuffling routine, and with more help from the ladies, I made it upstairs. Just climbing the stairs made my knee hurt. I walked into my bedroom and lay down on the bed for another short rest while Ann called Frank.

When I awoke, I was in my underwear under the covers of my bed. Sun darted through the window, hurting my eyes. I heard a voice talking on the phone. Things hurt, but not as bad as earlier. My knee worked a bit better and I was able to slip shorts on. A shirt stumped me, so I pulled on most of a bathrobe.

I walked out of my room to find Jenny on the phone in the living room. She waved at me, and I waited while she finished reassuring a client that I would be in touch shortly. The clock on the wall said four-thirty. I could only presume it was P.M., given the light outside and Jenny's presence.

"So what have I been up to?" I asked.

"Sleeping, since getting home from the hospital yesterday. You woke up a couple of times. Ann and I helped you to the bathroom and gave you some medicine. You were pretty groggy. Don't worry, we didn't take advantage of you."

"Have you been here all day?"

"Ann and I have been switching off. You probably don't remember, but we had a hearing in the Fernandes case. Somebody had to cover for you. And, by the way, we won."

"Nice job handling that."

"No need to thank me. The judge read your memo, gave the other lawyer a few minutes to spout off, then ruled in our favor from the bench without asking me a single question. Forget that, though. Are you feeling any better?"

"Better than what? I'm a bit livelier than roadkill raccoon, but I'll pass on a trip to the dance club tonight, if you don't mind."

"Will you ever give me a straight answer?"

"Maybe, if you ask the right question. In the meantime, while you're figuring out what that question is, I'm going to check the refrigerator."

"Whoa, cowboy. Before you move, I have a bunch of questions I have to ask about your condition to make sure we don't need to cart you off to another hospital."

Frank had obviously prepped her, and she went down a list of questions about my head, my vision, my chest, stomach, and limbs. When I gave her the answers, she said Frank would check me out later but I was okay for the moment.

"But stay there, I'll get something for you to eat," Jenny said. "The doctor from the hospital called, angry you left, and told me you'd better not move unless you absolutely have to. Ann and Frank gave me the same orders. We've stocked the refrigerator, so there's something there besides beer and ice cream. Ann and Frank will be coming over around six-thirty with dinner."

"Kind of a welcome home party."

"Yup. We have crackers, cheese, soup, fruit, cookies, and other stuff. What do you want now?"

"Granted I've been whacked on the head, but my memory is that I hired you to work in the office, not to be my nurse and nanny."

"I'm checking the office message system every half hour or so. I have some files here to work on. Believe me, I'm no nurse, but I've taken care of plenty of sports injuries similar to yours. Ann and I have both managed just fine. I won't charge any more for my therapeutic services, and the way I figure it, the more I do to get you back into the office, the less work I'll have to do."

I shut up and had some cheese and crackers. Beer wouldn't mix with my painkillers, so I went for ginger ale. Jenny wanted to hear what had happened, but she knew I would only have to tell the story again to the others at dinner, so we talked about how to retrieve my car and what work needed to be done.

I didn't have the stomach or head for legal papers. When Jenny went back to the phone and files, I went back to my bedroom and channel-surfed for a while, jumping from Brazilian beach volleyball to *Oprah*, MTV, and *Seinfeld* reruns.

Finally, I studied the insides of my eyelids some more.

Just after six-thirty P.M., Ann and Frank walked in carrying a pile of boxes of Chinese food. They conferred with Jenny for a few minutes. Frank took me into the bedroom and did a bit of his own questioning, poking and prying. He seemed satisfied with the diagnoses and care I'd received and the directions I'd been given.

While he examined me, Ann and Jenny put out the food. Finally, Frank asked me if I wanted to eat with them. "I don't know how this happened, but it looks to me like you're a lucky son of a bitch. You got beat up pretty good, but everything held up. The concussion symptoms seem to have passed. The knee and ribs will hurt for a while, the shoulder shouldn't take as long. Chinese food and ice cream might be better for you than anything I could prescribe."

Ann and Jenny seemed to have gotten to know one another in the hospital, but there was still a lot of small talk and good cheer at first. But good cheer turned to a more serious atmosphere as dinner progressed. All three started asking questions, until Frank told me just to start by telling them what happened. So I did, pausing a number of times when I got tired or, on occasion, when I had flashes of pain.

I described what I'd seen at the tire pile and all that I remembered of what happened to me. They made me repeat my description of the escape from the truck, since they didn't believe it.

Frank and Ann asked most of the questions. Jenny was mostly quiet. Finally, Ann and Frank insisted that I drop the case.

"We sure as hell don't want anything more happening to you, Dan," Frank said. "Something stinks there, but let the police have it. Ann and I have already talked about it. We'll fire you if we need to, we don't want any more violence, particularly against you."

"Sorry," I said. "You can fire me, but this has gotten too personal now. I'm on to something and I'm going to stick with it."

Frank didn't argue, but sat there looking down and drumming his fingers on the table. He finally spoke, without looking at me: "I don't like this at all. We never thought you'd get into anything this risky. Whatever's going on, you should get out before you're in over your head. I'm sorry we even asked you to investigate Aaron's death. It was a stupid idea and we should end it now, before any more damage is done."

Ann spoke next: "Dan, things have gone too far. You have to leave this to the police. You told us yourself that they'll do a good job. And getting yourself killed won't do a damned thing for Aaron or us."

"Ann," I said, "I understand you're upset, but I can't stop now. I'm not Sherlock Holmes, but I did come up with the helmet when the police didn't. This attack shows that there's something larger out there, something I think Aaron stumbled into by accident. I'll work with the police, but I want to continue as well. I can help figure this out, I know I can."

"How much of this is just your hurt, macho pride?" Ann asked. "I know you're embarrassed that somebody grabbed you and beat you up, and you want to get back at them." Unlike Frank, Ann looked right at me, her voice unyielding. "But that's not important, staying alive is. I'd forgotten just how stubborn and obnoxious you can be. Can't you leave it be? Jenny, you tell him. He won't listen to me."

There was silence for a moment. Jenny drew a breath and the others turned to look at her. I gazed through the window, not wanting this conversation to continue. Jenny spoke in a quiet, almost grave voice, looking not at us, but at her plate, or perhaps a reflection of herself. "No, I can't tell him that. We all have to draw our own lines in the sand, and I can't tell Dan where to draw his." I wondered if she was thinking about her ex-husband, Wayne Sharman, and all the other men she had to draw lines for over the years.

"Damn," Frank said, "I don't know what to think. It's true, Dan has found things the police didn't."

"Thanks for your words of comfort and support." I aimed at the jocular. Nobody laughed.

Frank turned to me and used a distinctly different tone of voice. "Wait a minute. I could go along with you, but only with conditions. You tell the police everything and cooperate with them. You work with them, rather than being some kind of Lone Ranger without a Tonto. And you don't do stupid or illegal things."

"Nice of you folks to let me make my own decisions," I said.

With that, Jenny jumped back in. "Don't you get it? You want to be a hero, fine, but these people care about you and are scared stiff that something's going to happen to you. They're trying to help you, and you're thumbing your nose at them like an eight-year-old kid. Maybe you've forgotten—you were attacked in the middle of nowhere just a couple of days ago and needed help from a little old lady. You're not quite the invulnerable superman you may think you are. Plus you were full of crap a minute ago when you said it's gotten personal because of the beating you took. This has been personal for you from the start. This isn't just a job for you—I don't know why, but it's like a cause or a crusade."

"Dan," Ann said, "haven't we had enough loss, enough pain?"

I paused for a moment, but couldn't make the words I'd said to Thompson come out in front of Ann, Frank, and Jenny, so I had to make do with what would. "I'm sorry, Ann, but this is important to me. I want to do whatever I can for Aaron, for you and Frank, even for Aaron's girlfriend, Sarah." I paused and took a deep breath. "You know there were times when you and Frank took care of me." They both nodded. "This is a time when, maybe, I can really help you, all of us, come to grips with what happened to Aaron."

Frank looked at Ann, who was fighting tears, her hands over her eyes. "Look," he said, "we'll talk about this later." Nobody disagreed.

Things quieted right down after that. There was a lull while we concentrated on our food and our roiled emotions.

Conversation slowly eased back to normal during the rest of dinner, although Ann remained subdued. There was a mixture of speculation on what the police were doing and what might be going on at the tire pile. The others cleared the table before dessert and coffee.

After a break in the conversation, Ann reached over, took my hand, and spoke up. "All right, I don't like it, but I got you started on this, so go ahead. It scares me, but I see it matters to you, and we all desperately want to know what happened to Aaron. But you have to be careful and promise not to take too many risks or be too stubborn."

Tension drained from the room. "Thanks, Ann. I'll be okay and I'll keep close contact with Randy Blocker and Richards. Last time I talked with Randy, the police hadn't done much to check out the tire pile, just a quick search of the trail area based on the discovery of the helmet. With what I saw the other night, they should have enough to get another warrant, do an extensive search of the area for more buried drums. It might not be related to the killing, but it's a start."

The doorbell rang.

Jenny stood up to get the door. "You'll have a chance to pass on the information sooner than you expected. Ann, you want to get the ice cream and pie?"

A minute later a familiar voice boomed through the front hall. "Anybody up for some hoops?"

Jenny showed up at the top of the stairs and smiled demurely at me. "Randy was one of your callers today while you were getting your beauty rest. I invited him for dessert."

"Thanks for the warning."

"Nice to see you looking so fit, buddy," Randy said. "And I told her not to warn you so you wouldn't head back to bed with some pansy complaint just to avoid me." Randy gave me a not-so-slight chuck on the shoulder. The one with the sling on it.

Greetings went around the table. Randy took about a quarter of the pie and a good portion of the ice cream. Jenny, Ann, and Frank pumped him about the investigation, but he didn't give away much. He said there wasn't much new and mostly he just wanted to have a few minutes with me.

After dessert, Frank said they would leave so Randy could do his job and I could get back to bed. Jenny volunteered to tackle the dishes, and Ann and Frank left, threatening to call me frequently.

"You stepped in it this time, buddy." Randy didn't waste any time.

I told him what happened. He asked a series of

good, detailed questions, tape-recording my story. He pushed me on whether I remembered anything that would identify the men doing the dumping, and whether I'd heard anything useful at the tire pile. Jenny joined us midway through, sitting quietly, but Randy didn't seem bothered by it.

When he was through with his questions, I asked him what he had that was new. "Not much," was the answer.

I gave a laugh. "I brought you the helmet, and now I give you a nice illegal dumping case at the tire pile. So the only thing you have is what I've handed you. That about right?"

Randy grumbled, then laughed. "Yeah, that's about it. I'll keep you informed, but damnit, be careful. We can't protect you and it's pretty obvious that somebody thinks you know something you shouldn't. We're looking at anybody we know in the area, drug dealers and whatever, and so far nothing's come up."

"Will you be able to investigate the whole tire pile based on what Dan saw?" Jenny asked.

"Yeah. I don't do the environmental enforcement stuff. I'll hand it over to the environmental strike force boys and girls, and I'm sure they'll turn the place upside down. Dan's right. It smells like some kind of an illegal dumping operation."

We talked for a few more minutes. Randy told us he would check in after the search of the tire pile. He knew better than to warn me off the case, but he did reiterate that I should, at the least, avoid the tire pile itself, check things through him and keep in contact with Richards.

Finally, Randy stood up to go. "By the way, they fix your jump shot while you were in the hospital?" he asked.

"Man, here I am a cripple and you have a heart of stone."

"Maybe," he said, "but I don't have rocks in my head like some people around here. Take care."

Randy left around nine-thirty. It felt much later to me. Jenny and I talked while she packed her briefcase and gym bag.

"Tomorrow I'll get out those letters," she said, referring to our earlier discussion about the office. "Then I'm going down to Southeastern Coastal to have a talk with Aaron's girlfriend Sarah."

"No, you shouldn't be doing that. Somebody's seriously pissed off about this investigation, you shouldn't get involved."

"Sorry, you lose. We agreed on this before, and I'm going. I'm not snooping around private property at midnight like you were, I'm just going to talk to a kid who's already talked to the police. Nobody's going to be interested in me. And you're in no shape to do anything but lie in bed."

"Jenny, I—"

"Party's over," she said, "after we get your medication and bandages squared away."

I sighed. "All right, I don't have the strength to argue with you. Promise to be careful and just stick with talking to Sarah?"

"Yes, and I'll keep my promise as long as you keep the one you made to Ann."

Before she left she gave me more pills to pop. I accepted them gladly. She checked and then changed some of my bandaging. She was cool and competent as she worked, but her fingers on my shoulder and chest still felt different than a nurse's. Not just different, better. Whether from the medication, exhaustion, or her fingers, I felt flushed and warm. Before I could analyze what was happening, my vision blurred and the lights went out.

CHAPTER ———

SEVENTEEN

I spent some time on the phone the next day with an investigator and an attorney from the Environmental Strike Force so they could put together affidavits to get warrants. I could hear them drooling by the time I finished with my story.

In the subsequent few days, the injuries did a lot of healing and I was able to do some work. I spent some time looking through two or three computer catalogues, fantasizing about new computers and printers for the office. But until I made progress sorting out my future, fantasies they'd remain.

Running was out of the question, so I could feel muscles atrophying by the hour. My downstairs neighbors, the Steiners, came up once, including Mike, who got upstairs with the help of his father and mother. Jessica romped through the house, we had a dinner together, and Mike had me tell the story of how I escaped about twenty times, with a different set of questions each time. For days afterward I looked for misplaced things in the house that had GOTCHA signs on them, placed there by Mike and his dad, but I didn't find anything amiss.

Finally, I managed to limp into Coolidge Corner to use a branch library and do some legal research. I put in some billable time, but more went into checking the Houghton family background.

I tracked down public reports of the environmental agencies. Using the computer data bases again, along with microfiche copies of old editions of the *New Bedford Standard Times* sent up by the New Bedford library, I also did some low-energy sleuthing on Jean Houghton.

Her background contained no hint of criminal activity. Al Thompson had been right. I found no evidence of illegal activity or serious environmental problems at the tire pile. Various inspections by state and local officials over the years unearthed nothing besides tires.

Jean had occasional tiffs with fire officials, who wanted the tires segregated into smaller piles or wanted alleys cut into the pile to allow access in the event of a fire. In most of those cases, though, it appeared she initially resisted but ultimately acceded to the requests. All in all, nothing I found indicated Jean would have engaged in either hazardous waste dumping or murder.

While the information on the boys also might not suggest homicidal instincts, their portraits were a little fuzzier. They believed the company had only a finite period of profitability. Jean had implied they didn't always agree with her methods or the compensation they received, and both men appeared to be financially leveraged to the hilt, perhaps beyond, with cars and houses. Maybe they wouldn't kill a teenager, but they might relish the extra cash obtained for dumping some illicit crap.

My bet was that the boys were diversifying Mom's business under her nose. They could pocket cash payments from companies eager to bury their chemicals and she would never know. Whether the boys' business ventures extended to killing Aaron and planting crack on him became the question before me.

About the daughter, Sandra, I learned little. From a series of hometown-girl-makes-good news clips and one interview in the local paper, I gleaned she had graduated from Jefferson University, a college in Virginia, and then the Wharton School of Business. Thereafter, she worked with a major Massachusetts computer company, Dynacomp, the one her mother had mentioned, before moving to New York. I found no reference to the scandal attached to her college career which Al Thompson had mentioned, so I made a note to follow up on it.

The usual parties checked in on a daily basis to make sure I was laying low. By the sixth day, I took off the chest and shoulder bandages to stop the itching. While the joints creaked, my knee moved better, and I went to the high school gym to work lightly on the stationary bike and to do some easy exercises. The knee hurt but did what it was supposed to do. On the way back I stopped at J.P. Licks and had an ice cream sundae, buttercrunch ice cream with butterscotch sauce and whipped cream, which made the knee pain disappear. By the time I got home in the afternoon, my mood was far better than it had been in days.

There was nothing of interest on television. With no more bright ideas about how to check on the other Houghtons, I decided to make some calls about the daughter. Nobody I reached in the administration of Jefferson University would talk to me about her, or they didn't know anything. My call to the local police went the same way.

I let it go for a day, until a shot in the dark occurred to me. I tracked down the student newspaper and placed a call one morning.

"Hello, this is the *Beacon* office," a young, chipper female said.

"Hi, I'm Dan Kardon, an attorney in Boston."

"Excellent," she said. "I'm Beth Woodward, and I'm prelaw. Did you graduate from here?"

"No, I'm looking for stories or information about a woman who graduated from there maybe fifteen years ago. Should I talk to you about it or somebody else? And what's your connection to the paper?"

"Well, I guess you'll have to talk to me," she said. "I'm the only one here. I'm the managing editor. I don't know if we'll have anything on somebody that old, but we can try to dig stuff up."

Old, I thought. "Thanks," I said.

"What's the woman's name?"

"Sandy or Sandra Houghton. She's—"

"Oh, everybody knows about her, she's a legend."

I settled back on the sofa and tried to get comfortable with the phone. "She is, huh? Tell me the story."

"The story is, she was really attractive. Her sophomore year, she started a bartending service that provided student bartenders, waiters, and waitresses to local people for parties and dinners. In her senior year she took a half a dozen or so of the best-looking girls and expanded the business. She set up an escort service, but the girls really worked as prostitutes. Supposedly she never worked any jobs herself. But she was pretty progressive about it."

"What do you mean?"

"Well, she didn't discriminate. She brought a couple of guys in so they'd be available for women. Word got around—there's some pretty rich people around here, the horse people. But one of the guys she used became angry, said he hadn't been paid properly for one of his jobs. So he charged her with an honors violation."

"What's an honors violation?" I asked.

"The university has an honor code. At the start of the first year of school, we all take a pledge that we won't lie, cheat, steal, or tolerate those who do. Only a student or a member of the faculty can accuse a student of violating the honor code. When a student is accused, an honors trial is held before a jury of students. A student judge presides and student prosecutors and defenders both prosecute and defend the student on trial."

"What happens if a student is convicted?"

"It's a single sanction system. If you're convicted, you're expelled."

"Wow, tough system. Hard to believe anything like that is still in place."

"It's worked for a long time. Some students bail out before being prosecuted and some go to trial, figuring a student jury will never convict on a minor offense. Most years, though, at least one student is expelled."

"But Sandy didn't get expelled?"

"Nope. A few weeks before she was supposed to graduate, she went on trial for violating the honors system by operating the escort service. The trial was closed to the public, but the whole school knew what was going on."

"What was her defense?" I asked.

"You gotta remember, I've only heard rumors and stories, but apparently she argued she hadn't violated the honor code since she never lied, cheated, or stole. She'd been honest with the students working as prostitutes and she paid 'em what they were owed. In the case of the guy who complained, she said that she hadn't been paid by the woman who hired him, and employees were supposed to be paid only when clients paid."

I laughed. "Either she had a good lawyer who gave her a slick defense, or she's pretty smart."

"It was clever but it wasn't true, people said. The student bartending service used university rooms, phone lines, and other stuff for a private business that was supposed to be only for student bartending. Technically, she was stealing from the school, but she became kind of a heroine."

"So the jury didn't convict her."

"Never got to the jury. The student judge ruled, after she testified, that there wasn't enough evidence of an honor code violation to go to the jury. So the case was dismissed. Story is, she got a standing ovation at graduation. She and a basketball star who stayed to graduate instead of turning pro are the only two students who've ever gotten standing O's here."

"Quite a tale," I said.

"Yeah, she was pretty cool. When people talk about honor code cases, that one always comes up."

I thanked Beth Woodward for her time. She asked if she could call me about Boston law schools sometime, and I gave her my number.

CHAPTER ————

EIGHTEEN

As I was getting ready to go to work the next morning, Ann came by to see me. She checked out my various injured appendages and grumped about the missing bandages and brace. She declared me mending but still on the injured reserve list.

Then I asked about her healing, and her face clouded over. "It's so hard, we miss him so much," she said. "And it's excruciating not to know why he died, if drugs were involved, how this could have happened. Explaining this to Linda and Greg has been awful. How do you make sense of it to kids who are twelve and nine? They know Aaron died and they miss him a lot, but they've also heard people talking about him using drugs. We've told them that drugs are bad, and the stories bother them." I had no bandages to place over her wounds. I could only listen.

We argued a bit over whether I should be going to work. She lost. I did take the banana chocolate chip muffins she offered, as well as a lift to my office.

Jenny was out when I arrived. It felt like months had passed since I'd last sat at my desk, not just nine or ten days. My mind worked sluggishly at the start. I could concentrate for no more than ten minutes at a time. Random images, fatigue, and occasional twinges and spasms pulled at the periphery of my consciousness.

After the first hour, I settled into a routine. Phone calls and short letters came more easily than turgid, lengthy legal documents. I stuck to the easy stuff and took some musing time at intervals. I was a model of inefficiency, but the work gave me a modest sense of accomplishment and normalcy. I had the muffins and a Coke for lunch, a minor reward for a few hours of effort. I talked with a few clients and told them merely that I'd been out because of illness.

Jenny was tied up meeting with a client. I'd hired her mostly to do the secretarial work, but at this point she was doing more legal work than I was, along with the office work. At the present pace, I'd have to turn the firm over to her in a month or two.

By three P.M. my spirits and energy had dissipated. I turned the phones over to the voice mail system, shut down the computer and copier, and threw out the lousy coffee I'd made for myself. Just before I walked out the door, Randy Blocker walked in.

"I called the house and you weren't in," he said. "Figured I'd stop here before going up to a meeting at the Attorney General's office, just in case you were fool enough to be working. Keep this up and I won't have the pleasure of whipping your butt on the court for a long, long time. Or maybe that's your plan, screw up your rehab so you can avoid any more humiliation at my hands."

"Randy, don't give yourself so much credit. The doctors assured me I'll be back better than ever. I plan to dunk over you by the end of the year."

"Man, that pain medicine's powerful. Only thing you ever dunked is a doughnut."

"Now you'll appreciate the miracle of modern medicine. With those fancy biotech drugs, a little physical therapy, and good-looking nurses, I'll be a new man. But you didn't come here to talk health care—what did you find at the tire pile?"

"We got some good stuff, but it may not help with the homicide," he said. "The Environmental Strike Force and some of the homicide investigators got a couple of new, broader warrants and went out to the site. Nobody was happy to see them. Apparently Jean Houghton wasn't there, but her boys and some of the workers were, and they became downright nasty. As soon as the search started, they called their lawyers.

"A couple of the environmental guys immediately identified the area where you'd seen the digging. It took time to remove enough of the chipped tires and then to dig out the pit, but they managed to do it while it was still light."

"What did they find?" I asked.

"Couple of guys jumped into those space suits to protect against chemical releases and they found some drums. The investigators closed the tire pile operation down when it looked like there were still more drums. They're analyzing the contents of the drums, but they're already pretty sure the drums hold some kind of toxic alphabet soup."

"That it?" I asked. "Just a few drums?"

"Naw. Next few days, they went back with more men and heavier equipment to do some serious digging. They pulled out a total of fifty drums from six different pits. Not a massive operation, but there's enough there that if the stuff in the drums is hazardous waste, people will be looking at jail time. Hurts to say it, but poking your nose where it didn't belong helped us."

"Again."

"Yeah, again," Randy said.

"Aw shucks, I'm just an honest, hardworking taxpayer trying to help out underpaid and unappreciated civil servants."

"Yeah, right, and I'm Michael Jordan."

"So what happens next?" I asked.

"They've questioned the men working on the site, and the Houghton boys have been taken for, shall we say, more extensive discussions. Since they're now investigating both the dumping and the murder, they'll talk to everybody at the site in connection with both investigations. Some of these folks, they'd already talked to after you found the helmet, but now they'll have much more to play with. So far, they haven't found out where the drums came from, or anything that ties the drums to the murder. When you talked to people, anybody know if Aaron ever talked about seeing any dumping there?"

"I've been wondering about that," I said. "Nobody's said he talked about dumping, but if he did show up at the wrong time, saw the dumping, and figured out something was wrong, maybe they discovered him, killed him, and planted the cocaine."

"I hear you," Randy said, "but there's a long way to go before we can prove any of that. We'll be checking it out, though."

We talked a bit longer, but Randy had little more hard information. Nothing tied the Houghtons, or anybody else, to the murder. And unless I found support for my speculations, illegal dumping at the site did not explain the drugs discovered on Aaron's bike. Randy said there had been no unusual drug sales reported in the area since, or around, the time of his death. None of the usual drug informants came up with anything, nor did the few dealers the police had arrested since the killing.

I tried out various theories on Randy. None impressed him. The answers might still be buried under the tire pile, but Jimmy Hoffa could be there and it still wouldn't be possible to dig the whole place up.

As the evidence accreted, we could only hope to narrow the field of candidates and put pressure on them to make more mistakes. Somebody goofed when they left Aaron's helmet, and again when they failed to knock me out of the picture. With more pressure from the law enforcement people, additional mistakes would happen.

As Randy was leaving I had a thought about how I could increase the pressure. The state investigators would look for the companies or individuals who had paid to dispose the drums at the pile, as well as inspecting the drums and their contents. The drums would yield nothing if they were simply reused by the dumping company, still labeled with the name of the original manufacturer. The drum contents might help more. A chemical analysis, for example, would show whether the drums came from an electroplating operation or a plastics manufacturing enterprise.

The investigators could then examine the records of the tire pile and determine from them which employees and customers were worth investigating. Even if no records on the illegal dumping were kept, the interviews and document review was likely to turn up somebody who would want to do a deal with the government. But the records might also help me.

"I expect you'll be looking at the records from the Houghton operation," I said.

Randy gave me a look. "You know, we do know how to investigate crime. You'd be surprised at how well we've done over the years without you."

I tried to be placating, without much apparent success. "All I want is to take a look at the records or summaries, if you've prepared them," I said. "Maybe something was brought to the site that we don't know about. Or maybe we can get a better idea of what Aaron saw if we know who was bringing materials to the site. I also think it might be worth tracking down the truck drivers who bring the loads in."

"Beat you on that one, pal. The strike force investigators are already doing that. On the records, I'll talk to the guy in charge about it, see about copies. Don't press your luck. You stay out of trouble, stay healthy, and we'll talk."

We shook hands and Randy took off, late for his meeting. I sat at my desk for a while, looking at the trees and the headstones in the Granary, the colonial burial ground outside my office in back. The light was dimming, along with my view of the Houghton family. A court might not convict them, but I'd seen them bury toxic chemicals illegally. I didn't believe that Aaron's murder, within a few yards of those drums, was coincidental.

Jean Houghton might still be a businesswoman of rectitude and honor, but her sons had chosen another path. If they had gone so far as to take Aaron's life, then all of Jean's efforts to turn her family's life around had gone for naught.

I sat, thinking through what I wanted to do, until a little after four-thirty. Again I was walking out of the door when Jenny walked in.

"What are you doing here?" she said. "You look terrible, like you're exhausted."

"Why, it's delightful to see you, too," I replied.

"Oh, stop it, I am glad to see you," she said. "I've been to see Aaron's girlfriend, went down after a meeting, so we have things to talk about. But you shouldn't have come to the office and you do look a mess. Why don't you head home, I'll do some things here, then I'll bring you something to eat."

"As long as it's barbecued ribs, I accept. And I'll pay."

"On the salary you're paying me, you're damn right you will."

I'd only gotten halfway through the first beer when the doorbell rang. Jenny walked in with a smile and an air of satisfaction. She had bumped into the Steiners, my downstairs neighbors, and gotten into a conversation with my young friend Mike. When she heard about his passion for sports, she told him about her own baseball background. He fell in love with her instantly and she promised to take him to a game at Fenway.

She entered with what looked like a seven-course meal. By the time Jenny had unpacked a large shopping bag, the pungent, sharp, sweet odor of barbecue filled the house. In addition to ribs, she opened packages of chicken, cole slaw, mashed potatoes, and corn bread.

The wafting odors ended any talk of work right away. Jenny, with her Tennessee heritage, was a barbecue fiend and had found one of my favorite places, the Blue Ribbon Barbecue in West Newton. The food she brought was great, but she swore hers was better. In trade for a vacation day to be named later, she agreed to prepare me some of her prized ribs. With the food in front of me and her promise, the mental and physical pains of earlier in the day disappeared.

Between ribs and chicken wings, I heard about her trip to the college. She had managed to track down Aaron's girlfriend, Sarah Burnham, with a minimum of fuss.

"Sarah told me that Aaron had been riding a lot," Jenny said, "building up to do some races. He'd been going on longer trips. One place he liked to go was Tern Point. He'd rest, have lunch, check out the windsurfers, some of whom he got to know."

"Did he talk to Sarah about the tire pile?" I asked.

"He didn't go there often, she said. Took him too much time to walk in and out, and he'd lose riding time. He took Sarah there once, but she got nervous so they left pretty quick. He told her he'd seen some weird things there, but never described them. She did say one interesting thing, though."

"What?"

"She and Aaron had a discussion early in the summer about drugs. She wanted to try pot. Aaron got mad, said he wouldn't touch it and he didn't want her to either. She agreed not to, I guess because he was so adamant. He said they didn't need it and it might hurt his cycling. And he walked out of a couple of parties when all the kids started smoking and snorting."

"Wish she'd told that to Richards," I said. "She know anything more about Aaron's plans on the day he was killed?"

"All she knew was that Aaron was planning a real long ride. She thought it was at least possible that he biked to both Tern Point and the tire pile."

I was silent for a moment, thinking about how much more Jenny learned from Sarah than I had. "How'd you get her to talk?" I asked.

"You wouldn't be interested," she said.

"Try me."

"It was sort of silly, girl stuff."

"What stuff?"

"Now, come on, I'm not going to tell you everything."

"Why not?"

"Are you annoyed?" she asked. "You are! You're annoyed that I got information you couldn't get."

"No, I'm not."

"Yes, you are, and I'm not saying another word until you admit it."

"All right, all right, you got me." She laughed, and I did too—sort of. "Nice job. What about Sarah's feeling that Aaron was pulling away from her? Did you talk to her about that?"

"Thought you'd never ask," she said. "I didn't push it with her, but Sarah did give me the name of a bike club Aaron had joined. I talked with a couple of people he'd biked with, two guys and one woman, all older, out of college.

"They had only good things to say about him, said he was a real promising rider. Turns out Aaron had developed a crush on the woman cyclist, started hanging around her a lot. She felt bad, guilty, knew he had a girlfriend, and she had no romantic interest in him. Just before he was killed, she talked with him, told him she was happy to be his friend but that he should stick with Sarah. She, the cyclist, felt Aaron understood, accepted it, and things would get back to normal."

"So adolescent hormones, not drugs or anything sinister, triggered Aaron's behavior with Sarah."

"Yup. Nobody who knows him believes he used drugs."

We didn't have much more hard information, but we had confirmation of his interest in wind-surfers and his disinterest in drugs. I'd have felt better, though, if we knew that the Houghton brothers were windsurfers who hung out at Tern Point.

As I had with Randy earlier in the day, I talked over the possibilities with Jenny. Investigating the Houghtons and the tire pile operation offered the most promise, but the Houghton boys would never talk to me. The obvious move was to contact tire pile employees, except that some would also be sus-pects in the illegal dumping. They wouldn't talk with me any more than the Houghtons would.

Jenny spoke up after a few moments of reflection. "So we look for ex-employees."

"We?"

She ignored me. "Just like I'm Wayne Sharman's ex-employee. If I knew he was connected to a crime, I'd want to nail the bastard."

"As best I recall, you want to nail the guy even if he hasn't committed a crime."

"Yeah, well you know what I mean."

At that point she started to put away the dishes and leftovers, dancing to Mary Chapin Carpenter as she did. From where I sat at the table, I watched her blond hair swing back and forth against her shoulders. She sang softly to the music and her hips moved to the beat. My hands started getting clammy; my head said it was time to send her home.

She saw me looking at her. I felt warm.

"You thought mountain girls can't dance? Or is it female lawyers? Come on, I'll show you. Only music better than this is good bluegrass."

She grabbed my hand to pull me up. Her hand felt firm and cool. Mine burned.

Jenny laughed as she boogied in the kitchen, pulling me along. She was a good dancer and would have made a great partner, except with her boss. The last time I'd danced with somebody from my office, we danced into her bedroom, and it was all downhill from there.

After a few halfhearted steps, I pointed at my

knee and said *"No mas,"* walking with an exaggerated limp back to the kitchen table. She finished the song by herself, a study in moving curves and lilting counterpoint harmony. I felt aches all over, particularly the inside parts that knew the knee felt okay.

When the CD stopped and the impromptu dancing ended, I told her I was fading fast and needed my beauty sleep. She took a quick, quizzical look at me and packed up her things. She shook my hand, a bit awkwardly, as she left. I thanked her and told her I'd see her in the office on Monday.

CHAPTER ─────

NINETEEN

Jenny's suggestion to look for an unhappy ex-employee was a good one. I wished I'd thought of it myself. At some point I'd go to the police to see if they'd compiled any lists of past and present employees, but there was a quicker way to contact unhappy former employees of the tire pile.

At eight o'clock a few nights later, country music played on the jukebox as I walked into a bar named Bill's. It stood by itself just outside the center of Wettamesett. On each side of the door there were small, rectangular windows displaying neon beer signs. One red sign had two letters missing in the lighted name, MILE instead of MILLER. The other blue sign also had two missing letters, MOON instead of MOLSON. For some, the bar probably did get them a mile from the moon.

Inside the bar, eight or ten green vinyl booths stood on the left along with a couple of tables at the end of the room, past the bar. Only a couple of people sat in any of the booths or at the tables. At each end of the bar televisions were suspended from the ceiling. One set had a football game on ESPN, while a James Bond movie played on the other. The fragrances of beer, pretzels, and cigarettes filled the air.

A bartender made some halfhearted swipes with a dirty cloth on the badly scarred bar. Three guys sat at the far end, all in blue jeans and sweatshirts. One had on a New England Patriots baseball hat. Each intermittently sucked on the neck of a beer bottle, no glasses needed. Each man stared at one television or the other, occasionally turning to talk briefly to his bar mates.

I'd dressed appropriately—blue jeans, Bruins sweatshirt, and denim jacket. I kicked myself for leaving behind my Portland Sea Dogs baseball hat, but at least I hadn't shaved.

The bartender had little hair and a sour look. I asked for a Rolling Rock and a bit of information. He came up with the bottle and stood there, elbow on the bar.

"Who are ya? Whaddya want?"

"I'm just looking for someone for a client from around here. I'm a lawyer, working on the case involving Aaron Winters, the college student who was murdered here a while back. He was a good kid, I knew him. I'd like to talk to any of the guys who used to work out at the Houghton tire pile, maybe equipment operators or truck drivers. I don't care so much about the guys working there now."

Silence followed for a bit, and the bartender went back to wiping the bar. Finally he looked up. "Look, I got a teenager myself. That kid's murder sucked," he said, "it pissed us all off. But I don't know what I can do for you. Nobody knows anything, okay? Guys I know worked the tire pile, but none of them would pull shit like that. Better push on, buddy. People come here to be left alone."

"Tell you what. Let me leave you my card. Anybody comes in who has worked there, if they're willing to talk to me for cash, just have them call me." I gave him a twenty-dollar bill with a business card and my home phone written on it, nodded and walked out.

I hit three more bars in Wettamesett and then four or five more in the neighboring towns. One place had a pool table. Two had corners set aside for bands. Otherwise, they all looked pretty much the same.

As the evening wore on, more people showed up and the smoke and noise picked up at each bar. The laughter and discussions had angles, edges, and points, nothing soft and light about any of it. Arguments over sports and politics and women all became more raucous as it got later.

At one place, a table full of boisterous women had most of the men in the bar eyeing them from other tables. It looked like the women had come from a sports event together—maybe a softball or soccer game, from their clothing—and were hoisting brews just as the men did.

The men in the bar regarded the women suspiciously. Maybe they didn't believe the women could laugh so much without them. Even the bartender commented on it to me. The women were the only ones I saw all night who really looked like they were having fun.

The bars were plain. Few windows, no ferns, no fancy tables and chairs or high-powered stereo systems. Damn little to distract the people of Wettamesett and Glassbury from their drinking.

My bar-hopping paid no immediate rewards. Besides the first bartender, two of the others clearly knew people who had worked at the site at some point. At the last place, the bartender's eyes gave it away. I could tell he was shielding somebody, but I couldn't pin down whoever he was protecting in the crowded, smoke-filled bar.

For my purposes, though, I'd done and heard enough. People still talked about the murder with anger. The killing undermined their sense of their town, their confidence in their neighbors, their notions of themselves, their hopes for their kids. Whatever else they felt about their hometown, they didn't want it to be a place of violence.

I stepped out of the foul, stale air and din of the last bar to a cool, silent, badly lit parking lot. The walkway led me to the right. After I took a couple of steps, a shadow came from behind the corner of the building. Then the lights went out altogether.

● ● ●

When I awoke, I was sitting in the driver's seat of my Chevy Blazer while a blue light flashed in my eyes. My car door was open and two Wettamesett police officers peered in at me. A few other people, presumably from the bar, stood in a clump nearby, watching.

"Sir," one asked, "are you all right?"

"Got a hell of a headache," I said, "but otherwise I seem to be okay."

"Then would you please step slowly out of the car, keeping your hands in front of you, then turn to face the car?"

"What's going on?"

"Just do as I say, please, don't give us any trouble."

The trouble came as I stepped out of the car. A small plastic bag filled with white powder fell out of my lap, onto the ground. Both cops noticed it, and one knelt down to take a closer look. "Looks like the real thing," he said to the other. Then they went ahead and frisked me. The only thing they found besides my wallet and some change was an 8 ½" x 11" piece of paper folded up in my shirt pocket. They took it out very carefully and unfolded it. We read it together in the beam of a flashlight. I'd never seen it before. The typewritten note said: DEAR SAM WATSON, LEAVE THINGS ALONE. HOPE YOU ENJOY HOW IT FEELS.

The cops then ran me through some tests to see if I was under the influence. I passed. Then one of them, the older one, asked me my name. I told

them, and they looked at each other. The older one
who asked the question said, "Oh, shit."

Another police car showed up and a cop
stepped out, took some pictures, and picked up the
plastic bag with a gloved hand. He opened it,
sniffed it, and put it in another bag. "Better read
him his rights and bring him in," he said to the two
who were already there, and then they motioned
him over for a chat out of my hearing. After confer-
ring for a while, they removed the keys from my
Blazer's ignition, locked up the car, and took me for
a ride to the Wettamesett police station. At three
A.M. on a Sunday morning they started to book me
for illegal possession of a controlled substance.

As soon as I'd been taken in the car, I started
protesting that I'd been framed. I kept it up at the
station. I asked to see Richards, but the officer on
duty, after hearing from me and talking to the cops
who brought me in, saw no reason to call his boss.
But because he knew who I was, he said I had two
choices. He could book me immediately and give
me a date for an arraignment in court, at which
point I could leave, or I could enjoy the hospitality
of the town jail through the early morning hours
and talk to Richards in the morning.

Richards came down around ten-thirty in the
morning. He didn't bother to say hello when he
walked into my cell, accompanied by the older,
lead cop from the night before.

"By all usual practices, Kardon, you should have been formally charged already," Richards said. "And I don't intend to treat you differently than anybody else. My officers would like to bring charges, and I'll back them up. Only reason they held off was because they know you've been involved in the Winters case."

"I'm not asking for special treatment, but I was set up." He didn't tell me to stop, so I kept going. I told them about my bar-hopping, and gave them the names of the bars so they could check them out. The cop with Richards confirmed the contents of the note in my pocket, so I told them about my earlier meeting with the Houghton boys, the only people in the world who knew me as Sam Watson. Richards's eyes narrowed and glinted, his face turned red, but he didn't say anything. I told them I suspected that somebody in one of the bars had called the Houghtons. The boys then decided on a little retribution—a bump on the head, dump me back in my own car, plant a little cocaine.

"You dust the plastic bag for fingerprints, dust the note, and I'll guarantee my prints don't show up. The lump on my head is real," and I pointed to it, "and if you check the note against a couple of old typewriters in the trailers at the Houghton tire pile, I'll bet the keys match the typing." I hoped, fervently, I was guessing right.

Finally, I took another flyer and asked if the police had received a call last night alerting them to a drug deal in the parking lot where I'd been found.

Richards didn't respond, but when I finished asking, the other cop turned to Richards with wide eyes, about to say something. Richards cut him off. On that point, at least, I scored.

Richards stood up, and the other guy followed. "We'll be back," he said as they walked out.

When Richards returned, he was alone. "You're a lucky man," he said, "but you're pushing things awful hard. My guys are fair, they want to do some investigating. We won't charge you now, but that doesn't mean a damn thing. We'll check on a couple of things, and if they turn out the wrong way, you'll get charged and we'll push the prosecution. Another tip for you, based on the games you played with the Houghtons without telling me. You do anything, anything at all, in my jurisdiction, which interferes with our investigation of the murder or the tire pile, I'll have you up on obstruction of justice charges. And just so you know, the Houghton boys have an alibi."

"What?"

He gave a sigh. "You'll hear about it soon enough. I want you out of this thing altogether, so I'll tell you some of what we've got. The boys gave us an alibi for the murder. About the dumping, they're not saying a word."

"I thought they weren't talking at all."

"They weren't, but I guess the prospect of a murder charge above and beyond a conviction for illegal dumping shook them up a bit. Now they're claiming they were running a little gambling operation on the night of the murder, at a renovated barn behind one of their homes."

"Seems pointless," I said. "There's plenty of legal gambling not too far from here."

"Well, they were running a high stakes poker game, complete with booze and some strippers for entertainment. High-class operation all the way."

"Good old American enterprise at its finest. But this is a small town. I'm surprised you hadn't heard about it before."

"So am I," he said, "but it was held in a real private setting. They had regular players who didn't want to screw up a good thing. They provided the facility, booze, entertainment, for a small group that included a couple of local officials, according to the Houghtons. They came up with people to corroborate their story."

"Sounds like you'll have some fun with these guys and their buddies," I said.

"Aw, shit, can't do much with it but embarrass some folks. But the Houghtons get something out of it. If their story holds up, they'll have plenty of people ready to swear that the Houghtons were the ones organizing and running the show. Of course, so far they still have no alibis for the night the hazardous waste was buried."

It wasn't what I wanted to hear, but even if true, the boys still might be tied in. Maybe somebody from the family was involved in selling drugs and had the killing done. I'd have to work with it. "From what I know of her, Mrs. Houghton won't be happy with her boys—except I suppose she'll be pleased they're avoiding the murder rap, at least for now."

"Yeah, she might chew their asses a bit," he said.

"So it looks like all the Houghtons are in the clear," I said.

"That's what we figure. Now we figure somebody tried to set them up, but more likely the kid met somebody there to buy some drugs. You and the Hastingses don't like that premise, but it's the simplest, the cleanest, and the only one we have right now." He looked right at me, and his face and voice hardened. "And now, for all I know, you were involved in the drug buy."

Richards's voice softened a bit. "I know you don't like to think about it, but you better start looking at Aaron and thinking about whether he wasn't in the middle of something that was too big for him. And you better hope our investigation on you comes up clean."

He stood up and opened the door. "Get out of here."

One of the cops gave me a ride to my car. Anger and fear kept me wide-awake on the ride home.

CHAPTER ———

TWENTY

It burned me, but I had to be prepared in case the Wettamesett police filed charges against me. On Monday, I pulled Jenny into my office and got her on the speaker phone while I called Randy Blocker. I laid out what happened and what I was thinking.

"Oh, Christ," Randy said.

"Will they really investigate?" Jenny asked.

"Normally, they wouldn't bother, they'd just prosecute," I said. "It's a chickenshit charge. Even if they win, which they'd probably do in district court, it'd be a first offense, and at worst I'd likely get some form of probation."

"What happens if they file charges?" Jenny asked.

"We go to district court for the arraignment, you plead not guilty for me, then we figure out what we have to do to get the charges dismissed."

"Yeah," Randy said, "but that wouldn't be your biggest problem."

"Don't I know it," I said. "There's a little matter of my license to practice, publicity, reputation, all that stuff."

"Not to mention the way this could screw up the Winters investigation, with some people wondering whether you were involved somehow," Randy said. "I'm sure the Wettamesett boys will look at it real close—they'll be desperate to avoid another mistake after you embarrassed them with the helmet. They won't bring charges against you unless they can sign, seal, and deliver on the conviction. The next few days, you'd better stay out of that town, keep your nose to the grindstone, and get down on your knees and pray. The longer it goes, I'd bet, the less likely they'll charge you."

"I know, it just pisses me off. Maybe the Houghtons have an alibi, maybe they don't, but this stunt sure as hell doesn't make them look any prettier from where I'm sitting."

"Yeah," Randy said, "I hear you, but if they were in the middle of a poker game and other people back 'em up, there's nothing you can do. Maybe they just saw a chance to retaliate for your little tour of their property. Now be a good boy, okay? And Jenny, don't let him off the damn leash."

She didn't. We even had lunches in the office every day. I did some billable work, stayed close to the office, and jumped whenever the phone rang. For the most part, I kept to myself. Ann called and I told her I had nothing new. Jenny inquired a number of times about how I was doing. Fine, I told her.

I was grateful when Friday came. I went home and headed out for a run. Mike Steiner was home, so I took him with me. He kept up a happy commentary on everything and everybody as we moved along. It was cool and dark, with couples, families, and small herds of students out on the streets.

It was the first decent run I'd had since the attack. The knee acted up, so I went slow and stopped well short of my regular distance, but it still felt great. To celebrate, for dinner I had a peanut butter and jelly sandwich and a pint of ice cream, although I skipped the beer. It did nothing for my cholesterol count or my waistline, but it improved my outlook immensely.

Just after midnight, when I'd switched from *Nightline* to ESPN for a late Friday night college football game—Arizona against Stanford—the phone rang. When I picked it up, there was nothing there.

It happened again, and then again.

The third time, I got mad. I had a phone service I rarely used. Press the right number code on the phone, and for half a buck—plus the toll charges, of course—my phone automatically called back the phone that just called me, even if I hadn't picked up the call. Perfect gimmick for moms who walk in from the supermarket just as their kids calling from college are hanging up the phone. I'd started using it when a guy whose case I refused to take kept making nuisance, hang-up calls to me. I used the service a few times, told him I knew what he was doing, and made clear I would take it to the police. He stopped.

This time, when the phone rang, a male voice answered: "Sea Oats Motel."

"I'm in Boston, I'm trying to reach somebody who's called from there a couple of times in the last few minutes."

"Yeah, the jerk keeps putting long distance calls through me and hanging up. I'll put you through."

"Who's doing—"

Before I finished the question, the phone rang again and someone else picked it up. First I heard a cough. Then a slurred, deep male voice I didn't recognize spoke.

"Hello?" he said.

"This is Dan Kardon in Boston," I said. "Have you been calling me?"

"You're Dan Kardon?"

"Yes."

"No shit," the slurred voice said, "I was just trying to call you." I shook my head and thought about hanging up. The guy was too far gone to even wonder how I'd gotten his number. There was a pause and heavy breathing on the other end. "But shit, man, they never told me they were going to kill anybody."

"You calling about Aaron Winters?" I wondered if my bar-hopping had paid off.

"I don't know, man. I'm in the middle of something heavy, they told me to get out of town, but I talked to them a while ago, and I don't know what the fuck is going on. Need somebody, maybe a lawyer. They told me you're a lawyer. Always hated those scumbags." I chose not to ask which "they" he hated. Words came out of him slowly, disjointedly. I could almost smell the booze through the phone.

"Look, I'll try to help you, but you've got to give me a little information. Just try to answer my questions. You with me?"

There was another silence and more heavy breathing, followed by a belch. "Yeah, man."

"What's your name?"

"Jeff Grizek," he said.

"How did you get my name?"

"Friend of mine works a bar in Glassbury. I call him regular, see if anything's happening. He gave me your name and number, said you're a lawyer. Said it was up to me if I wanted to talk. This thing's driving me crazy, so I called."

"What's your connection?" I asked. "Do you live up here or did you work for the Houghtons?"

"Hold on, I gotta piss." There was a loud crack as he dropped the phone on something. Silence, then I heard the toilet flush followed by a glass clinking. He was making room for another beer, I guessed, and a mere phone call wouldn't deter him.

"Sorry, man, but when you gotta go, you gotta go." A drunken philosopher, no less.

"Look, Mr. Grizek, or Jeff. I know you need help. You need money?"

A laugh close to a giggle came out of him. "No, fuckers gave me plenty of cash."

"All right, can you tell me how you're involved in this and where you are?"

The story came out with lots of digressions. "I worked in Wareham, near Glassbury. Drove trucks and heavy machinery, did other shit for a construction company. Did some special jobs, trucking jobs, for the lady, brought some crap down south a few times. Then I helped with this other thing, a nasty deal, and all of a sudden they gave me money, told me to rent a car and head down here." There was another pause. "Oh, man, I'm feeling pretty shitty. Might have to barf."

"Jeff, where are you?"

"Crappy little place, the Sea Oats Motel, in Avon on Hatteras. They told me to hole up somewhere. Man, I did. This place is the pits. You'll have to meet me. I need some help here. My car's fucked up, in the shop, can't get parts in this goddamned town."

"Why not call the police?" I asked.

"Hell, no, not till I know what's going on, get somebody on my side. Those guys'll chew me up and spit me out, I screw up. No police, not yet. I can always head out with the cash."

"All right, Jeff, I'll be there tomorrow night if I can," I said. "Otherwise, I'll call. You sit tight, don't move anywhere, and I'll be there as soon as possible. You understand?"

All I heard at first was an enormous groan. Then Grizek blurted "Oh, God, I'm sick" and belched. The phone clicked and the connection ended.

Where the run and the ice cream had put me close to a comfortable sleep, the phone call left me wide awake. First off, I hauled out my one expensive book, a beautiful National Geographic atlas. On occasion, when things get boring, I pull it out to try to remember all the places I've traveled to, as well as the places I still want to visit. Tonight, I had to find Avon, North Carolina. Not a foreign country and not on my list of top ten places to visit, but my next destination nonetheless.

For a few moments I thought about not going, calling the police in. But Grizek wanted me, otherwise he might bolt. And, if I was honest, I wanted to find another piece of the puzzle for myself, take another step to find whoever killed Aaron and now haunted his family and friends.

The map showed Avon sitting on the coast of North Carolina, on Cape Hatteras Island. It appeared that the closest major airport was in Norfolk, Virginia. From the map, it looked like I'd have to drive east through a bunch of small towns, past Albemarle Sound on the way to the Outer Banks and then head south. A long bridge led to Hatteras Island from the north, across Oregon Inlet. It would be a full day of travel to get there, between flying and driving.

I had a regular travel agent, but she wouldn't appreciate being contacted at home after midnight, so I called the airlines and stayed on hold for ten minutes. I finally got through to an agent who, with remarkable good humor for somebody working the late-night shift, booked me on a direct flight from Boston to Norfolk the next day. The earliest flight I could get a seat on left at noon. I had a hard time believing there wasn't an earlier flight. The agent listened politely to my frustration, and then listened even more politely when I learned it would cost over five hundred dollars for the round-trip flight.

After booking the flight down and a return flight on Monday, I called and arranged a rental car. I also took the precaution of writing up what little I knew and left it on my desk. Grizek hadn't given me much, but I wanted to preserve what little there was.

The next morning, I had to think about who to call about my plans. Randy would keep me home and send the cavalry down there. Ann and Frank would insist I call Randy immediately. Instead, I called Jenny and asked to drop by her apartment on the way to the airport. Given that she was still my employee, I thought maybe she'd give me at least a little deference and respect.

I packed a shoulder bag with a notebook, magazines, and books. My small point-and-shoot camera case was already in there, and I left it. If I didn't bring Grizek back, I'd at least get a picture of him in case it would help the police. I packed a second small bag with clothes and toiletries. If I'd had an Uzi, I would have taken it, but instead I packed my only weapon, a Swiss army knife. So long as I was attacked by an apple needing peeling or a fish needing gutting, I'd be safe.

I left in plenty of time to stop at Jenny's and still get to the airport. She greeted me with a smile in blue jeans and a Kansas City Royals baseball shirt, along with fresh corn bread she'd just pulled from the oven. I'd have thought more seriously about being an agent if ballplayers filled out their uniforms the way she did.

I told her about my phone call from Grizek. As usual, she listened intently, asking little until I finished the story and told her my plans. Then she looked down at the table and up at me, her smile long gone.

"I don't like this. Why not tell Randy, let him pick Grizek up?"

I tried to stay calm, but on a short night's sleep it was hard. "Oh, come on. Pick him up for what? He didn't tell me anything coherent or solid. All he said is that he did some work for Jean Houghton and then somebody gave him money to leave. He says he wants a lawyer—I can't represent him, I know that, but I can figure out what kind of trouble he's in, and fix him up with a lawyer down there."

"He also said something about somebody getting killed. There's no need for you to go to Hatteras," she said.

"I know, I know, but as my old friend, King Lear, said, 'Reason not the need.' Grizek may take off if he doesn't talk to somebody, and he said he won't talk to the police on his own. I found the helmet, I found the dumping when the police didn't—they're good, but not perfect."

"And you want to go, to nail the guys who jumped you," she said.

"Yeah, and I want to help Ann and Frank, and I want to find out what happened to Aaron. And I want to clear my name now. Anything wrong with any of that?" I asked in a rising voice.

"No, but there's also nothing wrong with backing off, letting somebody else do it. You've already done a hell of a lot, you don't need to do more to prove yourself." She looked at me and put her hand on my arm, a placating gesture. "But if you have to go, you've promised us you'll be careful, you won't follow in Aaron's footsteps. We just want you to come back in better shape than you did after your last foray to the tire pile."

I looked at her, felt the weight of her hand on my arm. "I'm sorry I got riled. Nobody has answers yet. I have to know I've done everything I can, for the family and myself, to find them. With Grizek, all I want to do is see what this guy knows, get him to a lawyer or the police. If we leave it to Randy to coordinate with the police down there, it may take too much time. It's a weekend and it's not as if this is a high priority for them. I want you to call Randy this afternoon and tell him what's going on. I don't want him thinking I'm tampering with the police investigation."

"You're doing just that, and Randy's going to think it."

I smiled at her. "I knew I hired a smart assistant. You're right. But by the time Randy and I talk, I'll have Grizek talking to somebody else about whatever he knows."

She gave me a worried look. "You don't have any idea of what you're walking into. It may be a trap."

"I don't think so. Grizek was pretty far gone last night, he couldn't have faked that. And whoever's behind this could have lured me into any number of ugly situations a lot closer to home."

She didn't look convinced, but she didn't argue the point. "Look, I'll go along with you partway. You gave me a chance as a lawyer, the least I can do is let you act out your own fantasy of Columbo or whatever. But I am going to call Randy and tell him everything you've told me and let him do what he wants."

"Fine." I got up to leave before she could change her mind.

Jenny gave me a big, final smile. "Of course, if Randy ends up throwing your ass in jail, remember to give me a call. I'll be happy to represent you, and I'll even give you a break on the legal fees."

"Aren't you a grateful employee." I trotted out my best John Wayne imitation. "Now, ma'am, if you'll excuse me, I've got some miles to put on my trusty steed. If I'm not back by Monday, just call in the cavalry."

"Not on your life, buster, this little woman back at the fort is calling the cavalry this afternoon, after you get your damned head start, and you'd better call or send a smoke signal back tonight, let me know what's going on. We like you better as John Wayne, not John Wayne Bobbitt." She reached out, grabbed my shoulder, pecked my cheek, and said, "But if you have to chase after this guy, make sure you nail the sucker."

CHAPTER ————

TWENTY-ONE

A slight bump in the air woke me near Norfolk. I read a magazine for a while, then reached into the shoulder bag to pull out the camera to see if it had film in it. The camera felt like a rock. When I opened the case, I discovered I was right. The case held a New Zealand adze, a small chisel-like tool hand-carved from greenstone jade. Stuck on the adze was a yellow sticky note which said GOTCHA—Mike Steiner and his dad had struck again. They must have substituted the adze for the camera when they'd visited while I was recuperating. I laughed and cursed at the same time.

The adze was shaped like a heavy, thick wedge with a sharp blade. Maoris, the indigenous people of New Zealand, used adzes for carving and cutting wood and plants and, on occasion, other Maoris, as well as the colonizing Europeans. This adze had been discovered on a sheep farm where I worked for a couple of months on the South Island of New

Zealand. When I left, the farm owners gave it to me. I'd smuggled it out of the country and carried it with me back to Boston.

I threw the adze back in my bag. While I missed the camera, on the brighter side, I was now fully prepared to go for a long hike in the New Zealand bush or to take on any enemies left over from the Stone Age.

On my way through the Norfolk airport, I passed pay phones and thought about calling Grizek. Fearing that now, sober and more rational, he would tell me not to show up, I decided against phoning. I could only hope he would still be there when I arrived.

At a car rental outlet, I grabbed a small Pontiac Sunbird and headed south. A highway runs most of the way, through a gauntlet of small towns. I went through Rocky Mount, Robersonville, Jamesville, and then Columbia, sitting on Albemarle Sound.

Just before reaching the coast, I passed over Roanoke Island, where a small band of colonists had completely disappeared a couple of hundred years before, a mystery that remains unexplained. I hoped Jeff Grizek hadn't followed their path.

The Cape Hatteras National Seashore consists of a thin string of sandy barrier islands stretching out into the Atlantic on North Carolina's northerly coast. On the map, it looks a bit like a breast; I was headed down to the nipple. To get there, I had to drive south down the main road and then take the long bridge to get to Hatteras Island. Avon sits in the middle.

Hatteras Island has long, clean beaches backed by large sand dunes and tall grasses waving in the breeze. Much of it is protected in a National Wildlife Refuge. Tourists to the area face an eye-popping menu of recreational activities. The open ocean and surf lie to the east, with the warm and shallow Pamlico Sound to the west. Great for swimming, surfing, windsurfing, and fishing. North, in the Nags Head section of the Outer Banks, there's hang-gliding and much more development. I'd spent two weeks in Nags Head one summer and done all of those things and more.

Admittedly, there are long stretches without much shade, and it gets brutal in the sun. It's also more than a little exposed to hurricanes. Some say a good hurricane would be welcome in the Nags Head section if it took some of man's handiwork with it—the T-shirt shops, schlock souvenir shops, theaters, miniature golf courses, bars, soft ice cream stands, beachfront condos and small cottages crammed in next to each other. All creations of entrepreneurs catering to people craving the wild, untrammeled ocean, so long as they have plenty of other amusements at hand. But still, there are the beautiful beaches, dunes, and marshes. Egrets fish the water's edge, and occasional stands of oak and cedar adjoin the road.

Upon reaching Nags Head, I still had some driving to do, but my empty stomach demanded attention. I stopped and grabbed some fish and chips while the waves crashed on the shore. The afternoon light faded slowly while I sat at a picnic table outside, the temperature around 80 degrees, with a slight wind off the water. I savored the smell of salt in the air. The ocean went from greenish to gray to cobalt as the sun fell behind me. Soon, out on the water, nothing was visible except a few pinpoints of light, bobbing and weaving, as fishing boats pulled their trawls and gathered in their silvery hauls.

I drove south, crossing the bridge with a steady but light flow of traffic. After a long stretch of nothing but beach, I reached a sign telling me I was entering Avon. I passed a few stores, but there was little of the commercial hustle of Nags Head. The attendant at a convenience store and gas station told me where to find the Sea Oats Motel. It was after seven P.M. and dark when I pulled up in the motel parking lot next to the blue neon office sign.

The lighting was weak and yellow around the motel, and it took a couple of minutes to discern the layout. The motel appeared to have three wooden buildings set back from the road, each containing about ten small units. Only about a third of the rooms had lights on and cars in front. Each room had a door and window, out of which hung old, rusting air conditioners. A small swimming pool sat in a courtyard between two of the buildings. From the debris on the surface of the pool, frogs would have enjoyed it more than people. The place lived up to Grizek's description of crappy.

Inside the office, the manager looked right at

home. Bulbous and bespectacled, he had long, thin, and frizzy brown hair and a red and green checked shirt that gapped hideously between the buttons. He sat at a small table behind the counter, eating what smelled like a tuna-fish sub in front of a small color television. From the sounds, professional wrestling was on.

It took a minute for the manager to turn his attention to me. When he did, he obviously begrudged the time away from Nasty Ned's epic confrontation with Boris the Brute.

"Wanna room?" His high, squeaky voice did nothing to enhance the first impression he made.

"No, just looking for one of your guests," I said, "a guy named Jeff Grizek. Can you tell me what room he's in?"

"Not supposed to give that kind of information out," he said. "Got to look at the book. Might not see his name, of course." A chiseler, to boot.

I pulled out a ten-dollar bill and put it on the counter. "This might help you read."

"Yup. Room 20, far end of the second building," he said.

"I thought you needed to look at the book."

He looked at me for a moment, grunted, and then turned back to the wrestling. I wanted an answer, just to be safe, so I pulled another ten dollars out of my wallet. It was the most expensive motel room I'd never rented.

"Did he check out recently? That why you know the room number?" I asked.

He stood, pulled up his pants, and grabbed the bill with a soft, flabby hand. He licked his lips as he put the bill into his wallet and sat down again, about a foot from the television screen. "Nah, he's still here. Some guy called for him about an hour ago and I put the call through. No big deal."

Maybe not to him, but something besides the tuna fish gave off an odor. I went back to the car and retrieved the pocketknife, but left the adze there. It was too heavy and clunky to be of any use.

I walked around to the back of the motel units first to do a bit of reconnaissance. It did me no good. Room 20 was an end unit. The one adjacent unit looked quiet and empty. Room 20 had a single small window on each wall, with light leaking out around the edges, but I couldn't see anything in the motel room itself. Skulking about, I heard the drone of the television but nothing else.

After walking back to the parking lot, I stood off to the side of the room. An old blue Chevrolet Camaro was parked to the right of the door to the unit, in front of the adjacent empty motel room. Grizek had said his car was in the shop. Nobody appeared to be in the unit next to 20. Between the Camaro and the call put through to Grizek, I guessed that Grizek had a visitor.

In case somebody was watching, I walked toward the road, around the office, and back to the Camaro by approaching on the other side of the parking lot. After crouching next to the Camaro, I pulled a pen out of my shirt pocket as well as a

scrap of paper from my wallet and jotted down the
Virginia license plate number on the car.

Next, I picked up a piece of two-by-four lying
next to the motel foundation and moved over adjacent to the door to room 20. With a deep breath, I
reached over with the lumber and banged on the
door.

"Who is it?" The voice answered over the background noise of the television, sounding like the
same wrestling match the manager had been watching.

"Dan Kardon from Boston."

"You the lawyer I talked to last night?" the
voice asked.

"Yeah. You're Jeff Grizek?" I replied.

"Yup, glad you came," he said. "Still feeling
poorly, but come on in. Sure can use your help."

The voice didn't sound strained, so I opened the
door slowly, ready to bail out. As I did, I also realized that the voice had a slight southern accent. The
voice on the phone the night before did not.

I heard something, maybe a movement, but saw
nothing ahead of me as the door swung. I slammed
my shoulder into the door, driving it back. I felt the
door hit hard and heard a groan. A gun went off,
then something clattered on the floor, out of my
sight.

As soon as I recovered my balance, I jumped
back out of the front door of the unit and dove
around the corner to the rear. I looked back around
the corner in time to see a skinny white male, about

five-nine with long stringy blond hair run out of the room. He jumped in the Camaro and the tires squealed as he took off in the night. The adrenaline rush subsided and I felt relief.

I stood up, brushed myself off, and walked into the unit. Somebody, presumably the real Jeff Grizek, lay on a bed at the end of the room, his hands bound by wire, a strip of cloth tied around his mouth, a bruise on his temple, his eyes closed and another wire wrapped around his throat. For a scene where so much violence had occurred, it looked remarkably normal. Wrestlers cavorted on television. A small suitcase sat on a bureau next to the door and a well-thumbed paperback lay on the nightstand next to the bed. Grizek looked almost quiet and contemplative, apart from the bruise and the angry red line around the throat.

The acid in my stomach gathered, but Aaron's death and all that followed had given me an edge and an anger that kept me going even as my legs shook. I walked over and took a quick look at Grizek. I detected no breathing and, feeling his left wrist, found no pulse.

A cursory look around the room revealed nothing more of interest. No pocket calendar, phone book, or wallet. Then the wrestling fan masquerading as a motel manager rushed in, out of breath.

"What the hell is going on here? Was that a gunshot? What are you—oh, oh . . ." He saw Grizek and his mouth stayed open, never finishing the sentence. Before saying another word, he put his hand over his mouth, walked outside, and I heard him throw up in the parking lot outside. I also heard the voices of other people asking him what was happening, so I went to the door, closed it most of the way and stood outside as others approached from around the motel.

It was still early on a Saturday night, so only a few people had been in their rooms. Two elderly couples in casual clothes, a couple of college-age women, and a young well-dressed black couple gathered in front of me, speaking to one another and to the office manager, who was still visibly sick and shaken.

I told them that there had been a shooting and that the gunman had taken off fast. I told them they should not enter the room. The young black man spoke up first, calmly and with presence, asking if I was okay and if I needed help. I thanked him, told him I was fine, but asked that someone call the police. I also asked that the group remain there until the police arrived, as the police might have questions for them.

I walked back in and saw a gun on the floor, behind the front door. I took a quick look in the bathroom, saw nothing, then walked back outside just as I heard a siren in the distance. I thanked the volunteer sentry, now reunited with his wife. Everybody turned to face the sounds of the siren. For no explicable reason, people talked softly, almost whispering to one another, as though they feared waking the dead man in room 20.

I looked out into the night, past the road to the sea, searching for the beauty I'd seen just an hour or two ago on the beach. Before the police arrived and my interrogation began, I pondered whether I could learn more from the scene.

Obviously the shooter had tied Grizek up, knocked him out, strangled him, and waited around to shoot me. Since he could have killed Grizek and escaped easily, he must have forced Grizek to talk and learned about his call to me. The shooter also took Grizek's wallet and anything else that might incriminate other people.

When Grizek called me, he said he'd just spoken with the people who sent him south. Perhaps Grizek was a great actor, but I'd bet dollars to doughnuts that his business associates had him leave Massachusetts so they could kill him a long way from Wettamesett. Presumably the gunman had orders to take out anybody associated with Grizek as well, so he waited for me. Or maybe the gunman had called his contacts after hearing about me from Grizek.

My contemplations ended with the arrival of a police car. Other sirens started up in the distance. A woman officer emerged, gun raised, and went right over to the manager, standing to the side.

"Darren, what's going on here? Someone called in a shooting. What happened?" the officer asked.

The manager's high voice quavered, and he didn't hold out for money from her as he had from me. "Guy inside has a wire around his throat, dead

I guess. I heard shots, came over, and found this guy inside." His finger pointed unerringly in my direction.

The police officer leveled her gun at me and walked over. She told me to raise my hands and patted me down, finding and confiscating the jackknife. She looked me over and put away her gun. She faced me squarely, up close, and I saw brown eyes and brown hair and a frown on what otherwise would have been a pretty, tanned face. She was about thirty years old and stood about five-five with broad shoulders, a narrow waist, muscular arms, and a confident air.

"You Dan Kardon?" she asked.

"Yes, officer. I believe a man named Jeff Grizek is inside, dead. I'll be happy to cooperate," I said.

"Yes sir, I bet you will. I'm Officer Andrews and I'm in control here until you hear otherwise. I'm putting these cuffs on you until I can figure out what happened. Stay here." She handcuffed me, turned back toward the group and spoke louder. "Now I'm going to take a quick look inside. I don't want anybody touching anything or going anywhere. As soon as I get back out, I'm calling in. You're all going to stick around here and give statements to the police and investigators who will be arriving."

Within two minutes she was back and another police car had arrived. Office Andrews went to her radio and called in for more help. She pulled a clipboard out of her car and then addressed the group while the male patrolman who had arrived planted himself at the door of the motel room.

"I'd like to get your names, home addresses, car license numbers, and room numbers right now. As soon as you give me that information, you can go back to your rooms. Either a police officer or an investigator from the county prosecutor's office will visit each of you shortly to get statements. After that, the officer or investigator will tell you you're free to go. I'm sorry for the inconvenience, but most of you will be free to leave within an hour or two.

"Darren, you can go back to the office, but don't leave until I say so, and you'd better call Ed and tell him about this mess. He squawks about us hurting business at his precious motel, have him speak to me. Mr. Kardon, you're staying by this car until the investigators or county prosecutor gets here."

"One thing, Officer," I said.

"What?"

"I've got the license number of the Chevy Camaro the killer was driving," I said, and gave her the number.

"What color and year was the car?"

"Blue, and old, an eighties model."

She called in the information on the car. With that, everybody gave her the information she wanted and then moved slowly off. I thanked the young couple who had helped out. They wanted to talk to me to find out what was going on, but in the presence of Andrews and with me in cuffs, they weren't asking and I wouldn't have told anyway.

I sat on the hood of the police cruiser while Andrews walked around the unit. As she came back I heard another siren in the distance.

A second cruiser came up, followed closely by a late model Ford Taurus sedan. Two police officers emerged from the cruiser and a tall, lanky, balding man in khakis and a University of North Carolina sweatshirt came out of the Ford. They all converged with Andrews and talked out of my earshot. Periodically Andrews pointed to the room or to me. The guy in the Carolina sweatshirt appeared to be in charge. When Andrews had finished talking, he started in and seemed to be handing out assignments. After about five minutes, the discussion ended.

One policeman went to his cruiser and made a call. Once he was done, he came and stood by me. The plainclothes guy went off in the direction of the office with the third officer, I assumed to chat with Darren, the wrestling fan. Andrews headed in my direction. First, she opened her car door and pulled out a battered Nikon F4 camera with a large flash attached to the camera body by a cord. Inside, I saw flashes go off through the windows as she took pictures. When she came out, she walked over to me.

"You got an ID?" she asked.

"In my wallet," I said.

"Where is it?" she asked.

I told her, and she fished it out of my back pocket. She looked through it and seemed satisfied.

"Come with me," she said. I tagged along as she took pictures of the front door and the parking lot. Then she went around to the back of the unit. She took photos of the back and side of the motel.

When she was done, we walked back to her cruiser. She began talking to me, with a little less of the formality that marked our introduction.

"You're going to give us the details in a bit," she said, "but give me a summary of what happened here."

I did, telling her what happened at the room and leaving out the background. When I finished, she stopped taking pictures and looked at me quite intently for a moment.

"You walked into this thing armed with a piece of lumber and a pocket knife, without telling the police?"

"Put that way, it sounds sort of dumb," I said.

"Not sort of," she said. "I was on the phone about three hours ago with a guy from the State Police in Massachusetts, Randy Blocker. He asked me to check on Grizek and to keep track of you. Told me you're one of the good guys but you stick your nose into places where you aren't wanted. He said you're about one beer shy of a six-pack when it comes to common sense. He also said you're large and ugly. So far, except for the latter, I'd say he's pretty much on target."

Officer Andrews did not fit the stereotype of a southern belle. And where was the famous southern hospitality I'd heard so much about? I tried to change the subject. "So what happened with Grizek? Did you check him out?"

"It's a small town, only a few of us on duty with a lot of ground to cover on a Saturday night. I had a couple minor emergencies and planned to get over here later. Blocker didn't say that either you or Grizek were in immediate danger."

"He didn't know. Neither did I," I said.

"That I don't believe," she said and shook her head. "Blocker gave me some of the background. I gather you're chasing some really nasty perpetrators. The guy who killed Grizek was obviously waiting around for you. From what I hear, this is the second time they've tried to take you out."

"Yeah. Sons of bitches are starting to get on my nerves." I gave her my best Clint Eastwood smile. Inside I felt more like Miss Piggy.

Andrews smiled back. "Sounds like a line from an old spaghetti western. You couldn't possibly be dumb enough not to be scared."

"No, I'm not that dumb," I said. "These guys have my full attention, not to mention my stomach in an uproar. I never thought I was walking into anything dangerous down here, so yeah, I'm concerned."

"Well, we'll need to talk with you about this mess, but as soon as we get back to the station you probably ought to call Blocker. He won't be happy about this, but he'll be glad you're okay."

"Thanks. And one question, if you don't mind."

"What is it?"

"Why are you taking the photos here? Don't you have people from a crime lab do that?"

"What's the matter, don't think a girl can handle a big camera like this?" I started to protest but she cut me off. "I know, it's just you've been in the big city too long, Kardon. We have a small force, but still have to get things done fast. I'm a good photographer, I sell some pictures on the side. I do the photos for most of the jobs around here, not that we get many homicides. Haven't had a murder for years. This way, I get the department to buy some of my film and darkroom supplies." She pointed the camera at me. "Smile." Her last photo captured me in front of room 20 with something less than a grin. That picture wouldn't bring her many sales.

At that point another cop and the guy in khakis showed up. Andrews introduced the plainclothes man to me as Assistant County Prosecutor Jay Wendell Greenwood, III. He shook my hand and told me to call him Jay. He told a couple of the cops to keep the unit secure until more investigators showed up, then took me back to the station with Andrews.

On the way I worried about how I'd be treated, an outsider in a small southern town. Visions of jail cells started me sweating. But inside the police station, the first thing Greenwood did was take the cuffs off me, and I immediately breathed more easily.

It was only 8:45 P.M. when we arrived. The police station was a small, single-story building of concrete, sparsely furnished. The dispatcher was alone in the building while phones were ringing off the hook. She waved us over as soon as we walked in.

"The chief's on his way in. People are calling wanting to know what happened at the motel. Lots of rumors about a drug raid, and a couple of the local reporters have called. What should I do?"

Greenwood stepped into the breach. "Doris, tell anybody from the outside that there was a shooting and a police investigation is under way. As soon as we have information, we'll pass it on, probably tomorrow morning. Anybody else, from the force or from my office, tell them to get in here, we need help. And Doris, see if you can scrounge up some coffee and cookies or something. Officer Andrews, Mr. Kardon, and I are going to meet for a while in the back."

Doris looked gratified and bustled back to the phones with new purpose and resolve. Her first call, as we walked back, was to the Blue Water Diner, where she bartered a delivery of coffee, pecan pie, and cookies in exchange for an exclusive the next day.

Greenwood, assisted by Andrews, was good. First off, he told me that the only thing keeping me from being a prime suspect in the shooting was the phone call from Blocker and the fact that Darren had indicated that somebody called earlier to ask about Grizek. Nobody else had seen the gunman or taken notice of his car.

From then on Greenwood carefully and thoroughly ran me through my paces. He started with my contacts with Grizek and went through all my movements and activities since then. I gave them a description of what happened at the motel and my glimpse of the gunman.

Once we went through the Carolina story, Greenwood wanted the background, which I gave him. Most of it, anyway. All of that, with numerous digressions and repetitions, took over an hour. At that point Greenwood told me to take a break.

I took the opportunity to call Randy at his house. Before I could get a word in, he dressed me down for having gone off without contacting him. Then, of course, he got really excited when I told him the latest developments. I didn't want an extended discussion with him, since I could predict most of what he would say. We agreed to talk the next day, when I knew more of what the police in North Carolina were thinking. Greenwood also talked with Randy for a brief interval.

After he hung up, Greenwood turned to me. "We found the Camaro, abandoned in a parking area near a restaurant."

"But not the driver?"

"Yeah, he's gone. Wouldn't surprise me if he stole another car and took off. No reports of cars stolen yet, but it's Saturday night, so if he took one, might not be discovered until later tonight or even tomorrow."

"Makes it much easier for him to get off the island."

"Yeah," he said, and walked away.

Since I'd promised her that morning, I phoned Jenny. I didn't tell her about the attack, but said I was tied up and couldn't say much. She wanted to talk, sensing something amiss, and made me promise to call later. It occurred to me at that point that I didn't have a clue where I'd be staying.

When we returned to the questioning, Greenwood told me that one of the local police was on the phone with Virginia police tracking down the owner of the Camaro through the license plate number. He then took me back again through my story, focusing on the events of the last couple of days. He wanted to nail down details, to ask a few more questions, and to give me a chance to remember additional material.

By eleven P.M. we had finished. Greenwood thanked me and, while not complimenting me on my detective skills, commended me for having avoided getting killed. Taking that as a sign of tolerance, if not approval, I asked if I could talk with him on Sunday afternoon to see about progress on the investigation. He told me that he'd be on the scene for the next day or two, coordinating the investigation, and would be happy to talk.

Finally, Greenwood said I could leave. I pointed out that my rental car was still at the motel and asked if he or Andrews had any bright ideas as to where I could stay, since the prospect of staying at the Sea Oats Motel didn't fill me with joy and rapture. Greenwood asked Andrews to help me with a room and then excused himself to go talk with the Avon police chief.

The air outside was cooler. Permeated with the mist off a salt marsh, it carried the pungent smell of low tide. Andrews asked me a few polite, social questions but my energy deserted me immediately after the interrogation ended. I gave only desultory answers. In truth, all I wanted to do was look up at the sky, where stars twinkled everywhere. We were a long way from urban smog or lights. Suspended over the implacable ocean, thousands of stars poured out of the night sky. Still no answers there, but what I saw was far more peaceful than the visions I had in my head.

Andrews saw me staring at the sky and recognized my fatigue. She offered to drive me to another motel and help me pick up the car the next day. I accepted.

When we arrived at the Sea Oats Motel, she stopped by my car and I grabbed my bag. There was still activity at room 20 and a few lights on elsewhere, but nothing revealed the violence that had occurred there earlier. Darren was probably still watching wrestling, where the blood was ketchup. My head went back and my eyes closed as soon as I returned to the passenger seat of the cruiser.

"You're looking fairly drained, Dan." Andrews sounded less like a cop now.

"Yeah, my system seems to be crashing. What's open this time of night? I'm looking forward to a beer and bed. I'd be happy to buy you a drink."

"There's a small, clean motel down the beach a ways. I can probably roust the owners out and get you in." She hesitated for a moment. "Sorry, I'm on duty for a while, with all the fuss you've brought with you, so I'll have to pass on the drink."

I looked over at her, her profile sensuous and smooth in the moonlight. Without the police hat on or the holster on her hip, with her hair down, she probably looked great. No ring on her hand.

"You did a nice job at the motel. I would have been delighted to show a little appreciation," I said.

She smiled. "The kind words are plenty enough. Don't hear 'em much down here."

"Can't be easy being a female cop in this town."

Her face looked pensive in the passing street-lights. "Oh, it's okay."

"I'm a lawyer, I've represented some female cops, female firefighters in sexual harassment suits. Stories they tell raise the hair on my neck. At least in Boston, it can get pretty ugly."

"Well, I'm the first one here, so there've been a few incidents, but it's not horrible. Most guys accept me, no outright harassment, but a few still don't like the idea, so it gets a little lonely. I grew up around here, though, and I love it. I keep to myself, mostly, and stay busy. Some guys, though, just don't care much for those of us with brains and tits."

"They have any brains themselves, they're only jealous. Why do you stay? There must be easier places for you, as well as friends elsewhere who'd be happy with your company."

She turned and glanced at me, smiling and sorrowful at the same time. "Call me Holly. I love the job, it's a good town, the ocean's here, and I can take pictures. I love to fish, windsurf. I haven't found anybody worth giving all that up for. And people come to visit."

At that point we turned into another motel and parked by the front office. True to her word, Andrews tracked the owners down and obtained a room for me. She came back to the cruiser in the parking lot and I got out as she came up to my door.

From a darkened side street just north of the motel, I heard the screech of tires on asphalt and the whine of an accelerating engine. Bursting out from a dark corner of the parking lot, a black pickup truck came right at us. In the light from the neon motel sign overhead, I saw a driver who looked like the guy who'd run out of Grizek's room.

I turned to Holly Andrews. "Damn, he's headed for us—shoot the truck."

But she had her hands over her eyes, blinded by the headlights. "I can't see," she cried.

I looked around for anything large, then grabbed the only useful thing close at hand, the adze, out of my bag. With all the force any New Zealand Maori could have mustered, I hurled it at the oncoming truck windshield. As I finished throwing, arms grabbed me and pulled me toward the cruiser.

The adze hit home, square in the windshield, just before the pickup sped by. It swerved wildly and went out of control as the windshield cracked and shattered. The car veered sharply to the right and crashed into a large cement-and-stone post standing to one side of the driveway entrance to the motel. The car hit head on and the horn immediately blared.

I stood up from the cruiser while Andrews called the dispatcher. We ran over, but as we drew close she motioned me back and drew her gun.

There was no need. The gunman who earlier had run out of unit 20 had now run out of luck. Blood covered the side of his face and he lay slumped over, his head on the steering wheel and his eyes closed. His hands still gripped the wheel. Andrews reached in and felt for a pulse at his neck.

She shook her head and holstered her gun. "Didn't make it."

"Can't say I'm sorry," I said.

We both looked up as we heard multiple sirens approach. Lights went on in the motel as the horn continued its wailing. Andrews and I walked a short distance away from the scene.

"Thanks," she said. It was warm but she shivered and crossed her arms. "I didn't catch on to what was happening there until too late, didn't react well. Greenwood was right, the son of a bitch must have stolen the truck, then followed us. Maybe picked us up back at the motel where we got your stuff. This was the first opening he had to nail you. And I gave it to him."

"Hey, nobody could predict he'd be this stupid.

Town is crawling with cops, and he sticks around. And anyway I owe you thanks, too, for grabbing me, hauling me away from the truck. We made a pretty good team there."

"Maybe, but I still screwed up and you saved my ass. Chief's going to love it when he hears that you stopped the car with a rock while my gun stayed in the holster."

I looked at her as two police cars and an ambulance wheeled in. "Officer Andrews, as far as I'm concerned, you did just fine in the line of duty."

We went through the whole routine all over again. This time Greenwood and other officers questioned Andrews before they talked to me. Back in the police station, the dispatcher took pity and found me more coffee and cookies. It was 12:45 A.M. and I sat down to snack in a quiet corner in the back of the building.

I thought about calling Jenny again, as I'd promised when we'd talked earlier. Her comments when I'd left came back to me—that I'd done enough and could back off. But I knew now that backing off wouldn't work for me. The awareness of things I'd backed off on over the years still remained piled in my personal attic, and I could feel the pile shifting, a bit unstable from all the recent, and unplanned, trips into that attic. Added to that, the things I couldn't do much about were legion— gangs in the inner cities, drug pushers who preyed on thirteen-year-olds, corporations that pushed cigarettes on adolescents and produced defective products, government agencies that jeopardized lives by polluting the ground with radioactive and hazardous waste, or husbands who beat their scared and scarred wives. The time had come to focus on things I could do something about and not back off. The first thing I could do was to help find out what happened to Aaron.

I didn't have the energy or stomach to discuss or debate all this with Jenny, so I put off calling her again, though I knew it would upset her. Part of me would have liked to have her waiting for me at the motel when I left the police station so that her warmth, her touch, her beauty, could help me purge my head and heart of what I'd seen that evening. But another part liked the feeling of being isolated and alone, far from anyone I knew and not responsible for worrying about anyone else. I had plenty to do to untangle the twisted tendrils of memory, fear, and anger left inside me by the night's events.

The police then summoned me back for more questioning. I answered for another half an hour. Meetings and activity finally ended. Andrews was still in conversation with a couple of people, so another cop drove me back to the motel. With the shooter dead, the police didn't bother with a guard at my new place.

I had just turned on the television after a fruit-less search for a cold drink when I heard a knock on my door. Two attempts in a night were enough. I stood by the side of the chained door.

"Who is it?" I asked through the door.

"Offi— Holly Andrews. You're right to be cautious. Let me slide my license under the door." It was the right license, so I opened the door only until the chain tightened and looked out.

"Hi," she said. She held up a couple of beer bottles in front of the door. "I needed one of these, and I thought you might like one, too."

"Great idea." Nothing could have looked better than the two bottles of Pete's Wicked Ale she waved at me.

I opened the door, she walked in, and I almost didn't recognize her. The uniform was gone. She wore a white cotton short-sleeve polo shirt over strong shoulders, and a denim skirt above sinewy, golden legs. Her brown hair, free of restraints, fell just above her shoulders. Her eyes smiled in a way I hadn't seen all night. I'd been wrong. She looked better than the beer.

She put the bottles down on a bureau and turned to face me. "Little late to buy anything," she said, "but I had a couple at home. And I didn't get a chance to say goodbye at the station."

"Now I know the meaning of southern hospitality. I was dreaming of one of these."

We popped the tops and clinked the bottles. Our fingers touched as we did. We each took a long drink and looked at one another. For an instant, remembering my earlier fantasy of having Jenny waiting for me here at the motel, I had an impulse to tell Holly thanks, but I'll just see you in the morning. I let the impulse pass.

"You know, I was feeling a bit abandoned by the police there for a while," I said. "No guard, and me, a marked man."

She took two steps closer. "Well, I'm just the one to keep you safe tonight. A hell of a guard, that's me."

I reached out and stroked her cheek. We set the beers aside and kissed, full of relief, spent adrenaline, excitement, and gratitude. We kissed long and hard, her hand pulling the back of my neck to her while my hands ran across her back and her thighs. Our fevered and hungry kissing escalated. I ran my mouth over her neck, and she stretched her head back. I pulled at her shirt and noticed she had only a beautiful tan, no tan line. Then our clothes were on the floor, we were in bed, and all the accumulated emotional sludge of fear, fury, and retribution dissipated with cries, whispers, and the syncopation of legs and lust.

After we made love the second time, a slower, sweeter union, I had no more words or energy. She sat up on the bed and brushed my forehead. She leaned over, her taut, firm breasts brushing my chest, and kissed me softly. "See you later," she said. The door closed and I fell asleep.

CHAPTER ————

TWENTY-TWO

The morning didn't start for me until after ten A.M., when I finally came up for air. The Atlantic Ocean was right outside my back window, about a hundred yards away. People fished and walked on the beach and two windsurfers in wet suits raced back and forth, powered by a brisk onshore breeze.

I put on shorts, a T-shirt, and my running shoes. Heading south on the beach, I ran about three miles, slowly. Running in the sand took my breath away far faster than running on the road, even if it was easier on the bad knee. Waves of two and three feet plopped on the shore, pushed by the wind. Sandpipers jumped in and out of the edges of the waves climbing up the beach while larger sea gulls calmly stood nearby, watching for a meal to wash up on shore. I passed by a small fish, species unknown to me, lying dead on the sand. The temperature felt warm, maybe 70 degrees or better, with only a few puffy clouds in the sky. I could taste and smell salt in the air. The world looked far better than it had the night before.

After running back, I took off the shirt and shoes and jogged into the ocean. The cold produced goose bumps all over, but I acclimated after a couple of minutes. It wasn't as bad as the water off the Maine coast in August, but it wasn't a bathtub. The waves, as I bodysurfed them to shore, raised my spirits even as they dumped me in the sand. I left the water chattering but eager to move on, to find out what Jeff Grizek and Aaron Winters had in common besides violent deaths.

I called the police station and asked for Holly Andrews. She came on after a minute over considerable noise in the background.

"Officer Andrews here."

"Getting formal on me now, Holly? I'd hoped I wasn't so easily forgotten. And given that it's a beautiful Sunday, what's all the ruckus behind you?"

She laughed softly. "Good morning, sleepyhead. I'm not supposed to tell you anything. Nobody knows where you are. They want me to pick you up and bring you in by the back door."

"Back door? Why?"

"You, my friend, are much sought after by the local members of the press, including a couple of television stations. Murders are big news, as are the people who catch the murderers."

"The press? For me? Damn," I said.

"No more for now. See you in ten minutes."

She showed up outside my motel room in her

uniform, but she still looked great. I brought her inside and we smiled at each other, laughed nervously, and then we shared a lengthy kiss.

"Last night was pretty exciting," she said.

"Yeah, and you were, too," I said.

She laughed. "I'd like to start over where we left off, but I've got to get you back to the station. Too many people want to talk to you."

"I'm sorry we don't have more time. You're a special lady."

"Thanks, but I proved I'm not a special cop."

"You did fine, in uniform and out."

"You're a little biased. You should have heard the chief this morning."

"I'll talk to him, put in a good word. Do you have anything new on the guy in the truck?

"I thought you only had eyes for me."

"Well, I—"

"Dan, don't worry about it. It was great, but we both knew it couldn't last long. Come on, we've got to get to the station."

Twenty minutes later I walked into a police station where phones rang, cops and investigators conferred loudly, and men and women with notebooks, microphones, tape recorders, and cameras hung out in the front hall. Altogether, there were more than thirty people buzzing around.

As soon as he saw me, Jay Greenwood pointed at me and waved Andrews and me into the office he was using.

First, Greenwood turned to Andrews and

asked, "Did you tell him anything?"

"Not a word."

"Good." He called in another man in plain-clothes, asking him to bring the pictures. He came in with a manila folder. Another investigator followed.

They all watched silently while Greenwood took the folder, pulled out a sheaf of photos and placed ten images in front of me. He arranged them in two rows of five. All white guys with full heads of hair, two with glasses. Three of the images were grainy, as if they'd been photocopied or faxed.

"I want to see if you recognize anybody in these photos," Greenwood said to me.

Without hesitation I pointed to a fuzzy but distinct picture. "That's the guy who was in the motel room. His hair is longer now and he doesn't have a mustache, but that scar is still there. No question about it. Same as the guy in the truck last night."

"Thanks. Just a formality, wanted to have you give a formal ID. Scum you just identified is—was—James David Henning," Greenwood said. "A career lowlife from Norfolk, Virginia."

"What else do you know about him?"

Greenwood leaned back in his chair, put his hands behind his head and gave me a grin. "Remember the clowns who tried to bust Nancy Kerrigan's knee? Well, this guy makes them look good. He was a punk with a rap sheet a yard long, mostly drugs and robbery, breaking and entering, a couple of assaults and armed robbery. No homicide convictions, although police there had him as a suspect on two a while back. Did a couple of stints inside. Right now, we don't know why he went after Grizek and you, but people from my office are going to Norfolk now."

"How did you identify him so quickly?"

"Fingerprints. Plus he was none too bright or maybe he was on coke. The car he crashed was his girlfriend's. Once the police tracked her down early this morning, she identified him. Seemed more upset about losing the car than losing him. She said she had no idea what he was up to. He'd told her he needed the car to visit a sick friend. The Norfolk police are still looking into his background, see if there's a connection with Grizek."

Greenwood looked like a Cheshire cat. "And we know what happened in the parking lot. You deserve a hell of a lot of credit for keeping your head. Be happy to tell the press about it."

Internal alarm bells went off loudly. "No, no, don't give me any credit for anything. I've got enough to worry about in Boston without that kind of publicity."

Greenwood picked up a pencil and started tapping it on the metal desk in front of him. "People want to know what happened; I've got to tell them something."

"Just keep me out of it, thanks. All anybody needs to know is that there was shooting and the guy who did it died later in a crash."

"All right, that's what I'll give them, but I have

a feeling you're going to be in this no matter what I say. This is a small town, everybody knows the motel. Darren will have made himself into a local hero by now, if I don't miss my guess. You think about it for a bit, but I've got to hold a press conference with the chief of police as soon as I finish making some calls. Holly here can fill you in on what's happening."

I groaned and turned to Andrews. She walked me back to a quiet corner. "How about just sneaking me out of here, and I'll grab my car and head north? I'd rather go hang-gliding in a hurricane than get a lot of publicity out of this."

She smiled sympathetically and shook her head. "The damage is done, Jay's right. Darren's already talked to the press. I don't doubt he got cash or a free meal or two from somebody. He's told them about you coming to visit Grizek. Rumors are out that you killed the gunman with an axe after the shooting."

"Oh, jeez," I said and rubbed my hand over my eyes.

"And I thought you were enjoying yourself here," she said.

"Holly, no, I mean, you're great. It's just so much has happened, I've got to get back, figure out how it all pieces together. I'll come back sometime, or maybe—"

She put her fingers to my lips, shutting me up. "Dan, last night was a bizarre roller-coaster ride. I'm glad it finished as it did, but the ride's over. You don't owe me, I don't owe you. We just have a wild and wonderful memory. It's okay. And thanks." She smiled.

"No, thank you. You're right, and anything I say will sound pretty lame." I shrugged. "But what about this notion that I killed Henning with an axe? Where did that come from?"

"People heard about the adze. Thought it was an axe. Nobody really knows what happened, so imaginations have run wild," she said.

Greenwood motioned us over at that point. I went into an office to talk with the police and investigators. We talked about what they would be following up on. Among other things, they planned to obtain the phone records from the motel room and Henning's apartment in Norfolk to see if he'd called anybody in the Boston area.

Finally, Greenwood told me I was free to go before he held the press conference, and that if I wanted to sell my story, that was okay with him. He laughed. I didn't.

Andrews volunteered to take me back to the Sea Oats Motel to pick up my rental car. Greenwood and I shook hands. He said he'd be in touch.

Just before leaving, I remembered to call Randy. I reached him at home, gave him a five minute synopsis of the events. He said he'd inform the D.A.'s office in Massachusetts and talk with Greenwood and the Norfolk police. He also insisted that I go straight home like a good boy and call him the next day.

Andrews and I went out the back door, both of us refusing to talk to reporters who circled and snapped like sharks at wounded fish. When I finally sat down in the passenger's seat and closed the door, I gave an exaggerated sigh.

Andrews looked over at me and laughed. "First lawyer I've ever known who went around kicking reporters' butts instead of licking 'em."

"I know they're just doing their jobs, but what a crazy way to make a living, asking any damn questions they can think of."

"Sort of like you conducting your investigation."

I laughed. "Score one for you. But on this thing, I've got enough problems with people at home without getting more notoriety."

Andrews nodded and thought for a moment. "You know, publicity about you may not be such a bad thing. It will be obvious you've talked with the police and given them what you know. The police up north will also be convinced that you're a target for somebody. Might make the bad guys less eager to go after you, particularly if they think you're tough enough to knock off a hit man."

"Maybe. On the other hand, it may also look like I'm even more of a threat." I hadn't told her about the drug charges being held over my head, and it was too complicated to get into with the time we had left.

"But they'll only want you if they know you've either got information you're planning to use against them or information you haven't disclosed. If they think you've already told us everything you learned from Grizek, maybe they'll leave you alone. Unless, of course, you continue to be a pain in the ass to them."

We turned into the Sea Oats Motel and pulled up next to my rental car. I turned to Andrews. "I hope you're right. It sounds good, and you're a smart cop, so you ought to know."

She blushed.

"Thanks for everything," I continued. "This trip was not my idea of fun, but I enjoyed . . . well, you. Last night, all of it, will be with me a long time."

"I've enjoyed it, too. If you get back this way, look me up." She reached across the front seat and kissed me, long and sharp, then tenderly. We looked at each other close up for a moment. She smiled and I touched her cheek. We could both recognize a goodbye kiss.

I grabbed my bags out of the car and watched as she drove away. I didn't wave and she didn't look back.

CHAPTER ———

TWENTY-THREE

I arrived back in Boston after a long drive and the last flight out of Norfolk. It was 11:45 P.M. I'd called Jenny to let her know of my schedule change, leaving a message indicating I might not be in until a bit later on Monday morning.

I'd forgotten to turn on the answering machine on the phone at home, thankfully, so no little red lights were blinking away. There were neither criminals nor reporters lurking about my front door. Only a couple pints of ice cream and the ending of a Sunday night football game on ESPN awaited. After the madness of the two days before, a good old American football game, with its contained, predictable mayhem, provided a comforting restoration of normality.

Normality disappeared in a hurry in the morning. When I walked into the office, Jenny was already on the phone with Randy. She waved to me and motioned me to my phone. I told them both what I knew of the goings on in Avon and Norfolk. I told Randy that the North Carolina authorities would be talking to people here about any connection between Grizek's murder and Aaron's.

"You're taking more of my time than most of the guys on our most wanted list," Randy said. "Never seen a man fall so deep in pigshit so often and still come up smelling like roses. But unlike some folks, I have real work to do. I'll be in touch with the people in North Carolina and get back to you. Assuming you aren't poisoned or machine-gunned before then." I couldn't tell if he was joking.

As soon as the call was over, I walked out to Jenny's desk. She smiled at me, but without much energy. My own internal radar on her was scrambled, and I felt defensive. I decided on a preemptive strike of warmth and cheer. "I never thought I'd be glad to get back to the office."

"You didn't call me back Saturday night like you promised, but I'm still happy to have you in the office. You look pretty good, no bullet holes or tread marks, but hearing about what happened on television didn't make me feel great. I'm sure Ann and Frank will feel the same."

"Yeah, I know, I'm sorry, things got a bit crazy. I'm tired of being the practice dummy for goons, but I'm fine and I know the police will make some progress now."

"I saw you down in North Carolina on a couple of newscasts. Looks like you made some friends," she said. "And I see they've got some attractive women on the police force."

I paused, and struggled to keep my face straight. "Officer Andrews did a good job. They all did—it's a small force, and I don't think they'd ever been hit with anything like the mess with both Grizek and Henning."

She was silent for a minute and gave a barely perceptible shake of her head before looking at me again. "I'm afraid we're not going to provide you with nearly the level of excitement and stimulation you've come to expect, and there is some legal work to be done. It won't get you killed, only paid."

"That's okay, boredom and compensation might be just the ticket. About time I paid for some things around here."

With that, she pulled a small stack of messages off her desk and laughed, with just a hint of malevolence. "You and I need to talk about what needs doing around here, but before you do anything for your clients, counselor, you might want to take a look at these messages." At that, the phone rang and Jenny grabbed it.

Calls had come in from about a dozen reporters from local newspapers and stations in Boston, North Carolina, and Virginia, as well as one national network. They all left the same message— they wanted an interview. Some reporters wanted to talk over the phone. The locals wanted to send camera crews to my office. My shenanigans over the weekend had sparked their interest, but I threw all the messages out. Talking to reporters wouldn't pay the bills or make the police happy.

Meanwhile, Jenny had another reporter on the phone. She put her on hold and asked, with a smirk, whether I had any interest in talking to this one. I replied with an epithet, but told her to ask the reporter what she wanted from me and why.

The media had seized on the unusual stories coming out of North Carolina. According to the reporter on the phone, they wanted to talk to me because I had bumped off a gun-toting, career criminal using a Stone Age weapon.

Just the thought of talking to reporters while I was trying to make a living and finish the investigation put my stomach in knots. Jenny only laughed again and said she had always understood that a lawyer's credo was that any press, even bad press, was good press. I cast my evilest eye at her, with little visible effect.

I told her to switch over to the answering system so we had a chance to figure out what to do. The only response that made sense to me was silence. Like all crime stories, it would pass in a day or two, when something more grotesque came along.

Jenny was much more rational about the situation. "You can't stop the attention, and, as Andy Warhol said, we're all going to have our fifteen minutes of fame."

"I thought Andy Warhol was before your time."

"He was, but even those of us who are not old and wise can read," she said.

"It's not the fifteen minutes I'm worried about. I don't want publicity getting in the way of the investigation. And I don't want it to complicate my life with Richards."

"Should have thought of all that before you went charging off." My near-death experience hadn't dulled her tongue. I could only look at her with frustration. This was one argument I knew I wasn't going to win. I agreed to try and work out something small to give to the press.

First, we went through our workload. After all, we wanted our clients to be happy. The last thing I needed was to be splashed all over Boston television as some kind of Indiana Jones when my clients thought I was doing their legal work. We figured out what needed to be done and who would do it, and I agreed that we might have to hire some temporary help, farm out a few cases, and in one or two cases hire a private investigator to check certain facts out. The firm's budget would go further to hell, but adze carriers of the past hadn't bothered with budgets, so I'd try to do so as well.

"By the way," Jenny said, and looked at me closely, "I just want to check on one thing. You have any particular private investigator you want to hire, like maybe see if Officer Andrews does off-duty work?" She gave a little laugh, but it had a dark bite to it.

I made a small sound, halfway between a cough and choking. "No, we'll use Ralph Franklin, a guy I've used a few times."

For a moment Jenny kept an intense gaze on me, but then she turned back to some of the case files in front of us and we finished discussing how to handle them.

Next, we talked about the publicity. Jenny played devil's advocate and, much as I grumbled about it, pointed out the benefits. Echoing what Holly Andrews told me in North Carolina, Jenny said the publicity might make any further attacks on me less likely. And if the press linked up the murders of Grizek and Aaron, it could pressure the police up here to finish the investigation.

But I didn't want to link Grizek and Aaron publicly unless the police and the D.A. wanted me to do so. Even Randy was beginning to view my activities with a jaundiced eye, and I had no desire to antagonize the police further.

We also talked about what needed to be done in the investigation. The cops would be all over Grizek's background, and Henning's as well, so there was no need for my snooping in their neighborhoods.

A still glaring hole was the missing motive for Aaron's murder. All we had was an effort to silence people—Aaron, Grizek, and me—who apparently knew something that scared the hell out of somebody, but I had no idea what the something was.

And we still had no connection between Aaron and Grizek. The only potential tie I had was the tire pile. Aaron had died there, I'd suffered a beating near there, and maybe Grizek had worked there.

The tires had squealed for me before, but I couldn't go back there to check things out.

"You know," she said, as if reading my mind, "since you're so notorious now, maybe I should do more to look around, talk to people about Aaron."

"No," I said quickly, and watched a frown cross her face.

"Why not?"

"I appreciate the offer, but this has turned pretty ugly and I don't want you or anybody else put at risk."

"Nobody knows me. Only a few people even know I'm working for you. I can do things quietly, carefully."

I paused for a moment, trying to figure out what to say. The image I had of Wayne Sharman, her ability to figure me out, my night with Holly Andrews, my fear of anything happening to her, concern about the already shifting relationship between us—I couldn't tell her about any of it.

"Jenny, you're doing great work around the office. That's what I hired you for, that's what I want you to do."

"You don't think I'm competent to help, do you?"

"No, that's not it."

"It looked like you relied pretty heavily on Officer Andrews."

"Jenny, she was a cop, investigating Grizek's death. The next thing we knew, a madman tried to run us down. She was just doing her job, but neither of us expected to be taking on a murderer. You can't compare what she did and what you do, or what you're competent to do."

"I don't understand. I'll do the office work, but I just want to help a little in the investigation so it's not all on you."

"I'm sorry, but no. That's the way it has to be. There's plenty of other work to do around here, and that's what I want you to concentrate on."

"I'm not talking about doing anything danger-ous. The least you can do is explain to me why you won't let me get involved."

"Sorry, no explanations. I'm still the boss, so a no on this is all you get."

Her face, usually so sunny and open, stiffened and filled with lines and dark patches. The air cooled between us.

"Now I know why some people call you a prick," she said, and stood up. "I need to go out to get some coffee, I'll be back in a while." She walked out of my office, but then came back. "That is, if I'm welcome."

I'd never fired anyone for telling the truth, and I wasn't about to start now. "I meant what I said, I'd like you to do the work we have here."

She left. At one point or another, I thought, I'd managed to piss off just about everybody—Ann and Frank, Richards, Randy, and now Jenny. And all I'd developed were small clues and a belief that even if I didn't know where I was headed, it was in the right direction.

CHAPTER ————
TWENTY-FOUR

Normally, I hate working at my desk, but the legal work I did for a few hours to catch up on some cases was a welcome respite, in a perverse sort of way. At least I wasn't in danger from punks or reporters. The phone burped steadily, Jenny kept answering, and only when established clients called did she give me written phone messages. She didn't say much to me for a few hours.

None of the clients who phoned seemed upset at my antics. One client told me that he liked the fact that even though I was a lawyer, I could do something useful.

By the afternoon, Jenny could not stave off the outside world any longer. The D.A.'s office wanted to interview me, and I agreed to meet with them late in the day. With Randy vouching for me, I hoped the prosecutors and the investigators on Aaron's case and the Grizek investigation might let me look at some of what they had.

The D.A.'s office was in a county building in Dedham, south of Boston. It was a nondescript brick structure built fifty years ago. The offices inside were no more remarkable than the outside, including the conference room we met in. The wooden table was scarred and nicked from the hundreds of objects thrown on it. Stains from endless spilled cups of coffee over the years covered the surface. The books on the walls containing statutes and cases looked just as used and abused. Even the people wandering around the office appeared rumpled, strained, and frayed around the edges.

The meeting went smoothly, although not quickly. The D.A. himself stepped in for a time to hear part of the story and, I thought, to take my measure. There was considerable overlap between what I said and what I'd already told Greenwood in North Carolina, but there were some additional twists because of the Massachusetts angle.

The D.A.'s office was assisting the North Carolina and Norfolk police in their inquiries, and a transcript of my interview would go on to them. In addition, the D.A. wanted any more information I had accumulated concerning Aaron's death or any linkage between Aaron and Grizek. They perked up when I reported what Grizek told me over the phone, and pushed me to recall anything else he might have said. Nothing came to me.

After the questioning, they told me that the investigation of Aaron's death had not moved very far or fast. In other words, they had few leads. They found no record that Grizek had worked at the tire pile. They were intrigued with a potential connection between Grizek and Jean Houghton, but Grizek had no close family so nothing would come quickly.

Down south, the investigation of Henning was also proving to be a dead end. Other than an unusual deposit of $7,500 in cash in his bank account on the day before he ventured to Hatteras to kill Grizek, the investigation uncovered nothing significant about Henning.

It was easy to conjecture that somebody in Massachusetts sent Grizek away and then sent a killer after him. Presumably having him killed outside the state would make it tougher to tie him to Aaron's murder. Without the phone call to me, the connection might never have been made, even if Henning, a remarkably dumb felon, had been caught. But when Henning died, that lead died with him.

After the conference with the investigators, I asked for access to the tire pile records. First came a lecture about staying out of the way of the investigation, as well as a reminder about confidentiality. But the D.A.'s people made oblique references to Randy Blocker having good judgment and they acknowledged that I'd helped in the investigation of Aaron's murder and in the illegal dumping case against the Houghtons.

I also played the violins a little, pointing out that I'd received a beating and free truck ride, and had been a victim of attempted murder by Henning. Surely I had some right to see what the authorities had for evidence.

The assistant D.A. and the investigator went out of the conference room to talk, and a few minutes later the assistant D.A. returned alone. He gave me copies of two typed lists and asked me to get back to them if I saw anything helpful. One list contained the employees whose names had shown up on the Houghton business payrolls for the last few years. The police had already talked with all of those on the list they could find. Grizek's name did not show up on that list.

The other document was compiled from the records of the tire pile and supposedly included all of the companies that had sent tires to the Houghton pile. The document included one long list taken from the regular operating records and a very short list taken from a separate, smaller log or journal. The illegal dumping I'd witnessed at the site, though, gave me little comfort that the records kept on the tire pile were either accurate or complete.

I got home just in time to turn on the local news. Just as I feared, the story was still playing, not among the lead stories, but at the end. Interviews of various police officials from both Virginia and Massachusetts came on followed by a clip of the North Carolina press conference and a blurb and a photo of both me and an adze. They'd also found an acquaintance of mine, an attorney, who opined that

if anybody was likely to go after a gunman armed
only with a rock, I was a good candidate. It was not
clear he was complimenting me.

The report depressed me, but no more so than
the steady stream of calls I'd received. I left the
answering machine on to screen additional calls.

Frank called from the hospital, unusual for him.
"Damnit," he said, "what foolishness have you gotten into now? Call me immediately, you lucky jerk."
Ann's message was gentler. "Dan, we can't believe
what we've seen. We're worried about you. Please
call us right away." I noted the names of the others
who left messages so I could call them back later.

I did call Ann and Frank. They were, by turns,
concerned, scared, angry, fascinated, and pleased.
The shooting appalled them but they were impressed to see me on television. Nothing could
reassure them completely, but I did my best.

Mike Steiner from the unit below called me. He
was thrilled to have a celebrity as a friend, even if I
wasn't a baseball player or his newest heartthrob,
Jenny. And he'd figured out that he had helped me
by substituting the adze for the camera. On a whim,
I asked him if he wanted to go for a run.

We took off and ran through Coolidge Corner,
down Harvard Street, and up Route 9 to the
Brookline Reservoir. Mike told me in detail about
how he and his dad had switched the adze and the
camera.

We ran past The Country Club, one of the most
hallowed private golf clubs in the country. Mike

asked for a complete accounting of everything I knew about the place. Ironically, golf in American became a much more democratic sport when a former caddie and amateur player, Frances Ouimet, beat two well-known British pros in a playoff to win the 1913 U.S. Open at The Country Club. The 1988 U.S. Open had been played there and won by Curtis Strange. The Ryder Cup competition was scheduled to take place there in 1999. Mike was mildly disappointed when I told him that I couldn't describe the course since I'd never played there and almost certainly never would.

That topic quickly exhausted, Mike moved to something else.

"Dan," he said, "they said on television that the guy in the truck was trying to kill you."

"Yeah, I guess that's true."

"But the guy that tried to kill you, he got killed instead, right?"

"Right."

"That means you killed him, right?"

I'd always answered his questions honestly, but no answer had hurt like this one did. I stopped running, walked in front of the carriage and leaned down so I could see his face.

"Well, Mike, you could say I killed him, or at least helped to kill him. I'm not proud of it. It's sad, but I did it. He drove his truck at me and a police-woman. He was trying to hurt us badly, maybe to kill us. I threw the adze into the windshield just to stop him, and because of that he drove into a stone gate and was killed. I didn't mean to kill him, I just wanted to protect myself and the policewoman, but still it happened."

"Was he a really bad guy?"

"I think so, Mike, but I still wish it didn't happen."

He paused for a moment and I straightened up to start running again. The conversation brought to mind the line from *Macbeth*, "What's done cannot be undone." I'd have liked for Aaron's murder, Grizek's, even Henning's death, all to be undone. Instead, it would take me a long time to sort through all that had been done.

I could see he was puzzling on something, so I waited.

"Dan, were you scared when the bad guy drove the car at you?"

Honest answer, I reminded myself.

"Yeah. Very scared."

"Are you scared now? I mean, you've gotten into two fights. Aren't you afraid that more bad guys will try to get you?"

"Well, I'm a little scared, but the police know what happened, and they'll find the people who are doing these things. And if you're worried about something happening at the house to you or your family, you'll be safe there, nothing's going to happen."

"No, I'm not worried about me. I'm just scared about you. I don't want any bad guys to kill you."

I put my arms around him and hugged him.

"Thanks. I'm going to be okay," I said in a husky voice. "You and I have a lot more places to run to."

I went to the carriage and started running hard, hoping that sweat from my brow would ward off tears from my eyes.

CHAPTER ———

TWENTY-FIVE

Back in the office the next day, only a few messages had piled up. My reign as a media celebrity was ending.

With the door to my office closed and a Miles Davis tape on the stereo, a things-to-do tape ran through my head over and over again. Most of the rational steps available to me were small and incremental. What I wanted was to take big steps.

At some point soon I'd have to take a close look at the lists from the D.A.'s office, but I simply didn't have the patience to do the thinking and analysis the task would require. Instead I wanted to keep moving, poking, prying, to unsettle people as I pursued the tire pile connection. With that in mind, what the hell, I'd head south and visit Jean Houghton again. I didn't expect to get any meaningful information from her, just more of a sense of her response and involvement while legal and familial tornadoes whirled around her. At best, I'd provoke a reaction that would bring her out in the open.

Before leaving for her house, I returned a call from Chief Richards. The message from him made me jumpy. It didn't say whether he was calling about the drug charges or just to chime in on my latest adventure. When I called back, he wasn't in, so I left a message that I would stop by later.

Jenny was on the phone when I emerged from my office. As I opened the door, she put her hand over the phone and asked where I was going and when I'd be back.

"Out and I don't know, but I'll call later."

She spoke into the phone. "Nancy, hold on a minute. Dan, can you please stay for a few minutes? I need to run some things by you, you've got a bunch of messages here, and I want to know where you're going."

"Sorry, Jenny, I can't sit still, I've got to get out of here. Going to stop by and see Richards and maybe Jean Houghton."

Her mouth dropped open and her eyes went wide, but I merely waved and walked out the door. It felt good to have the last word.

My mood didn't stay elevated long. I harbored no illusions about the prospects for talking with Jean Houghton. Deliberately, I had chosen not to call ahead. With the criminal proceedings pending and police sniffing around about the second murder, I knew she wouldn't say much, if anything, to me. She might not like what her boys had done with the illegally buried drums, but that didn't mean she'd appreciate my uncovering it. Richards wouldn't like my visiting her either, but technically she didn't live in his town, so I wouldn't be doing anything in his jurisdiction.

I gambled that she wouldn't be at the tire pile and got lucky. When I arrived at the house, her pickup truck sat in the driveway.

Jean Houghton answered her door. Her eyes went cold and opaque and her lips narrowed into a tight, straight line when she saw me. "Kardon, you may think you have big balls for showing up here, but you have shit for brains. You're not off my property in thirty seconds, I'm calling the police."

"I just have a couple of questions," I said.

She practically snarled. "I've seen you on television. Maybe somebody thinks you're a hero, but not in this family. I talked to you once—it won't happen again."

"Ms. Houghton, you have every right to be upset. But two people have been killed, I've been beat up and almost run over. All I want to know is what happened to Aaron Winters."

"Damn you," she said. "Whatever happened has nothing to do with me and my boys. I already told you we weren't involved."

"But Jeff Grizek, the guy killed in North Carolina, worked for you," I said.

"You're a liar. That fool Grizek never worked for me. He came looking for a job, but I knew he was a no-good drunk, never came close to hiring him. Leave us alone. I'm sorry he's dead, but as for you, you keep butting in, I won't be sorry if they use you for a speed bump next time. Get out." She slammed the door in my face. I was happy to leave with only my pride wounded.

Based on how she had run her business, on her history and character, I could only accept her statement that she'd never hired Grizek. It was also consistent with the list of employees I'd seen. The boys, though, had presumably acted without her knowledge when they buried the hazardous waste. They might well have hired Grizek without her involvement as well.

As I drove away I replayed in my mind my original conversation with Jean Houghton and compared it to today's brief confrontation. The only thing missing was any reference to her daughter. She'd protested that she and her boys were clean. In the first conversation I had with her, Jean said that her daughter and the boys did some things together, but today there was no mention of Sandra. It was probably meaningless, but Grizek had referred to a woman in his drunken phone call with me. Jean Houghton had convinced me she was aboveboard, but there was another lady Houghton to check out.

From the Houghton house it was only a few miles to the police station. By the time I arrived, there were only two or three officers still around. Chief Richards finished a phone call and waved me into his office. I took a deep breath and walked in, not knowing whether I'd leave with a court date.

He didn't waste time with small talk. "We're not bringing charges," he said, but he didn't smile when he said it.

"Thanks," I said, and unclenched my sweating hands.

"One of your hunches paid off, though you know we could have nailed you for possession anyway," he said. "Found fingerprints of George Houghton on the plastic bag, and we dug up a bartender who made the call telling us you were around that night. We figure that's enough to back up your story."

"I appreciate the work you did."

"I told you, my men are fair. If I have to choose between your version of how the drugs got there and George Houghton's, it's not much of a choice. Now tell me about this latest mess you got into."

Richards sat on the edge of his chair, elbows on his desk, and listened intently as I told the story. When I finished, he sat back in his chair a bit and seemed to relax.

"So apart from the phone call from Grizek," he said, "you never had a chance to talk with him and he didn't leave anything in writing?"

"That's right."

"And the only hint in the phone call was that he'd worked for a woman? No name, nothing to indicate who else might be involved?"

"Nothing. I tried to get him to talk, but he was pretty drunk."

"So we can't be sure that Grizek's death and the

kid's are related," he said. A statement, not a question.

"No, but Grizek suspected something," I said. "So do I, given that people have gone after me twice, once while I was investigating Aaron's killing and then when I contacted Grizek. And while I'm a target, I don't intend to sit still. I'll be looking for Grizek's mystery lady or anybody else who'll talk to me."

Richards looked at me without moving a muscle in his face. "I suppose, given what you've been through, I can't blame you," he said. "I just wouldn't rely much on what Grizek told you."

"You knew him?" I asked.

"Oh, yeah, not well, but I pulled him in myself a couple of times for drunken driving. He wasn't a regular drunk, but he'd go on a bender now and again, like a few others around here. If he didn't get violent or crazy, we took him home on occasion when we got calls from bartenders. As best as I know, he didn't have much in the way of either friends or family."

"You know anything about where he worked, what he did?" I asked.

"No, just that he did some construction work, drove some heavy machinery, various things," Richards said. "I never knew him to stick with anything for long."

"Did he ever work for Jean Houghton?"

"Not that I know about, but like I said, I don't know much about him."

We talked a bit longer, but he had scant more information to offer. I expressed surprise that the police had so little to work with despite the two murders, probably linked, on their hands. Richards agreed that something larger and nastier than he initially expected was going on, but he threw up his hands when I asked if he had ideas about what it was.

"Yeah, I have ideas, but you won't like 'em," he said.

"Try me. I'm past the point of getting upset at ideas."

"Aaron was into something, probably drugs, that got him killed," Richards said. "Maybe he was part of a group, Grizek, too. They could have each been couriers or small-time dealers. Something bad happens. They both piss somebody off, both end up dead. Stranger things have happened. The investigators are looking again for anything we might have missed. And we're going back to every drug informant we can find."

"I'm happy we're beyond the notion that Aaron's killing was a drive-by shooting, but other than the cocaine on the bike, you don't have a shred of evidence tying either Aaron or Grizek to drugs," I said.

"Not right now, I agree, but it's the only scenario that makes sense."

I'd said that ideas wouldn't upset me, but this one still did. "You're wrong about Aaron, and anybody who knew him will tell you the same. He wasn't involved in drugs."

Richards looked at the ceiling. "Don't let your heart get in the way of your brain on this one, Kardon. And maybe you get off on seeing yourself on television, but that stuff isn't going to help you find the killer."

He was the second one in a few hours to tell me that my instant fame didn't impress him. Any chance of a swelled head was diminishing rapidly.

At the end of our chat it was too late to go back to the office so I drove home. The phone was ringing as I walked in the door. When I didn't answer, it simply rang again in a few minutes. Instead of answering, I took off for a short run. I headed down Beacon Street, over to the banks of the Charles River, where lights reflected on the water and lovers held hands.

Back at the house, equilibrium restored and a Killian's Irish Red in front of me, I went through the messages on the answering system. Most could wait for the next day, including one from Jenny telling me she had a deal that I couldn't refuse.

The most interesting call had come in from Al Thompson. His message said that he'd been away fishing and hadn't seen any news about me until he returned. He wanted me to call him right away. Thompson trumped Jenny and I called him at his home.

Thompson picked up the phone. "You sound in pretty good shape for a Stone Age warrior," he said and laughed. "Ought to take you with me on my next hunting trip. Maybe you could teach me some things."

"Yeah, well, I'm an expert with the weapons they used back when you were a kid," I said.

After giving me a brief description of his raucous salmon-fishing trip to New Brunswick with a group of old drinking buddies, he was all business, the retired cop back on the crime scene. He wanted to know about my conversation with Grizek as well as the events with Henning. We talked about the absence of suspects for Aaron's murder and the trouble the police were having linking up the two murders. I told him about my meeting with Richards and his suspicion about drugs. I also mentioned my interest in Sandy, Jean's daughter.

There was silence for a bit. "I just don't believe it was Jean," Thompson said. "Maybe Sandy could have been involved, but it still seems unlikely."

"Al, did you know Grizek?" I asked.

"Yeah, I knew him, a bit like Richards knew him," he said. "Only I took him home over a lot more years and probably from more bars. Guy was never nasty or obnoxious, usually just morose. He'd carp about his job or his boss or his ex-wives. A few times I had to arrest him for driving drunk. He had his license suspended once or twice. He was a lucky son of a bitch, never got in any serious accidents I knew about."

"Did he ever talk about the Houghtons or the tire pile?" I asked.

"I remember one time, sometime in my last year or two, I picked him up one night. He squawked about not being paid as much as he'd been promised for a trucking job taking tires from a tire pile. Didn't say from where, but could have been the Houghtons' tire pile. Lot of what he said I didn't catch, but I do recall him saying something like, 'She may be a looker, but she's also a bitch.' "

"So maybe the daughter employed him for something," I said. "You think he talked about taking tires away from the site, not trucking them into the tire pile?"

"Yeah, I remember that because it seemed to make no sense," Thompson said.

"You ever talk to the Houghtons about him or that particular project?"

"No, just had that one conversation with Grizek about working there. Never thought more about it. But I still think you got a ways to go to make that connection."

"Yeah, but you've given me a little bit more than I had," I said. "And nothing you've said tells me I'm on the wrong track."

"Could be you're right, but I hope not," he said. "I've always admired Jean, and I have a tough time believing she's connected to this. She's been through so much, she's worked damn hard to get where she is, and she's got plenty of money. Why would she or her family get involved in this kind of a nightmare? But I know you can't argue with two dead bodies."

"No, and I'm just as happy there wasn't a third."

"I'm glad you mentioned that. I know this

means a lot to you, but you better be careful, son, real careful. I don't have good feelings about what's going on."

"I'll keep my eyes wide open."

"All right, it's your scalp. Maybe literally. But you need help, you call me."

We talked for a while longer. I promised to let him know what happened. I could hear the tension in him. On the one hand, he cared about Jean Houghton and her family. On the other, he still had the blood and instincts of a cop coursing through him. I wouldn't bet against those instincts.

CHAPTER ——————

TWENTY-SIX

First thing in the morning, Jenny bounced into my office. With a smile I hadn't seen since our small dispute, she waved a letter at me. "I think you're going to like this."

"Don't tell me, let me guess. I've been offered a permanent spot on *American Gladiators*."

"Not even close."

"An axe manufacturer wants to start a signature model using my name on the handle."

"Aren't we clever this morning? You're wrong again, and no more guesses. The Red Sox have invited you to throw out the first ball for the Patriot's Day game at home next season. And you get four front-row seats. They're having a day to honor people who helped prevent crime, and they want you and three others they've selected."

I had to smile at that one. Patriot's Day is a state holiday in April, celebrating Paul Revere's ride, the first battle of the American Revolution, and (if we're lucky) the beginning of the end of nasty New England winters. The Boston Marathon is held on that day and the runners go right by Fenway Park. The baseball game starts at eleven A.M. When it ends, the spectators wander out into Kenmore Square and watch the end of the marathon. A big party all around. "That would be kind of fun. I can bring Mike Steiner. Man, would he love that scene."

"Are you trying to tell me you wouldn't love to throw out the first ball, that you're doing this only for Mike?" Jenny asked.

"No, that would be cool, so long as I get to pitch off the mound and not from the stands."

"I already figured that out and the Red Sox have agreed."

"You're pretty good at this agent thing, aren't you? Unfortunately, no money in it for you."

"No, but I'm holding out for one of those four seats."

"Sounds like a fair deal to me. So long as I haven't fired you by then."

She made a face at that. "The way things are going around here, buddy, we may both be fired. With the checks I've seen come in this month, you've got a shot at being sent down to the minors, or maybe we'll just skip your paycheck altogether." She could take on any general manager in baseball, no problem.

Jenny then gave me capsule descriptions of the work that needed doing, some of which I promised to take on. I plugged some depositions and hearings into my schedule and agreed to call some clients.

We talked about the investigation for a brief, awkward period. Again I told her the best thing she could do was to keep the office going. Her eyes went flinty, but she didn't say anything.

Randy Blocker had called a couple of times. One voice in my head told me to call him back and tell him of the potential Grizek-Houghton connection. But I heard another voice, too, one I'd never heard before, telling me to finish what I'd started, clear the slate for Aaron, pay the bastards back. That voice scared me, but not as much as the thought of handing it all over to the cops and walking away. I didn't make the call.

Usually when I had to scrutinize business and financial records for a client, it bored me silly. In this case, I had more enthusiasm for the process. I began with the lists the D.A.'s office had prepared.

The three lists each had different headings. The first, titled "Employees," was six pages long and had a column of names and addresses on the left and a column of dates on the right. The dates appeared to be the dates of employment for each of the employees. Some individuals were missing start or finish dates. None of the names on the list meant anything to me, and Grizek's name didn't show up on it.

A second list, captioned "HTTI," had a column with names and addresses of companies, towns or government agencies, and a few individuals. The list went on for over forty pages. My rough estimate indicated that it contained over four hundred names. The list apparently included firms that had sold and shipped tires to the tire pile over the years of its operation. It also included service stations; car dealerships; trucking, construction, and rental car companies; manufacturers; and state agencies from all over New England and a few from New York: the kind of places that would own or operate cars and trucks and therefore have old tires to get rid of.

The third list, titled "TEI," was much shorter, only three pages, and was comprised of approximately thirty names and addresses. Almost all of the names were towns or municipal authorities along the eastern seaboard from Florida to Virginia. It made no sense until it occurred to me that the names might include some of the towns and enterprises that had created artificial reefs with Houghton tires. In that light, I took a look at the few other names. One of them was a power company; perhaps exploring the possibility of creating a facility to burn tires for energy in the Northeast. The other names had no meaning, but the list gave me something to work with.

I started by calling the assistant D.A. who had given the listings to me. He didn't exactly gush when he heard who I was, but he didn't hang up on me either.

"What can you tell me about the lists?" I asked.

"We made up the employee list from payroll

records we found on the site," he said. "Don't have a
clue if they're accurate. Records were pretty messy."

"What about the other two lists?"

"Made 'em up from billing logs. Whole operation there was manual. Amazing, no computers."

"Why two sets of names?" I asked.

"Simple. Two sets of records," he said. "One
large set of records was under the name Houghton
Tire and Trucking, Inc. The second log was under
the name of Tire Enterprises, Inc."

"What have you done with the lists?"

"Interviewed some of the employees, that's
about it. Looked at the customer records and tried
to cross-check for any known bad actors. That's
about all I can tell you. We don't do a lot of these
cases, so we're working with the state and federal
environmental folks."

I changed tack. "Any luck identifying any of the
companies sending waste to the site?"

He grunted, then said, "Man, I can't get into that
stuff."

"Look, I've been in the business," I said. "I
know the drums themselves don't tell you much,
they're often reused by different companies. And I
know the folks who run sites like this one don't
keep great records for the IRS or anyone else. I'm
not trying to solve your hazardous waste case, I just
want anything that will help me on the other cases."

"All right, Kardon, I hear you. We figure the
waste came from a few small companies that accumulated their crap, paid cash, and didn't sign any-

thing. But right now, no names. That'll take time."

"So you'll have to work it back through the operators, nail them and see if they give anybody up."

"Probably," he said. "Once the enforcement team and lab guys have the analytical work all done and we can show that the stuff is hazardous waste, the Houghtons will be charged for illegal possession and disposal, I imagine."

At that point, if Jean wanted to avert a jail sentence, she'd have to establish that she knew nothing about her sons' actions. She might succeed if the boys had run their little operation without telling Mom so they could keep the cash for themselves. But Jean would have to make the choice of saving herself by pointing a finger at her sons. Or the boys would have to protect her by giving themselves up. And if they did, they would also likely give up the companies that shipped the waste in order to plea-bargain lighter sentences.

After we finished discussing the records, the assistant D.A. wanted to know what I was following up on. Truthfully, I told him I was on a fishing expedition and I had no idea if there was any significance to the lists. He seemed mollified but told me to call if I came up with anything.

Two hours later, most of which I spent staring into space, an idea occurred to me. I went over to the Secretary of State's office in the state office building at One Ashburton Place. The building sits across the street from the gold-domed state capitol. But proximity to elegance has done nothing to improve the appearance of One Ashburton.

The building is twenty-five or so stories high, boxy, with a boring and minimally maintained lobby area. In addition to people, mice work in the building. I should know. I lost countless packages of junk food to them when I worked in the Attorney General's office, just a few floors above the Secretary of State, where I now sat.

The Secretary of State's office keeps records about Massachusetts corporations. By looking through index cards and microfiche, I could check out corporate records that companies were required to file when they were incorporated or filed annual reports. The files I looked through did have data on the Houghton companies.

Not surprisingly, the president of Houghton Tire and Trucking, Inc. was Jean Houghton. Her sons were treasurer and secretary. The three of them and Sandra Houghton owned all of the stock, and they were all directors. But Jean owned seventy percent of the shares, giving her a more than comfortable margin of control. The company's records dated back to the late 1960s, about what I expected. As updated over the years, they gave the addresses of the officers, which matched the addresses I had for the Houghton family.

Tire Enterprises, Inc. was a much younger company, set up in 1987. Again, the Houghton boys were secretary, treasurer, and directors. The surprise, though, was that Sandra Houghton, not Jean, was listed as president, holding sixty percent of the stock. Jean was neither an officer or stockholder. I jotted down the New York City address and phone number for Sandra Houghton included in the company records.

For a few minutes, I sat there, working through what I'd discovered and contemplating how to make use of it. Jean Houghton might not have much to do with her daughter anymore, but her sons did. It looked like Houghton Tire and Trucking, Inc. brought the tires in and Tire Enterprises, Inc., on a much smaller scale, sold and shipped tires out. The sons were involved with both companies, but shipping the tires out must have required others to do some of the work. Time to forget Mom and focus on daughter.

Walking back to the office, I thought about the differences between the companies. Jean Houghton controlled the tire pile and a trucking company that picked up tires and brought them to the tire pile. People paid her to take the tires, or for trucking services, or both. The trucking company's customers were people or firms with tires, period. A simple, low-tech company with substantial profit margins.

Somewhere along the line, the sons became greedy for more and didn't want to wait until Jean retired or died. They realized they could generate easy cash on the side by taking on customers Jean didn't know about. They put the word out to small companies that wanted hazardous waste buried for less than the legitimate disposal companies charged. Buried waste under the tire pile would take years to be discovered. Ultimately, though, the chemicals would leach out into the groundwater or the nearby stream, and the neighbors or authorities would figure out what happened. Maybe the boys didn't know that, or perhaps they planned to be gone by then. Jean Houghton would not have approved, so they didn't ask her. They just set up a few extra truck runs to service the clients with the illegal cargoes.

Meanwhile, Sandra Houghton saw an asset just sitting there, which she converted into a marketable product. Jean Houghton was paid to take the tires. Sandy and the boys were paid to deliver the tires and make artificial reefs elsewhere. Either Jean didn't care because she knew the sales of the tires were small compared to her business, or she liked the fact that her daughter had some tie to the family business.

Perhaps Sandy had done with the tires as she had with her coworkers and bartenders at Jefferson University, simply diversified the corporate opportunities. The burning question was whether her new corporation had gone beyond setting up reefs to doing something else, something that ended in violence. Something that killed Aaron.

All of that, of course, left me no closer to figuring out what happened to Aaron or why Grizek was killed. If Richards was right and Aaron had been involved in buying drugs, we had no evidence that the Houghtons or either Houghton company had any drug connections. Nor did Grizek turn up on the list of employees of Houghton Tire and Trucking, which corroborated Jean Houghton. And we had no list of the Tire Enterprises, Inc. employees.

At the same time, if Tire Enterprises only performed occasional projects, it might not have regular employees and might hire outside drivers. One like Grizek.

Grizek, in turn, in his travels to southern seacoast towns carrying tires for the artificial reefs, could have become acquainted with Cape Hatteras, a place that would have appeared safe and serene. There were, in fact, two North Carolina towns listed on the Tire Enterprises list.

All of this was speculation, but it was as plausible—or more plausible—than anything else we had. And it gave me a shadowy outline to work on.

When I arrived back at the office, Jenny remarked upon my good mood. In an act of indulgence, I told her we were closing the office early for drinks and dinner. She protested, saying she had work to do and there was mail I should review. In a fit of self-aggrandizement, I told her it would all wait, that I had more important things to discuss.

Over a pint of strong red ale at Boston Beer Works near Fenway Park, I told her what the corporate records showed and what I thought the information meant. Toward the end of my beer, and before she'd done much damage to her beer, she looked at me across the table, no smile.

"Maybe I said a bit too much the other day, but I just wanted to know what's going on and to help," she said.

"Don't worry about it, I could see I upset you. When you go over the line, I'll let you know."

"Well, you may have to do that now. I'm still trying to figure you out. You've turned up a lot, and now you're out there, putting yourself more at risk. Maybe you're closer to tying Grizek to the Houghtons, but you still have nothing about Aaron." Her tone was not sharp or argumentative, more cool and analytical.

Cool and analytical was not what I wanted. I gnawed on a chicken wing while trying to come up with an answer. "If you're asking why I'm doing this, we've been over that," I finally said. "It's important to a lot of people, me included. And I'll be careful." I went back to my beer.

She took a drink of hers. "This really isn't about Aaron, is it?"

"What are you talking about?" I tried to keep the sharpness out of my voice, with only marginal success.

For a moment, I watched as she fiddled with a napkin, looking at it intently. Finally, she edged forward in her chair, clasped her hands on the table in front of her and looked at me.

"You know, while I was with Ann at the hospital waiting for you, she told me that when you were in college and your sister committed suicide, you pretty much crawled into a hole, wouldn't talk to your parents or anybody. She and Frank were the ones who kept you going."

"Yeah," I said. "I wasn't a real happy cowboy back then. For a few weeks, they kept me grounded in reality, I'd guess you'd say."

"So maybe you think you owe Ann and Frank something big."

"They've been great friends." I shrugged and took another swing of beer.

"Yes, but I think there's something else, too, like maybe you feel guilty about your sister."

"Is this therapy for free or do I get a bill later?"

"You know," she said, ignoring my comment, "teenage girls are a little more complicated than you might think. Things happen inside them that can be pretty damn painful and mysterious. I know, I've been there. Television, movies, tell us to have smooth skin, skinny legs, and big boobs, while our teachers and parents want us to be bright, go to good schools, get good jobs. But you learn that it's not always great to be as smart as the boys, or to do better in school, or to want the same jobs. The girls that do the best, they usually aren't too popular with the other kids, and dates are hard to come by. And sometimes people don't listen quite as hard to girls as they do to boys. The girls who play on teams don't have the bands, the cheerleaders, the crowds that the boys who play football and basketball do." She stopped for a breath and a sip.

"I don't know what—"

"Hold on, let me finish, then you can tell me

you don't know what I'm talking about, argue with me, fire me, whatever. Nobody's to blame, or maybe everybody is, I don't know, but it's tough trying to figure things out when you're a teenage girl. You throw drugs, sex, alcohol into the mix, it gets even crazier.

"What I'm trying to say is, I'm guessing you still blame yourself some, maybe your parents, too, for what your sister did. Maybe you and your parents weren't as responsive as you could have been, but you're burying yourself in guilt. You need to get past it. You didn't kill her, your parents didn't kill her, and blaming yourself won't bring her back."

"Right now I'm not trying to get anyone back, I'm trying to find out what happened to Aaron, that's all."

"Ann also told me about your fiancée, Elaine, how she died and you took off and traveled right after that."

"I think maybe Ann said too much. I'm not doing this for either my sister or Elaine."

"I know, that's what I'm saying. It's for you, because of how you define yourself, how you see yourself falling short when it comes to people you care about. You've got to let go of the burden of your sister's death. And nothing you could have done would have saved your fiancée from a drunken driver either. You can love people as much as possible, but still you can't protect them from all the evils of the world or the flaws in themselves."

"Believe me, I understand all too well there was

nothing I could do to save Elaine."

"Maybe you understand it, but do you accept it? Do you forgive yourself for it?"

I had good answers for a lot of questions, but not for that one. I just sat there, staring into my beer.

She gave me a small smile. "Sorry, I'll get off the soap box. I don't mean to give you such a hard time. It's funny. When I came to work with you, not long ago, I was looking for my own kind of redemption. I wanted to rebuild my confidence, pump up my self-image, all that classic pop psychology stuff. I'm doing that slowly, with the things you're letting me do.

"Could be that's you, too, in some way I don't get. Maybe I'm way off base and I've missed the questions eating at you. But you've got some powerful demons driving you in this investigation. I can't be sure what it's about, but I hope you find whatever it is you're looking for before you get yourself killed."

I did feel a powerful compulsion to keep going, despite my fear, convinced it would satisfy something inside I'd never identified. I'd seen Aaron rebound from his losses and find a dream of riding and racing. His capacity to dream contrasted sharply with the emptiness that filled my life after Jacqueline, then Elaine, had died. My visions for the future seemed to dry up and blow away. Completing the task of refurbishing Aaron's memory and the integrity of his dreams might restore a piece of me as well.

Jenny gave me the chance to say all this but the words wouldn't come out. I sucked on a new beer to pass the time, make the silence at our table less conspicuous, and ease the tension I felt. Jenny seemed to sense my discomfort and let me off the hook.

She reached up, pulled her hair away from her eyes and smiled. "Hey, I didn't mean to lay a heavy trip on you. You've treated me well, given me some good stuff to do. But I worry about you. It's like you feel compelled to walk into a hurricane. The violence around you is escalating. You may not be able to avoid it next time."

"I appreciate the concern. I'm really not looking for a hurricane—I want the truth. But if a hurricane comes along, I plan to walk out the other side."

We drank and ate for a while before turning to office talk. Jenny told me about various cases and asked my advice on a number of issues. Other cases held little interest for me, but I focused as best I could.

After a couple of hours, I left her at the Kenmore subway station. "Thanks, boss," she said. "See you in the morning."

For a moment I thought about asking her whether she wanted to go back for a beer or three, go to a club, catch a movie, anything. But apprehension froze my tongue. I told myself I was just being the appropriate employer, but at another level I couldn't face the prospect of having Jenny lay bare more of my insides.

The subway ride and walk home in the cool night brought a small measure of rationality. At home, with beer, Jenny, and legal cases left behind, I resolved to approach Sandy Houghton directly, just as I had her mother, this time knowing something more about the companies and their activities.

Out of my briefcase, I pulled the yellow pad on which I'd copied the New York phone number for Sandy Houghton from the corporate records. My call reached an answering machine that had a cool, utterly undistinguished female voice telling me the number I'd reached and to leave a message. With nothing to lose, I did. I had no idea if I had the right number. If there was no return message in a couple of days, I'd go into my computer data bases and try to locate Sandra Houghton.

As I hung up the phone I realized it was just as well I hadn't reached anybody. The odds of my being cogent and convincing on the phone were slim. I walked into my room, lay down fully clothed on my bed, and fell asleep.

CHAPTER

TWENTY-SEVEN

My courtroom appearance the next morning began with a major headache and a minor motion that I argued in court. Apart from a few snide comments from the judge about what some attorneys would do to get publicity, and the snickering of my lawyerly brethren, everything went smoothly. The familiarity of the session, with conferences outside in the hall, lawyers whispering in each other's ears, and the judge chastising each set of lawyers before him, felt comfortable. Life's unpleasant little surprises and controversies played out in moderately orderly courtrooms, not at tire piles and motel rooms.

The messiness of real life asserted itself as soon as court ended. I crossed town and went to the Boston Public Library. In the next few hours I quickly scrutinized back copies and microfiche of major newspapers in Boston, Providence, and

Concord, New Hampshire, during the month or so of Aaron's murder. I checked out headlines for criminal activity and then copied any articles that looked interesting. Articles about crimes involving drugs, robberies, or truck transportation all went into my pile. Anything involving domestic shootings or random street crimes I let pass.

I wanted to spend some time on a similar search for articles about the Houghton family. But by the time I'd finished my sweep of the remarkably inventive ways in which conservative, puritanical New Englanders had perpetrated crimes, I needed to get back to the office. The Houghton family saga would have to wait.

After making some overdue calls to assuage a few anxious clients, I sat down with over two inches of articles and excerpts I'd assembled. Jenny poked her head into my office just after I settled in.

"What's all that?" she asked.

"Articles about criminal activity around the time of Aaron's murder. Have to go back another day for stuff on the Houghtons."

"That's a big pile. You want some help? It'll be quicker with two of us looking it over, and then you'll have time for other things." Eagerness spilled out of her, lending high tones to her voice and glitter to her eyes. I didn't like disappointing her yet again, but I still wanted to use my own personal net on this fishing expedition. "No thanks. I know it will take more time, but I'll get it done."

The glitter vanished and her voice dropped.

"Dan, I know you'll get it done. I'm just trying to be helpful."

"I know. I appreciate the offer, but I want to look through these myself, categorize them, see if there's any one thing or maybe a pattern that stands out. It's a long shot, but it's one of the few things I can think of to do. If you could hold the fort out there for a couple of hours, that'll be the best help. I'm sorry—I know you want to help and you've already done a lot. I'm just doing this the best way I know how. And, of course, if you do some paid work, maybe we won't be evicted." I gave her my best shot at a charming smile. She gave me a combination grumble and sigh. As a gesture of conciliation, if not approval, she went out and came back with a cup of coffee and cookies, then closed the door.

First, I skimmed the articles as best I could to categorize them. Simple shootings, gang violence, and murders in which the police had identified a prime suspect I put in one distressingly large pile. Drug crimes or violence apparently related to drugs went into another. Burglaries, bank robberies, corporate crimes, and miscellaneous articles went into another. Only one article focused on a truck. Some kids had broken into a dump truck on a hill and released the safety brake and clutch. The truck ended up in somebody's living room—unpleasant for the homeowner but not likely to precipitate a murder.

Once the articles were sorted, I went through

the piles again, looking for anything that Aaron might have seen or become involved in. There were no significant violent crimes reported in the towns he'd have visited on his bike. No big drug busts occurred in his area during the month in question. For a time my long shot had no legs.

Midway through the last pile of miscellaneous articles, it picked up steam. One article set alarms off in my head. It described a large theft of computer chips from a computer company in eastern Massachusetts which had occurred the day before Aaron was found dead. I vaguely recalled the heist, which had appeared in some papers because of its unusual nature.

The article's significance didn't hit me for a minute, but then the name of the company kicked in. Dynacomp, located in Westborough, was a well-known, large Massachusetts computer company. One of the catalogues I'd been drooling over a short time ago featured their computers and work stations. And the company was also a place where Sandra Houghton had worked. I banged my desk and gave out a loud "Yes."

Jenny burst into my office. "What's the matter?" she said. "What are you yelling about?"

"One of these articles. I have some more checking to do, but I'm on to something."

"What is it?"

"Let me check it out first," I said. "It's just a hunch, but I think I may have a connection. If I'm right, Aaron saw something he wasn't supposed to see. More important, his murder had nothing to do with drugs."

"What are you going to do next?"

"Do more research, make some calls, and dig up another article or two. If I find anything, I'll take it to the cops or the D.A."

"No more being a hero? You'll call Randy or Richards?"

"Yeah, I'll try and be a good boy."

Jenny gave me a piercing glare. "Trying won't cut it, buddy," she said. "This time, you get no slack. No head start like you had in North Carolina. I'll call Randy, Richards, or the damn FBI right away if I have to." She waited a beat, then gave me a smile, sort of. "After all, you're a celebrity now, your adoring public wants you safe and sound. And, of course, you pay my salary, so I want you to stick around, too."

I smiled back. "Fair enough. I don't want to let you or the Red Sox down. In the meantime, though, I want to get back to chasing the bad guys. Or girls."

Jenny gave me a little mock curtsy. "Yes, master, I know my place. I'll return to my quarters."

"Oh, give me a break. Be careful, you might get your wish—if this ends quickly, I'll go back to doing real work cranking out long, boring legal documents for you to type." She tossed her hair, swiveled, and left me alone.

I read the article I'd isolated one more time. The theft of computer chips from Dynacomp had occurred at night. Two security guards were clubbed and tied up. Crates of chips were then stolen from a locked storage area in the facility. The article speculated that insiders had been involved since the armed robbers knew a great deal about the guards' schedules and the layout of the facility.

Somebody must have known the computer industry well or had good instructions. Garden-variety felons wouldn't know a potato chip from a computer chip, and would probably prefer to steal the former. I'd learned enough through my own reading and computer explorations to know that a gray, and sometimes black, market exists for computer chips. The component makers—Intel Corp. is the best known, but many others exist, large and small—sell enormous batches of chips to computer manufacturers. They also sell chips to authorized distributors, who sell them to other manufacturers. In the distribution process, chips are often diverted, sometimes legally, sometimes not.

The article about the Dynacomp theft said that companies in Silicon Valley had suffered thefts amounting to as much as forty or fifty million dollars in chips per year. For a select few in the distribution business, the work was no less lucrative than selling drugs.

Stolen chips command high prices because shortages inevitably develop. Supply bottlenecks, manufacturing problems, or unexpected surges in sales of particular computers or components can quickly affect the prices for specific chips.

Memory chips, logic chips, chips for video displays, Pentium IIs, MediaGXs, 6x86MX, Alphas, K6s, 15406s, DRAMs, SRAMs, or transistors, all have differing characteristics, manufacturers, serial numbers, and prices. If someone knew which chips were in high demand and could obtain those chips at low or no cost, a tidy profit could be turned quickly. A single chip may not be worth a lot, but crates or boxes of them are. In their own market, chips are commodities, like soy beans or coffee. For some people, the chips stolen from Dynacomp would be a commodity just like gold. Or tires.

Even better for the crooks who hit Dynacomp, the crime was new to New England. The police might not react quickly or knowledgeably.

Sandra Houghton would have had easy access to information about the company, as well as to trucks, a site for transferring chips to other trucks or vans, and the people required for stealing and transporting the chips. And she'd never show up as a suspect to the law enforcement agents or the company.

It was late in the day when I called the police in Westborough, where Dynacomp was located. I didn't know anybody in the office, so I didn't get much information. The officer named in the article would tell me only that the crime was still under investigation and no arrests had been made.

As soon as that call ended, Jenny walked into my office. "There's a call you might like to take," she said.

"I'm still working on this thing. Can't it wait?"

"Oh, I think you'd like it."

"Why? Who's on the phone?"

"Sandra Houghton." I almost got whiplash looking up from the articles. Jenny went on. "Remember, you promised you wouldn't do anything stupid."

"Yeah, I remember. I'll take it."

Jenny walked out and I stared at the phone, willing Sandy Houghton to stay on the line.

It rang. "Hi, this is Dan Kardon."

"This is Sandy Houghton returning your call."

"Thanks for getting back to me."

"My—well, pleasure, of sort. Your adze-wielding fame precedes you, Mr. Kardon. Nobody I know would turn down the chance to talk with you. You can be sure I will put this call to good advantage at cocktail parties for months. I expect, though, that our family discussions about you may be more heated." The tone was flat, not hostile. Her voice was low and without an accent, carrying no trace of Jean Houghton or New Bedford.

"You've talked to your mother, I assume."

She hesitated. "Not recently. My mother and I don't talk much. I'm in touch with my brothers and other friends in the area. I don't understand your role in all that's been going on, but I gather you're looking into a connection between our family business and the college student who was killed last summer. And I've also been led to believe you might be linked to the investigation of some dumping at the tire pile. You seem to be fairly industrious."

"Yes, I've been investigating the killing of Aaron Winters. He was a good kid and a friend."

"Why do you have my family under scrutiny?"

She was cool, she was good, giving nothing but pumping me instead. "I can't tell you much, Ms. Houghton, but you probably know there's evidence that Aaron had been at the tire pile not long before he was killed."

"But that evidence does not implicate my family, does it, Mr. Kardon? Or someone from my family would have been under arrest by now. I know little about criminal investigations, but I do know that murderers are usually caught quickly if they're caught at all. The police are satisfied that we are not involved in the murder at this point. I can only view you as a dark cloud, a pestilence jeopardizing my family's future. Why should I have anything to do with you?"

Good question. Part of me wanted nothing to do with her, but rather to pursue what I had and not give her the chance to cover her tracks. But I also had a competing sense, a feeling that if I kept the connection with her, I might accelerate the pace of things.

"Refusing to talk with me won't stop me," I said.

"Neither will talking with you, I expect."

She paused, and I let the silence fill the phone.

"What do you want to talk about?" she asked.

"How the tire pile and the family business operated. Your brothers are suspects in the illegal dumping investigation, we both know that. Their lawyer, quite properly, wouldn't let me near them. Instead, I've contacted both you and your mother."

"What did my mother tell you?"

"Not much."

"So I represent your last hope?" she said. "And if I say no, your investigation of my family will have reached a sizable barrier, I would assume."

"Maybe, but I understand you're a pretty sharp businesswoman. Always have to watch your assumptions."

There was a pause and her voice turned a notch lower and harder. "Are you threatening me, Mr. Kardon?"

"Nope. I want to talk to you because it may get me to certain places faster. If you won't talk, I'll just find other ways to those places. I've always wanted to visit Jefferson University, for example. The school has a fascinating history, I understand."

A soft sigh came across the line. Her intonation changed slightly, her words became more clipped. "Mr. Kardon, I don't know yet if you are legitimately investigating or hoping to blackmail me. Blackmail won't work, I promise."

"I'm not trying to blackmail you, but I'll go anywhere and talk to anybody to get useful information. And anything I find will go to the police. So far, we have the murders of Aaron and Jeff Grizek as well as the illegal disposal of hazardous waste, all with some connection to your family's tire pile.

Your background, your brothers' background, anything about your mother, it's all fair game now. You can stick your head in the sand and hope this is just a bad dream, or you can give me information that might help us figure out what happened and clear your family. Your choice, Ms. Houghton. I should point out, though, that for the family of Aaron Winters this isn't just a bad dream and I'm not going away."

"You don't mince words, Mr. Kardon."

"So I've been told."

The line was silent for a moment, then Sandra Houghton responded. "I need to think about whether I want to talk with you, and I'll talk to my family as well. Anything that happened in Virginia is completely irrelevant and from a distant past, but perhaps I need to convince you of that. As for the other issues you raise, you won't find anything on me or my family, Mr. Kardon. We are not angels and we may not qualify for high society, but we all worked long and hard in our respective businesses. You're wrong to pursue my family. I have my differences with my mother, but she raised us with integrity. That integrity will allow us to persevere, Mr. Kardon, and we will emerge unscathed."

A stirring speech, beautifully delivered. I almost believed her.

"Ms. Houghton, I would be delighted to find that none of you were involved in any of this. Can I call you back about a meeting?"

"As it turns out, I am scheduled to fly to Boston

later tonight for a meeting first thing tomorrow morning. If I have a chance, I'll talk to people and get back to you. But no promises."

"If your meeting ends early, how about meeting me here in Boston?"

She laughed. "No, Mr. Kardon, not with the weather reports I've seen. It's supposed to be a warm and windy day. I love to windsurf, and if the weather is accommodating, I will head directly to Wettamesett. Even if I decided to meet you, which I haven't, I'll be windsurfing tomorrow."

"I'd never stand in the way of fun," I said. "But I can also meet you in Wettamesett tomorrow evening if you like."

"You are persistent, Mr. Kardon, I give you that. I'll be in touch. Goodbye."

I looked at the phone as I hung it up. Windsurfing at Tern Point—an activity that had attracted Aaron, perhaps unwittingly to his death. The outline remained shrouded, but a pattern lay below the surface, a web of activities and interrelationships I could only barely distinguish. Sandy Houghton had been involved in something. Aaron had stumbled upon it or upon her. I still had to make the case, but at last the pieces were coming together.

After the phone conversation, Jenny was eager to hear it replayed. I laid it out without embellishment, explaining for the first time what I'd learned earlier about Sandy Houghton's college escapades. Jenny vacillated between moral outrage and feminist pride. She also expressed concern about my meeting with the younger Houghton, but I brushed it off, promising to check in with the D.A.'s office or Richards if a meeting did occur.

Finally, I asked Jenny to cover a couple of matters in court for me the following day. I didn't know if Sandra Houghton would call, but if she did, I wanted to know all I could about who she was.

CHAPTER ———

TWENTY-EIGHT

Friday dawned as promised, unusually warm and with a westerly breeze. The morning weather report said that temperatures would hit the mid-seventies and the weekend would be a slice of true New England Indian summer. Walking to the Boston Public Library, people everywhere had smiles and talked to one another, hardly routine for a workday, or most days, in Boston. The confluence of a Friday morning and unexpectedly warm weather gave everybody more of an upper than coffee could.

I spent the morning going through newspapers, to no avail. If the Houghtons or the tire pile had ever shown up in articles, I couldn't find them. I was hamstrung because the library didn't have microfiche for local papers from smaller southeastern Massachusetts cities and towns. After a couple of hours I retreated to my office.

From there I called the *New Bedford Standard-Times*. The paper had a library where they kept back copies. The woman working in the library would help me do a search, I was told, if I specified what I wanted. But not today, since she wasn't in. No quick help there.

Then I located and called a couple of other papers located in smaller towns in the area. None could give me immediate help or information; I'd have to visit or write each one separately. By noon I knew nothing more about Sandy Houghton or her family than when I'd started.

Finally, with no other bright ideas coming to me, I remembered Beth Woodward, the managing editor of the Jefferson University college paper.

"Hello, this is the *Beacon* office," a male voice said.

"Hi, this is Dan Kardon, an attorney in Boston. Is Beth Woodward there?"

"Just a minute."

"Hello, Mr. Kardon, how are you?" a familiar female voice said.

"I'm fine, Beth, how's school going?"

She gave a laugh and sounded a little embarrassed. "Well, to be honest, between the paper and some other things, I haven't worked too hard. But we've got exams soon, so I'm going to have to start cramming."

"I hope things go well. But I called about getting some research done. My first question is, how old is the paper?"

"It started in 1967 as one of those alternative papers," she said and then giggled.

"I guess it's not so alternative these days."

"No, pretty mainstream."

"How would you like to make a little money?" I asked. "I'd love to hire you to review back copies of the paper from the spring of 1980 to look for some articles."

"Awesome. When do you need it done?"

"I'd like it done today or over the weekend, if possible."

"Thing is," she said, "I have a biology lab this afternoon and then I'm going out of town over the weekend. Plus, you know, we don't have back copies here, they're off-site in storage."

"None at all?"

"Nope."

"Damn. Well, I appreciate your time and—"

"We do have all the old copies on a computer here instead."

"You mean they're copied onto a computer data base, or a CD or something?"

"Yeah, a rich alumnus who used to work on the paper gave us a big chunk of money, so one thing we did is have all the back issues copied and put on a computer and then we moved the old papers to a storage place. Cleared up a lot of space, allowed us to put in some new equipment, and meant people could find stuff quicker."

"Well, is there anybody around who could check the data base this afternoon?" I asked.

"Can't say. The two of us here are about to leave."

"Nothing's working today. How about over the weekend? Is there anybody—"

"You could check things out yourself, if you have a modem and can get on the Net."

Bingo. It took a half an hour of horsing around with my computer system, which had me swearing I'd replace the thing, but with Beth's help I finally hooked up through my on-line subscription service and the Internet.

I checked out a number of issues, but had trouble reading some of the text on the computer. In hopes of improving legibility, I had all the weekly issues from the spring of 1980 downloaded into my computer and then had my computer print them out. Between the downloading and the printing, the process was slow and painful to watch and I all but ordered a new system from a catalogue on the spot.

I had a long list of things that clients needed done, and making calls, scratching out letters, and reviewing a contract took most of the remaining afternoon. Jenny's meeting was running late and she hadn't come back, so I had to cover the phones. Just after five P.M. the phone rang and I picked it up.

"Hello, this is the law office of Dan Kardon."

"Hello, is this Mr. Kardon?" There was static on the line and the voice had a tinny, distant tone.

"Yes, it is."

"This is Sandy Houghton. I've conferred with

my family, and I'm willing to meet with you, tonight if possible. I'm calling now from a car phone. I had a wonderful afternoon windsurfing and I'm just going to shower and change."

"Great day for it."

"Yes, it was a beautiful afternoon. If you wish, I can meet you in Wettamesett later for dinner."

"I'd like that."

"Do you know the area?"

" A little. I know some of the restaurants."

"Initially I thought we might eat at the Wettamesett Inn. But then I thought that it's warm enough to eat outside, perhaps with some take-out seafood."

"Sounds good."

"Do you know the Oxford Creamery on Route 6? Perhaps we could meet in the parking lot at seven P.M. If the weather becomes a problem, we can always go elsewhere."

"Sure. How will I recognize you? I'm—"

Even over the car phone, the laughter was distinct. "Mr. Kardon, I saw you in a clip on television. Believe me, I will have no trouble recognizing you."

"Okay. One other thing, feel free to call me Dan."

"Fine, Dan, I'll see you at seven."

Normally, the trip from Boston to Wettamesett would take only an hour and a quarter, maybe an hour and a half. Friday night at rush hour would mean a much longer trip so I had no time to play around. I changed into casual clothes I kept in the office to cover just this kind of social emergency. A suit might work at the Wettamesett Inn but it wouldn't work for a moonlit feast. More important, I might not get much information out of this meeting, but I could expect juicy fried clams, greasy french fries, and tartar sauce, all of which would look better on blue jeans than on suit pants.

Before leaving, I took a quick look at the back issues of the *Jefferson Beacon*. They were a little easier to read on paper than they had been on the computer, so I stuck them in my briefcase, along with the lists I'd gotten from the D.A.'s office. With luck, either I'd get to Wettamesett a bit early and have a chance to look at everything before I met with Sandy Houghton or I'd get stuck in traffic on the Southeast Expressway with some good reading material.

Finally, I switched the phones over to the answering system and left a message for Jenny, telling her where I was going and what I was doing. I thought about calling Randy, but I still had only suppositions and inferences to pass on. I'd call him after the meeting.

In the parking garage, cars battled their way down the spiral ramp, each one fighting to advance inches at a time. I'd parked in the garage late and so had the curse of a parking space on the eighth floor. From experience, the wait looked to be about five minutes, enough to have a quick look at the back issues.

I opened the folder with the papers at the seventh floor of the spiral exit ramp just as the driver behind my car honked at me for insufficient aggressiveness in the exit line. Skimming through to the end of the issues, I found a small headline announcing that Sandy Houghton's case had been dismissed. The article indicated that most honor trials were confidential, but knowledge about this one had become widespread.

By the time I'd read the article, which confirmed in more detail the story I'd heard about Sandy Houghton's college scandal, I was near the bottom of the exit ramp.

The article told me little new. A picture accompanied it, though, fuzzy but clear enough for my purposes. The caption under it said that the female student in the photo was Sandra Houghton celebrating after her case had been dismissed by the student judge.

The caption did not name the young man in a judge's robe standing behind her, but I didn't need a caption. I'd seen a picture of the same young man, only in football gear, in a photo sitting on a filing cabinet in Wettamesett.

A pay phone hung on a pillar at the bottom of the parking ramp. I raised the ire of every driver behind me in line by parking at the base of the garage ramp and running back to the phone. The parking attendants yelled at me. I yelled back that I had to make an emergency call.

I tried to reach Randy Blocker, but he was out, so I left a message to have him call me at home.

Based upon what I'd learned, I didn't want to take a chance on a more substantive message. The cacophony of horns behind me grew. I called my office and left another message for Jenny, telling her quickly what I'd found. A parking attendant approached me as I called Al Thompson. He, too, was out and did not have an answering machine. Then I got back in the car to the accompanying urban automotive choir.

Traffic was miserable heading down the expressway. To counter my frustration, I put on some vintage Bruce Springsteen and cranked it up high.

Once clear of Route 128, the highway encircling Boston, I picked up Route 24 heading south and pressed the accelerator. Speeding ticket or not, I didn't want to miss dinner with Sandy Houghton. Whatever else was served, I planned some surprises for her. I hoped to see her nervous and off balance. Just as I'd been for too damn long.

CHAPTER
TWENTY-NINE

I pulled into the Oxford Creamery parking lot just after seven P.M. It was still warm, and a line of people stood at the ice cream window on the side of the small restaurant. Families sat at picnic tables, downing their lobster rolls and clam plates. I stepped out of my car and stretched my legs, looking around to see if I'd recognize Sandy Houghton from the old newspaper picture I'd seen. I was gazing toward the restaurant when a voice came from behind me.

"Dan?"

I turned and faced a slender brunette, about five-five with short hair, stretch pants, and wearing a blue windbreaker with lots of zippers and pulls over a multicolored sweater and cream-colored blouse. She had a narrow face with round, gentle cheeks, a shapely mouth, and something of her mother around the eyes.

I hadn't seen Jean Houghton before the years of supporting a dissolute husband, a family, and a business added flesh to her frame and carved channels of worry in her face. Perhaps years ago mother and daughter looked more alike. All I could tell now was that Sandy Houghton's attractiveness had matured and become more compelling since the college picture I'd seen. Cute had become beautiful.

"Yes. I assume you're Sandy?"

"That's right. I appreciate your willingness to accommodate me on short notice and I apologize for not having called earlier." Her voice was a little higher in person than on the phone and her hand was firm, almost hard, when I shook it, maybe from windsurfing. From what I could see, the rest of her would probably be much the same.

"No problem. Thanks for meeting with me. And I admire your interest in sailing on a day like this. The air is warm, but the water must have been cold as hell."

"I wear a dry suit, gloves, booties, a hood, all sorts of things to keep warm. It sounds crazy, I know, and most of my friends cannot understand it. But once you windsurf in strong winds and waves, it's enormously exhilarating, almost addictive. I will not venture out in the coldest winter weather, but usually until Thanksgiving I can sail."

"How do you get your equipment up from New York? And where do you keep it? From what I've heard, most places in the city don't have room for their inhabitants, let alone windsurfing equipment."

She laughed, soft and trilling. "No, I don't keep the equipment in New York. I have a friend in this area who keeps my equipment for me. I also borrow his car."

She pointed to a red Jeep Cherokee with roof racks on it. If I hadn't seen it before parked at the Wettamesett police station, I'd eat the roof racks.

"Sandy, what did you decide about dinner?"

"I failed to stake out a picnic table here. How about grabbing some dinner here and eating over at Tern Point? I have a six-pack I thought might entice you. We won't have many more nights like this one, so I thought dinner outside would be nice. But if you'd prefer, we can go to the inn or elsewhere."

"No, beer and a clam plate would be great. Why don't you tell me what you'd like and I'll get it?"

"We can drive to the park in my car. How about a plate of scallops, please. Let me give you some—"

"No, you brought the beer, dinner's the least I can do." I held up my hand to stop her from going into her purse. "I'll be over to the car in a few minutes with the food."

The small interior of the restaurant held a horde of people waiting patiently. The good moods I'd seen earlier in the day in Boston had permeated here, too. Even the kitchen workers behind the counter, accustomed to the din of shouted orders, harassment by customers, and the heat of the frying vats, had smiles on their faces. Investigating armed robbery and murder in these surroundings made no sense.

Bags of food in hand, I walked back to the car. I climbed into the passenger side after a quick, suspicious look in the back of the Cherokee. The light from the restaurant sufficed to see there was nobody crouching behind the front seat. Chiding my overactive imagination, I climbed in.

At Tern Point we left the car at the water's edge and walked back to a picnic table. Only a few clouds were overhead while we looked out over a calm sea and a rising moon. A gentle wind off the ocean brought the taste of salt and marshes, the perfect dinner condiments.

We each opened a beer. The only light was from the moon and a single floodlight, but it was enough for us to see one another.

After we settled in, she came right to the point.

"I'm well aware that we are not here to discuss fried clams or windsurfing. Why don't you tell me what you want?"

"I'd like to know more about the operation of the family business, what it involves, who does what, that sort of thing." I tried out a gentlemanly smile. "No need to discuss illegal dumping, of course."

"What illegal dumping?" she replied.

"Fair enough, but my question still stands."

"And if I don't answer," she said, "you start throwing around my little business enterprise in Virginia?"

I held up my hands in a shrug. "Haven't thought that far ahead."

"I don't believe that." She gave me a flat, level look for a moment before speaking again. "Well, in general, after my brothers got out of the service and settled back into the business, my mother gradually let them build up and run the trucking part of the operation while she dealt with the customers and the operation of the tire pile. She developed the tire pile and really does not want to let it go. Funny to think about someone having sentimental attachment to a tire pile, but I suppose that's what it is."

"She still contacts customers, markets, controls the finances, hires and fires, deals with government agencies, all that?" I asked.

"She still does most of those things, at least when she's around. There is no marketing to speak of. By now, people who want to dispose of tires find her. Many of the day-to-day operations she has turned over to the boys, but she still retains overall control. Except when she goes to Florida in the winter, she still visits the tire pile most workdays. She still looks over the books and deals with employees. Even with the truck operation, she insists on discussing any major decisions."

"Such as?"

"Oh, major new equipment purchases, different lines of hauling, other things."

"Can't be easy on your brothers, still having to answer to her," I said.

"I'm sure there is occasional friction."

"What about compensation? Are your brothers paid well?"

She gave a little shake of her head and smiled, staring down almost sadly at the table before looking up to speak. "Some areas are private, Dan, and that's one of them. I will try not to be annoyed when you pry into these things, but it is hard."

Under the circumstances, I didn't care. "You've never been involved in the tire pile or trucking operations?"

"No. The boys started early, working in high school. They were expected to get involved. They tried other things, but neither one found anything else they really wanted to do."

"That doesn't explain why you're not in the business," I said. "From what I've learned, you've got more business acumen and entrepreneurial spirit than either of your brothers."

Her mouth drew tight and her eyes half closed. "My mother never wanted me in it. She did not share your assessment, did not think my talents lay in business, so she kept me out of it."

"She wanted you to go to college, become a professional, that sort of thing? She must feel pretty good about how you've turned out."

She looked at me without seeing me, perhaps seeing something in her memory or herself. Her face gave away little, but a shadow seemed to pass across her eyes. "You'd have to ask her."

Jean and Sandy had given me remarkably similar descriptions of the tire pile, as well as similar stories about Sandy. But they had each given the story precisely the opposite interpretation. Jean said she didn't think the business was suitable for women and didn't want Sandy in it. Sandy took it that she was not suitable for the business.

"You and your mother don't get along too well, I gather."

"Gather as you will."

At that point Sandy Houghton became the cross-examiner. "How did you get involved in this case?" she asked. "Investigating a murder is hardly a routine activity for most of the lawyers I know."

"I knew Aaron and his family," I said. "None of us believe the killing was drug-related, as the police thought. The family desperately wants to know what happened, to clear Aaron's name. They also felt the police might not have the personnel to follow things up closely, so they asked me to get involved. We're making progress, slowly."

"Oh, from what I've read, that's a little false modesty. You seem to have accomplished plenty, including staying alive. How long do you intend to keep on with this?"

This time it was my gaze that was cool and level. "Long as it takes."

"What is the reward for you in this case?" she asked. "Do you get a rush from the hunt? Surely you can make money in easier ways." There was irony in the tone, but she watched me intently, as if this was a test question.

"No money," I said. "Just the hope I can help some friends sleep better at night, maybe clear a name or prevent another killing. Take your pick. Whatever, the reason's good enough to keep on keepin' on, as Bob Dylan would say. And no, I'm not a hunter. This isn't about an atavistic need for blood or vengeance." I tried to keep my own annoyance in check.

Sandy continued in a more challenging, edgy tone. "Maybe. But of course, the publicity must be attractive. Going on with the investigation might just add to your notoriety. I can see the headlines now—'Stone Age Warrior Gets His Man.' And from what I've gathered, your law practice could use more publicity."

"What makes you think my law practice needs any help?" I'd come for information about her, but so far I had nothing new and she'd turned the interview around.

"Oh, I've done some research recently," she said. "That's one of the things that has made me successful—learning as much as I can about prospective new partners or adversaries. I prepare, Dan, as I gather you did with me."

"There are plenty of people who'd look at my practice and think I'm pretty successful." I'd said the same thing to Ann Hastings.

"True. There are also some who say you could be doing much better for yourself."

Another woman analyzing my life and finding it wanting; this was getting tedious. This time, though, I had some analysis of my own to pass on. "I'll bet preparation helped when you started your small business in college."

"Certainly. I found a nice little market. Then I found some colleagues willing to help me service it.

It was a perfect enterprise until one person got greedy. We provided value and quality, everybody involved profited in one way or another. I ran the business, and others handled the clients. Good money, good fun. And I was an equal-opportunity employer, both boys and girls. Nothing fairer, more American than that."

"Sounds rational, logical, the way you set it out. And you even got a standing ovation for it."

"My, you do thorough work. But you're right, even if you're being sarcastic. And the people who carped about the immorality of it were the most hypocritical."

I laughed and reached for a new beer. "Oh, shit, no sarcasm from me. I don't care much about the morality of your brothel operation. Governments raise money by hooking poor folks on lotteries and gambling. Corporate executives get absurdly rich by cutting the benefits of their workers and turning them into part-time workers. Churches cover up sexual abuse by priests and ministers. Bank and real estate executives steal millions of dollars.

"You can accuse me of plenty, but I'm no crusader for morality—it's already long gone. People want to buy and sell a little sex, I won't partake, but I won't throw a nutty over it either." I took a drink as the silence welled up between us.

The night had a warm glow to it. Other cars drove in and parked by the water. Doors opened and closed. Sometimes cars drove in, no doors opened, and the people inside looked at the moon or whatever. I heard waves lapping on the boulders lining the shore. Oarlocks creaked as someone rowed a dinghy just off the shore. A high-pitched whine came and went as an outboard boat ventured out for some night fishing.

Sandy gave a small laugh, leaned over the table and touched my arm. "Dan, you surprise me. I thought you were a bleeding-heart liberal. But underneath, perhaps you bleed less than I expected."

Rather than answer, I finished off the beer and tried to understand what was going on. I hadn't learned much, while she now figured I had a moral core like hers, a vacuum. If our chat was going anywhere, it wasn't forward.

Sandy seemed to sense my uncertainty. She sat up straight at the table and looked at me intently, almost quizzically. "You never did answer my question about your law practice."

"You mean, about how well I do?"

"The very question," she said.

"You didn't want to talk about certain subjects. This one I don't talk about. I make enough for beer, potato chips, ice cream, and cable television. 'Our basest beggars are in the poorest thing superfluous,' said an old friend of mine. I have everything I need."

"Well, well, well—quoting from *King Lear*. You are full of surprises. I was an English major in college and loved Shakespeare, in case your research did not go that far." She had it right. The only literary allusion I had at hand didn't slow her down. She went right back on the offensive.

"I have friends, business associates, and lots of acquaintances. Some love to chat. Others want cold, hard cash in return for information. In your case, it was easy. People want to talk about you, claim you as a buddy, now that you have a bit of notoriety. From what I was told, you have a good head on your shoulders, considerable trial skills, independence of spirit, and a way with words. With that, you've built an undistinguished law practice providing a modest income.

"You have no family, not much real estate, and little prospect of change. Your ability and intellect exceed both your clients and your assets." Her eyes were hard and bright, and her right hand tugged at a spray of hair over her ear. I looked back, struggling not to give away any of the roiling inside me.

"Sorry, I'm not the guy to comment on my ability and intellect, and the rest of my life is fine, thanks."

"Dan, I told you earlier I get to know the people I'm dealing with. I'm certain that you're capable of doing more than you do now. I think, in fact, that you're a lot like me—smart, impatient with fools, easily bored. I'm trying to see what you're made of, see what makes you tick. Maybe there are things I can do to help you."

Sitting there, looking at me with a hint of a promising smile, she adroitly shifted from trashing me to praising my potential, switching from the stick to the carrot. If she were a car, she'd be a Porsche—great lines, breathtaking acceleration, able to turn on a dime. Next to her, I felt like an old, battered Volkswagen beetle.

Sandy's voice softened and I had to lean toward her to hear clearly. "I'd like to spend some time talking with you. I'd want you to back off my family, of course, but I can generate some very lucrative and challenging work for you. Big clients, big cases, and big retainers.

"I'd like to have you come to New York to discuss things," she went on. "Come for the day, I'll pay your way. Or if you prefer, come down for dinner and we can go to a show or a jazz club, whatever you'd like." The voice softened even further and she gave me a real smile.

I sat back, putting a bit more distance between us. "Hold on, this is moving too fast for me. You're transforming me from a two-bit shyster in Boston to a high-powered New York corporate litigator. You must be a damn good magician to pull that one off. Maybe even good enough to make some computer chips disappear?"

I paused. Her face showed nothing, but her fingers tapped on the table, not my forearm.

"Or maybe you're proposing a bribe?" I asked. "Maybe you want me to become the highly paid lawyer on retainer to Tire Enterprises, Inc.?"

The corners of her mouth turned down just a fraction. She rocked back a little on the bench. Her hands abandoned her beer and crossed her chest as if she felt cold. The eyes, wide and sparkling with interest and excitement just moments before, became narrow and sharp.

"You're not a law enforcement officer. I'm simply talking to a prospective business associate. No bribery, just mutual gains," she said. "But I must say, you really do your homework, Dan. And you play your cards close to your chest."

"You're not the first woman to tell me that."

"I take it you know more than you've told me. And all this time you were setting me up."

I didn't bother to respond.

She glanced over at the Jeep for a moment, as if making up her mind. She looked back at me, her face cold in the moonlight. "You're more difficult to deal with than I hoped. Let me suggest something. The air is becoming a bit chilly. Why don't we drive back to the restaurant and grab some coffee. We can talk a bit longer."

It wasn't just the air that was chillier. I had a feeling our discussion of mutual gains had ended.

While Sandy cleaned up the table, I picked up the last of the beer I was working on and the remaining bottles. I couldn't expect more from her, but I still had hopes, so a trip for coffee wouldn't hurt.

Walking back to the car, Sandy took a sudden right turn and we walked over to the lighthouse. She stood at its base and placed her hand on the cool white stone wall. "I sometimes wonder," she said, "what it must have been like to live here through the winter, riding out nor'easters, keeping company only with birds and the ocean."

How we got on to the lifestyles of lighthouse keepers, I didn't know, but if she wanted to talk, I'd listen. "Lonely, I suppose," I said, "but you can't beat the view, and there's always fresh fish. Just have to be sure you can live with the company."

"You mean, the lack of company."

"No, I meant what I said."

"Ah, living with oneself." She paused and looked up at the top of the lighthouse. "There is that." Then she turned and looked at me. "I only wish we met under different circumstances." She whirled around and walked away. "Enough laments. Time for coffee." She led me back to the car, past couples sitting on boulders, arms intertwined and eyes on the moon.

CHAPTER ————

THIRTY

Sandy got into the car and opened the door for me as I approached from the side with the remaining beers. I sat down inside, put the bottles on the floor, and closed the door. When she pulled out, I grabbed the bottles to keep them from falling over. We headed out of the parking lot and back to the main road.

Bottles safely stashed on the floor, I sat up and turned back to grab the seat belt over my right shoulder. My right temple bumped into an object that felt like the barrel of a gun. Which it was.

"Hey, Bruce, I'm not surprised to see you, but I can't say it's a pleasure."

Wettamesett police chief Bruce Richards pulled himself up from the floor behind the front seat, where he'd been hiding. He rested the gun against my cheek. I'd been one, sometimes two, steps behind him all the way. My chances of catching up were diminishing rapidly.

"Wondered if you'd catch on. Still, nice to see

you again, Kardon. Only sorry it's under these cir-cumstances." A loud laugh, almost a bark, fol-lowed. "Sounds like we're at a family funeral. Might be fitting here."

The gun barrel felt cold and sharp on my neck. "You might want to sit back and put on your seat belt, Richards," I said. "In this state, the police can fine you if you're not wearing one."

"Bad jokes won't save your ass," he said.

The gun didn't move, although the cold spot on my neck began to burn. I bent down to pick up a beer. Richards grabbed my shoulder and pulled me upright. Sandy Houghton was startled and the car swerved for a moment.

"Sit the fuck back and keep your hands at your sides," he said.

"The law-abiding citizens of Wettamesett wouldn't think much of your language," I said. "I was just going to grab a beer. There's an extra, if you like."

"Kardon, you must think I'm a moron," he said. "I let you pick up the beer, next thing I know either you whack Sandy with it or we have beer in our faces and you're making some foolish escape attempt. You bicycled out of a goddamn dump truck on me once, you got away from a hit man, you think I don't know what's going on in your head? You're like that damn pink battery bunny, you just keep going and going. Now, stay still. I like the inte-rior of this car as it is, just as soon not have to clean your brains off the seat covers."

One less mystery to solve. Richards and a crony had jumped me. I'd figured out most of it, except for the part about how I'd stay alive to tell somebody else what had happened.

Keeping my arms still, I turned toward Sandy Houghton. Her mouth was taut. The cords in her neck stretched like wires down her shoulders to the rigid talons gripping the wheel. Her silhouette appeared chiseled in stone. Her arms and a little vein under her jaw, rhythmically pulsing, were the only parts of her moving. Lights played on and off her face as we drove down the road.

Richards stopped talking for a moment, so I tried to engage Houghton. "That bribe still available?" I asked.

Her mouth tightened even further, but she didn't say a word. Instead, Richards spoke up, his voice a rasp. "Jesus, you'll try anything. Give it up. She didn't want to kill you, just to pay you to drop it. I'm not such a nice guy. But you blew your chance, so don't waste your remaining breath trying to get us upset or off guard."

"So how'd you work it? You couldn't know what I was going to do until Sandy and I talked."

"You're so smart, Kardon, you tell me."

I thought for a moment. "You watched from another car. When she took me over to the lighthouse, that was a signal you'd worked out. Then you slipped in the backseat."

"You've got good instincts for this kind of thing. Close. Only one difference. I wasn't in another car. I rowed over from the town pier. Didn't want to be seen driving in."

The oars I'd heard had been his. "Isn't it a bit risky, you, the police chief, hanging around Tern Point at night?"

"Less risky than letting you run around loose much longer."

We turned off Route 6 and headed north on Route 107. I was pretty sure I knew where we were headed. "Long as I'm out here, maybe I can pick up a new set of tires."

Sandy spoke for the first time, her voice firm and cold. "We thought it might be poetic justice to take you back one last time to the tire pile. After all the misery you have visited on my family, 'The wheel is come full circle.'"

"Another *King Lear* allusion, if I'm not mistaken," I said. "You're not just an ex-madame and a felon, you're a woman of uncommon learning."

She nodded slightly, although she continued looking straight ahead. "Nice you picked that up," she said. "Most people don't know Shakespeare these days. In my business I hear the quotations of Bill Gates, Rush Limbaugh, or Beavis and Butthead, not necessarily in that order. Too bad you're such a Boy Scout. We could have used you."

Route 107 had little traffic on it. I thought about grabbing the wheel or stamping on the brake pedal, but I was pinned by the pistol and the seat belt. After this was over, I'd write to the National Transportation Safety Board and explain that seat belts don't always improve personal security. In the meantime, my mouth was the only thing I could move safely.

"Yeah, it's too bad I won't be on the team to rip off some more computer chips. Maybe if I'd met you earlier, in college like your buddy Bruce, things might have worked out differently."

Richards sighed and spoke. "Kardon, all you've done is buy yourself a permanent tire mausoleum. We hoped to find another way, but now there isn't one. You want to take the high ground, that's your choice. But tell me how you figured this out."

"Should have sorted it out much earlier. Just today I found the last piece, a picture of the two of you after the honor trial at Jefferson University. Then it clicked. You went there to play football, messed up your knee, and ended up majoring in criminal justice. You got to be a student judge, and whose trial do you end up presiding over? A great-looking student from near the old hometown. Why do I think that maybe you guys fixed that trial and have gone on to greater glories since? With Tire Enterprises and your respective positions and knowledge, you two are in a position to pull off some great scams."

"Yeah, we're a damn good team," Richards said. "Go on."

"Aaron, I figure, happened to bike to the tire pile just after you hit Dynacomp. You did some kind of transfer of the chips from one truck to others, maybe, and somehow you stumbled onto Aaron. How'm I doing?"

Richards spoke in an almost approving tone. "You really ought to be in a different line of work. But others won't make the same connections. Once you disappear, investigators will find crack cocaine in your car, along with the gun that killed Aaron. All sorts of confusion and speculation. And Sandy and I will be long gone."

"Tell me about Aaron," I said. "What happened?"

"You got it about right," Richards said. "We were transferring pallets and boxes of stolen chips from a truck to a couple of smaller vans at the tire pile. None of the regular employees were around. Aaron had been out for a bike ride and wandered in to check things out. He had a coughing jag and we heard him. Didn't know who he was, so I had to go after him. He ran, I chased him, and finally caught him when he fell.

"Unfortunately, when I brought him back, he recognized both Sandy and me. He knew me and he'd seen Sandy windsurfing. He didn't know exactly what we were doing, but the boxes were labeled and he heard us talking about transferring the stuff and selling it. I had no choice but to kill him. I took his body and his bike out by truck and arranged it by the side of the road."

"And you planted cocaine from your evidence room in the bike bag when you went back to look over the scene in the morning?" I asked.

"Yeah. I also went out and fired some shots in other places so we had the additional cover of a drive-by shooting."

For a moment all I could hear was the road noise and the tires screeching as we rounded a turn. I looked over at Sandy Houghton. As I did, an electronic ringer went off.

"That's my portable phone," she said. "Probably calling me about the meeting earlier today. It's in my jacket pocket on the seat," she told Richards. "Reach in and turn it off, okay?" He did.

I turned to Sandy. "I see you fit right into the Houghton family—gambling, illegal dumping, an occasional homicide. Good use of your education, Sandy."

That got a rise out of her. "You don't have a clue, Kardon. We—"

"It won't work," Richards cut in, his voice harsh and rough. "You can't make her feel guilty, asshole. I killed Aaron, she didn't have any part in it. I didn't want to kill him. That was never part of the plan. He just blundered in where he didn't belong. Just like you.

"We had chips already sold to three different companies and had millions coming to us on the deals. No way we were letting anybody take that away."

I stayed silent, breathed deeply, and willed myself not to turn around. I concentrated on keeping the conversation going, not on the grotesque story I was hearing.

"What about my being nailed in the bar parking lot with the planted drugs. That your idea?"

"Hell, no," Richards said. "George Houghton

got a call from a bartender that you'd been around, and he improvised a little payback. I would have loved for it to work, but he made all sorts of mistakes, and I couldn't afford to have you make us look bad."

"You said that the two of you are leaving tonight," I said. "Where to?"

"We'll be leaving you behind, probably rent another car. Take separate late-night flights out. Bought the tickets with cash under assumed names and we have fake IDs. A series of one-way flights from New York will get us to a South American country. No extradition treaty, and a prominent businessman and a cabinet secretary are only too happy to have my security expertise and Sandy's computer and business knowledge. We'll be safe and sound, but I will say this, Kardon—you've cost us a hell of a lot, forced us to abandon some exciting plans."

Sandy Houghton finally spoke, her voice firmer. "For what it's worth, Kardon, I'm sorry about Aaron. I never wanted that kind of violence. I've always loved to gamble, and my dad taught me well. How to get in the big games, when to pass, when to stake everything. He always went for the big play, never made it. But we, Bruce and I, we made the big hit with chips. And it's been much bigger than we could imagine, millions."

"I'm sure your father would be proud of you."

"I never thought the killings would happen, did not want them, but you know the clichés—no risk, no reward—and the money is just too good," she said. "I hate the thought of leaving New York and the business. Our new life will be boring. We'll have to wait it out for a few years. But as soon as you called me the other night, we knew we had to make plans to leave."

Richards chimed back in. "My turn with some questions. What about Grizek? What did he tell you about the operation?"

"Not much. Said he'd been involved in something, I inferred Aaron's murder, and he'd been sent off with some money. He did say he'd been involved with, and I quote, the 'Houghton bitch.'"

Sandy Houghton didn't flinch. She gave a short, mirthless laugh. "Yes, Grizek never liked me."

She took the turnout on Route 107, that served as the head of the trail into the tire pile. As we stopped, Richards grabbed the back of my shirt collar and told me to hold still.

CHAPTER —————

THIRTY-ONE

There was no streetlight near the turnout. The sky was clear, the moon high and bright. I looked forward and back for oncoming traffic. One car passed going in the opposite direction, too fast to notice anything amiss. In the rearview mirror on the passenger side, I thought I saw a metallic glint or a reflection well behind us. When I wriggled closer to try to see better in the mirror, the only thing I saw was part of my face. The picture didn't cheer me up.

Richards kept the gun trained on me as he got out of the car and ordered me out. Then he shoved me toward the trail. Sandy Houghton pulled on her jacket, grabbed her bag, then led the way with a flashlight.

No more cars passed as we headed into the woods. I glanced back toward where I thought I'd seen a light, but nobody appeared. I'd seen a chimera born of hope and fear, nothing real. No John Wayne, no cavalry to the rescue.

Houghton walked fifteen or twenty feet ahead of me on the trail, using a small flashlight. Richards walked just behind me, using his flashlight on the trail in front of me.

I'd answered their questions, but still had my own. "Why go in the back way?" I raised my voice a bit so they both could hear me.

"Keep quiet." Houghton's voice sounded tight and stressed.

"What are you going to do if I don't, kill me twice? The least you can do is answer some of my questions."

Richards grunted, then said, "It's a nice touch. The environmental and criminal investigators have been all over the tire pile. There are new gates, locks, security cameras to prevent midnight dumping, all that stuff in place so nobody can go in the front door. But there's no security in back, because they're only worried about trucks bringing in more hazardous waste."

"Why dump me at a site with government officials all over it?"

"That's the best part. Killing you is easy. Making you disappear is harder. We leave your body in a field, in the woods or in a pond, somebody out walking their dog or kids necking in the woods will find it.

"But the tire pile is the last place anyone would look. The investigators have pretty much finished. They dug a whole bunch of test pits and wells and pulled up sections of tires. They'll leave the existing wells in place and do some monitoring, but no more digging and no more disrupting the tire pile while it operates as an ongoing business. Anybody buried under the pile won't be found for a hell of a long time."

"Nice work if you can get it," I said.

Richards continued without any prompting. "Yeah, chips are a great business. Sandy knows about the computer industry, while I know people in the Southeast, mostly law enforcement guys, but in my business you get to know all kinds. Made it easy to hire help in various places when we needed it."

"Quality help like Henning," I said.

"Believe it or not, he came highly recommended. Turns out, he'd been pretty good until too much cocaine turned his mind to mush. I just wish I had that decision back." Richards was gushing, eager to impress me, almost wistful in his reminiscences—sad that things were ending and that he could never tell anybody about his accomplishments.

"It's a big step from stealing computer chips to murder," I said. "If it wasn't me, somebody else would have nailed you for it."

Richards almost brayed with laughter. "Ah, hell, we had a beautiful plan, damn little exposure, and lots of money to cover up the few holes we had. And as long as we didn't get too greedy, we could have gone after chips once, maybe twice more. But you just wouldn't let go."

"How was Grizek involved?" I asked.

"He helped out, drove a truck, did what I told him. I paid him well for it," Richards said. "He and I and a couple of others pulled off the robbery of the computer plant. Grizek didn't have much choice. Found him driving under the influence a few times. Told him I wouldn't prosecute if he did some little things for us. And once he got involved, each time I had more hanging over his head."

"I don't suppose you deliberately staked him out once you knew he drank."

"Could have."

"And me, how'd you know where to find me, that night you threw me in the back of a truck?"

"Shit, Kardon, you were so damn predictable. I knew about every damn shipment of hazardous waste the boys buried. Had to let 'em go since I didn't want any government scrutiny of the family, Sandy particularly, since she and the boys were in business together. Too much at risk.

"Once you showed up with the helmet, I knew you'd be all over the pile like a dog in heat. That convenience store was the closest place to the trail to park. I had a guy in the store looking for you or your car. I'd heard the boys were going to do another shipment but I hoped you'd give up before you saw anything.

"That night, once we knew your car was at the convenience store, I called Grizek, he brought a truck, and we grabbed you. Planned to dump you a long way away, discourage you, not kill you. Grizek wasn't happy about it. I had to, shall we say, encourage him. Just bad luck that you saw the dumping."

"And then," I said, "you sent Grizek off and had Henning kill him because he knew too much."

"Piece of cake. I went down to Norfolk, located Henning, and paid him the first installment. I sent Henning out as soon as we knew where Grizek's car had broken down, told him that if you were around, he should nail you as well. In any event—ouch, shit!"

Richards yelled. I'd grabbed a broken tree branch that had blocked my way, turned and thrown it at him. As soon as it left my hands I jumped off the trail and ran, crouching low to avoid tree limbs. In the darkness, though, I tripped over a root and grunted as I hit a tree with my bad shoulder on the way down.

Houghton came running back on the trail, swinging her light wildly as she searched for me. Richards stumbled at first but was quickly over me and hit the side of my head with the gun barrel as I struggled to get up. I went down again, and then he stood a few feet away, pointing the gun and flashlight at me as I tried to stand. We were both breathing hard.

"Kardon, I'd like to fucking shoot you now, but then I'd have to drag your dead ass back on the trail and to the tire pile. Get up and get moving."

I wiped my hand on my face and felt something warm and sticky. Probably not Sandy Houghton's lipstick. "Maybe I'll just take a nap right here."

Richards moved right next to me and shone the

flashlight directly in my eyes. "I told you, get up, stop screwing around before you push me too far. Let's go." He grabbed my arm, pulled me up, and pushed me back toward the trail.

Houghton stood back and let us go forward. She hadn't said a thing throughout my little escapade.

Back on the trail, I started talking again. "Sandy, when you started the company—"

"Shut up, Kardon," she said. "I mean it. And you too Bruce. Not a word from either one of you. You guys sound like high school assholes, 'How'd you like how I dunked the ball?'" Her voice dripped with anger and bile. Her normally precise, careful language went into the gutter. It worked. Neither one of us said a word.

Another couple of minutes passed and we emerged at the tire pile. Though I'd watched for it as we walked in the darkness, I had walked unknowingly past the clearing where Aaron hid his bike. I'd wanted to see it, acknowledge it, to say a silent memorial to Aaron and an apology for having failed him. Like so much throughout the case, I'd not seen it in time. And once again I hadn't finished something I'd started; one more time I'd failed to make a difference. Actually, not one more time—one last time.

The three of us emerged into the clearing between the woods and the tire pile. The pile itself was visible, particularly where it reached up high and blocked out the stars and moonlight. Here and there whitewalls shone with a soft luminescence.

Ordinary things, things I might not see again, looked magnificent.

At Richards's direction, I walked along the edge of the pile and then turned around. Richards walked over and stood next to Houghton, about ten feet from me. They had the pile on their left and the moon over their right shoulders.

The scene brought back a memory of my first view of the pile, when I saw it as a shimmering volcano. Now Houghton and Richards, backlit and visible only as silhouettes, appeared as Stephen King might have created them, spirits of the tires, deriving their evil and power from the spent petroleum and chemicals lying in waste behind them.

Houghton craned up toward Richards' and whispered something to him, her hand on his arm and her lips close to his ear. The light beam held steady on me from Richards's hand. They looked at each other, and both of them laughed at whatever she'd said.

"Turn around and kneel down," Richards said.

"Aw, come on. My pants are dirty enough already."

"Kardon, the clowning is over. Just do it."

"Sounds like a sneaker ad." Nobody laughed. "You killed Aaron Winters and Jeff Grizek, I'm next in line. You guys are upping the ante each time."

"Too late, Kardon, much too late," Richards said. "The stakes are already way too high. Right now, you're just part of the cost of doing business."

"It's a long way to travel, from greed to murder.

The sooner you stop, the easier it will be to cut your losses."

"Losses only matter if they catch you, asshole. Now kneel down."

I turned and knelt. As I went down I saw a small, rusty metal bucket in front of me, between two tires. Before landing on my knees, I reached for the can. With my back shielding my hands, Richards and Houghton couldn't see me grab it.

With both hands, I whirled and threw it at the pair. As soon as I let it go I jumped aside. The can hit Richards, spraying both Houghton and him with dirt. She yelled. I heard a gun go off, a thud, and a tire near me jumped.

Richards dropped his flashlight, grasping the side of his head where the can had hit with one hand and rubbing his dirt-spattered eyes with his gun hand. As he did, I jumped up and ran at him.

Just before I hit him, Richards saw me and brought his gun hand down. I went in low and hard under it. The gun went off by my ear. Before he fired again, I drove my shoulder into his ribs. After hitting him, I kept pushing upward. With my fist, I hammered his side. A lower rib seemed to let go and he let out a *whoosh*.

But he didn't fall. He tried to bring the gun inside, to fire into my chest. I grabbed his firing arm with both of my hands and jerked his wrist down over my knee. The gun fired again and dropped out of his hand.

The bullet went off into space and I heard a roaring. Some of it came from the outside. Most of it came from inside, from internal voids and fissures venting hope, anger, pain, and life. Yelling, I dropped my shoulder low again and drove Richards like he was a blocking sled until he slammed down against a bunch of tires.

While I was on top and forcing him down, he tried to slug me, but the punch lacked power. I picked up a small tire and swung it, cracking him in the temple, harder than necessary. Richards sagged back and his head fell into the center of a larger tire. I pulled a couple of tires around his feet and arms and threw another one on his stomach. Closest thing to a straitjacket I could find.

The sounds in my head started to subside, but behind me I heard movement. Sandy Houghton was running toward the trail, her flashlight beam bobbing along. She had a head start, but windsurfing did nothing to increase her endurance. I caught her quickly.

She fought with me, clawing my face, but I overwhelmed her quickly and wrenched the flashlight from her.

"We can do this easy or hard," I said. "Walk back with me quietly or I'll whack you in the head with the flashlight and drag you back."

She walked.

Once we got back near Richards, I heard him moaning, so to shut him up I threw a couple more tires on him. I told Houghton to give me her jacket and to lie down next to Richards. I piled tires on her, over her protests.

While she wrestled with the tires, I grabbed her cellular phone out of her jacket. I didn't know the emergency number for the State Police and didn't want to call the locals, so I dialed Al Thompson's number. I heard his voice answer, but then it turned out that some of the roaring I'd heard earlier had come from a pickup truck.

"Al, this is Dan—"

"Put down the phone," someone yelled at me, apparently coming around a mound of tires about twenty feet away. "Kardon, stop right there, don't move, or I'll shoot."

The moon was behind a small cloud, but it illuminated a figure approaching, holding something that gave off a metallic reflection. Jean Houghton with her rifle. I dropped my hand with the phone to my side.

"All right, Ms. Houghton, take it easy. Why don't you put down the gun."

Sandy Houghton gave a muffled cry. "Mom, thank God." Richards just moaned some more, but I heard Sandy Houghton scrambling amidst the tires.

"Ms. Houghton," I said. "Bruce Richards and Sandy brought me here to kill me, they're the ones who killed Aaron Winters and Grizek—"

"I've listened to too much already," she said. "I got here a few minutes ago, heard enough to figure it out."

"How did you know to come, Mom?"

"Had some sensors, motion detectors, put in on a couple of those trails at the back of the tire pile and didn't tell anybody. With all the stuff going on, I wanted to find out what was happening. The sensors went off, triggered an alarm in the house, and I came over. I never dreamed I'd find you here."

"Mom, you've got to help us." Sandy had pushed the tires off her and climbed to her feet. "Give me the gun, then we can get Bruce into your truck so we can get to our car."

Jean didn't take the rifle off me, but she didn't say anything either.

"Mom—"

"Ms. Houghton," I cut in, "don't do it. Hate me all you want, but this isn't about me, it's about you, how people will remember you. You've worked too hard for too long to blow it all now."

"Mom, we don't have time for philosophical discussions. I need help and we need to move quickly to get out of here." Sandy took a step toward her mother. "We never wanted all these things to happen, it was all a mistake."

"Hold on," Jean Houghton said. "Give me a minute."

"You've got a choice," I said. "You've always made the right decisions before. Do it this time. You want to kill me, or let Sandy do it, you want to choose to be a murderer, now's the time." I started walking toward her. "But how about giving me the rifle instead . . ."

"Stop right there, Kardon," Jean Houghton ordered. I did.

"You always tried to do the best thing for your family," I said, "and the best thing is to give me the gun, end this madness now." I took a few more steps.

"Give me the gun, Mom, or shoot him," Sandy said.

The moon came out from behind a cloud, and I could see Jean's face, contorted and tear-streaked. Her hands, holding the rifle, shook. I dropped the phone in my hand and closed the gap between us.

Sandy jumped toward her mother at the same time and we both grabbed the rifle barrel. The gun went off, high into the sky, and Jean let go of it. Sandy wrestled with me for a minute, but I overpowered her again and took the gun. "It's over," I said.

Jean was crying softly. Sandy turned to face her, unconsciously straightened out her hair and said "I'm sorry" to her mother. Jean stepped toward Sandy and embraced her. Her daughter's countenance cracked and she broke down sobbing. Over and over she said, "I'm sorry, Mom."

Her mother held her and rocked her, saying, "I'm sorry too, Sandy, I couldn't do it."

Noises came from where Richards lay, and I went back to find him wrestling with the tires. In the distance I heard sirens. I pushed Richards back down without much resistance and threw a couple more tires on him.

I sat down on a large tire and looked over the scene. I saw Richards's gun on the ground shining in the moonlight, felt the rifle in my hand, and thought about Aaron and Grizek. Everybody had warned me about rushing in. I'd been lucky to get out alive. And I was glad I had.

For a moment I looked up and admired the stars. They still didn't hold any answers, but now I had answered the questions about Aaron. And maybe I'd started on those about me.

Shortly, engines whined and cars burst through the chain-link fence guarding the tire pile. Horns wailed in the middle of the forest and car lights streamed from the entrance toward where I stood.

From the first police car, Al Thompson, Jenny, and two cops emerged. They ran over, flashlights waving wildly. I was relieved to see they were Glassbury cops—Wettamesett cops, seeing Richards under the tires, might have shot me on sight.

"Over here," I called.

The police pulled the tires off Richards and helped him up. Richards remained hunched over, clutching his chest. Al looked at Sandy and Jean and shook his head.

Jenny walked over to me and I gave her a hug. She shuddered, and I whispered in her ear, "Thanks, but no overtime for this."

She hugged me hard around the neck and clung, the energy draining from her. I felt a few tears course down her cheek and thought I heard her say "jerk" into my chest. After a long minute I opened my arms and she stepped back, clearing the tears from her cheeks. She didn't say anything but gave me a smile and nodded that she was okay.

"Son, for a pansy-ass Boston lawyer, you throw quite a party," Al said.

We walked over to him. Soon State Police cars poured in after the locals and cops swarmed over the site.

"Thanks, Al," I said. "I'm glad you guys showed up so quickly."

"You're welcome," he said, "but you did all the work. 'Course, you look pretty crappy now, buddy. How's Richards?"

"He was out for a bit, but he should be okay. I wanted him to make another move so I could whack him again. And I do regret I didn't take a hard shot at her." I pointed to Sandy Houghton.

I heard another roaring sound, and from nowhere a helicopter blew in, hovered for a moment, found a level clear spot with its searchlights, and landed. Two figures climbed out. A familiar voice boomed, "Kardon, you gonna leave anything for us professional crime fighters? You may recall, we're sworn to serve and protect and all that shit."

Randy came over and clamped a hand on my shoulder. The wrong one, and it hurt like hell, but I didn't bother to tell him. Other state troopers had their spotlights on and guns out. Human forms moved in and out of the light beams, appearing and vanishing as if we were watching a bad sci-fi movie. The police called out to one another, trying to make sense of the scene.

Soon state troopers escorted Richards over to a cruiser. Randy motioned a couple of others over, talked to them briefly, and they extricated Sandy from her mother and put her in a separate car.

Jean Houghton walked over to the cruiser where her daughter sat in the back. I heard her tell Sandy that she would call a lawyer and join her at the jail. Then Jean walked past us, looking frail and bruised. She stopped at her pickup and climbed in. In the bobbing lights, we could see her bent over the wheel, her head on her hands. It appeared she was crying.

Al Thompson walked over to the pickup, opened the door, leaned in and put his arm on her back. He spoke into her ear for a minute or two. She turned to him and grabbed his free hand.

Somehow, I didn't think Jean Houghton would thank me for reuniting her with her daughter and with Al.

When Al came back, he was shaking his head, his eyes downcast. "What a waste. After all her struggles to protect and save them, those kids of hers have done their best to destroy the whole damn family. But I think she'll be okay. I'll check in with her tomorrow."

Whatever Jean Houghton had done, she didn't deserve the Greek tragedy that had engulfed her. And whatever evils had plagued the family, I knew

I'd always hold a special place in the pantheon of Houghton enemies.

I gave a brief statement to Randy and a couple of troopers and investigators. Randy knew I was tired and a bit shaky, but he wanted a more complete statement immediately, so we agreed to meet him back at the Glassbury police station.

In the car, Al and Jenny told me their story.

"I returned to the office a while after you called in. The minute I heard your message, I got scared about your meeting," Jenny said. "I grabbed my car and headed toward Wettamesett. With my car phone—a recent invention which you might consider for yourself, Mr. Kardon—I tried to call Al and I couldn't reach Randy."

"Sorry about that," I said, "my cell phone died and I've been meaning to get it fixed."

"Anyway, I came down," she continued, "and didn't know where to go, but I finally reached Al just before I got down here, and he told me to come to his house."

"Lucky she did," Al said. "Smart thing you did there, son, leaving the phone line open while you talked to Jean and Sandy."

"Thanks for not talking back. That would've screwed things up royally."

"Yeah, at first I was just confused, couldn't figure out what was going on, but then I recognized the voices and just listened. After I got a handle on it, I called some of the local boys I trust to come over, and they called the staties. Got to tell you,

Dan," Al said, "you need a full-time bodyguard, the kind of people you attract."

By the time we were through at the police station, the adrenaline rush was long gone, leaving me with a headache, bruises, and an aching shoulder. Randy offered to have a trooper drive me home, but his people had plenty to do at the tire pile and in Glassbury and Wettamesett, so I told him I'd drive myself.

Al drove Jenny and me back to our cars, dropping Jenny off first. She and I didn't say much, just that we'd talk over the weekend.

Then, alone with me in his car as he drove me to mine, Al asked, "How you doing?"

"Guess I'm okay," I said, "Shoulder hurts a bit and—"

"I'm not worried about your shoulder, son. How's it feel inside?"

"It's weird, hard to sort out. Figuring things out, getting some answers for Ann and Frank, for Aaron's girlfriend, Sarah, that's good. They'll sleep better, feel like Aaron never betrayed them. But . . ." My voice trailed off.

"Yeah?"

"It's just depressing as hell to see how amoral and violent people can get, particularly these two with so much going for them. I feel like I got slimed by Sandy and Richards, and some of their crap won't come off."

"Yeah," he said. "I've been there. The normal-looking ones, the smart ones, those are the scariest. They really make you shake your head."

"Makes me wonder how far away any of us are from pulling stunts like this."

"Give it a little time. You see a few of 'em like this, it gets easier to understand these people are nothing like you and me. But, hell, I understand; I'd never have believed these two would be doing this kind of stuff."

"Well, for now, I'm just glad it's ended. I'll leave it to the pros from here on out."

Al laughed. "Yeah, maybe you will. But in a day or two you'll feel better about how things ended up. You'll think, hey, nailing the bad guys wasn't half bad."

When we were by my car, before getting out, I thanked him. "You've been a big help," I said. "I appreciate it, and I'll talk to you soon."

"No, thank you. Felt good to get back in the saddle a little. Happy to help out. You were damned lucky, but you also did a real good job."

In the car, I cranked up Muddy Waters and Jerry Jeff Walker tapes. A stop at the Burger King drive-in halfway, where I grabbed a milk shake and french fries, helped, although my arm hurt just putting the fries in my mouth. For a while my mind was on cruise control, but then I thought about Aaron. Memories came back in a torrent, memories of games we played, conversations we'd had, and the places we'd gone. The memories, unspoiled by uncertainty, made the drive go quickly.

When I pulled into my street in Brookline, there were no lights on in any of the houses. It was clear and cool. I had a fleeting thought about taking a short run as a step on the road back to normalcy. The thought retreated in the face of a vision of a warm bed.

As I opened the front door, a car pulled up in front of my house. Jenny climbed out, carrying a small paper bag. She stopped right in front of me on the doorstep.

"Hi, Dan, thought I'd check on you. You scared the hell out of us tonight. Then, by the time we left the police station, you looked a little gray and I could tell your shoulder was hurting. Thought you might want some help or company. I brought some ice cream."

"Um, sure, come on in."

"I should tell you one thing." She moved closer. She'd never looked better. Her eyes glinted as she smiled and took a deep breath. "I've had a sense, maybe it's a hope, that you're holding back with me, probably because of what happened with Wayne Sharman. Anyway, I just needed to tell you, I'm quitting."

To see her smiling while she said it sent a chill through me. Later, Jenny told me I looked like a puffer fish in that moment, my mouth opening and closing without words coming out.

"Jesus, Jenny, I'm truly thankful that you showed up earlier with Al, but you know, you could have waited to tell me. That's a surprise I didn't need tonight."

"You know, guys can be so damn frustrating," she said. "So damn black-and-white about things, no emotional subtlety. A villain shows up, and the hero has to go to the opposite extreme. You, you figure that Sharman harassed me, so you have to act like a robot. Or maybe like John Wayne, show all your emotions by how you tip your hat."

"I'm lost—what's going on here?"

"Dan, I'm sorry I've been so tough on you recently. I was pretty angry at you for a while for keeping me out of things."

"I noticed. I wasn't keeping you out because you aren't good—you're a fine lawyer. It's just, well, a lot of things . . ." I didn't know how to continue.

She gave a soft laugh. "We can talk about it later. Anyway, things got confused there for a while. I thought sparks were flying between us, then we got off track. I'd like to see if we can get things back where they were. I've heard all your damn Shakespeare quotes—I found one I thought fit here. 'Pray you now, forget and forgive.' "

"Not *King Lear* again. I can't believe it."

"What do you mean?"

"Never mind, I'm happy to forgive. And since I was, in your accurate description, a prick at times, I hope you'll do the same and that you'll stay on at the office."

"I can't. My dad just had a stroke back home in

Tennessee, so I need to go back and spend some time there. I'm happy to offer some nursing and therapy in the meantime, but I've got some things to do before I go. Besides, I have to quit since I know you'd never lay a hand on an employee. While I'd welcome the hand, I'd never want you to violate office policy."

I'll admit, it took me a minute before I figured it out, then another few seconds to recognize the building pressure in my chest. Yes, my hesitation with Jenny had been about Sharman, but it had also been about me. At that instant I had a recollection of my last bike ride with Aaron. Or maybe it wasn't a recollection, maybe it was him, reaching out from somewhere far away and giving me a spiritual kick in the ass.

As I looked at Jenny, smiling at me, I remembered what Aaron had said about his return to biking—that people don't forget how to ride a bicycle because of their muscle memory. I knew in that moment that I'd handled things badly for a long time. I'd suffered losses, but not of any faculties, abilities, or capacities. Instead, in retreat from pain, I'd let my heart, my emotional muscle, go unused, to wither and atrophy.

Once upon a time, though, I'd used it more and for better purposes. Maybe it had its own memory; perhaps the expanding force in my chest was not anxiety, but my heart pushing to escape the walls constraining it, like an Alaskan husky in a pen bursting to haul a dogsled. The time had come to let it loose; to let my heart's muscle memory lead me to things I'd shunned for too long.

I pulled Jenny close, hugged her as hard as I could. We looked at one another for a moment, then kissed, long and deep. My chest released and then filled again with lightness and warmth. Walking inside, holding her hand, the house didn't feel lonely at all.

Jenny showed me a full complement of nursing skills. They helped. I didn't feel pain in the shoulder or my knee all night long. And the best thing was, I still needed nursing the next day.

CHAPTER

THIRTY-TWO

The newspapers, predictably, had a field day with the case. My favorite headline read: ADZE MAN TIRES OUT TOP COP. A television station called and asked me to be its regular courtroom commentator. My legal brethren gave me unmerciful grief. Happily, though, one colleague belonged to The Country Club, with its sacred golf course. While I'd never be welcomed as a member, I was something of a trophy guest for him to bring around a few times, and Mike Steiner loved hearing about the golf course.

When I told Ann and Frank all that I'd learned, it was as if a dam burst within Ann. She hugged me, sobbed and whispered Aaron's name over and over again.

"Oh, it still hurts so badly, but it feels like a hand has been holding my heart, and now it's eased up, I can breathe. We can let go, feel good about who he was, know we didn't fail him and he never failed us," she said. "Thank you, Dan, I can't tell you how much this means to us, how much it helps."

"Thanks," Frank said. "And we're damn glad you came out alive as well." He gave me a hug as well, the first we'd ever exchanged.

We talked for a while, going over things, reminiscing about Aaron free of fears and doubt. Ann and Frank insisted on paying me. I refused. We compromised on their paying for dinner and a party at a local bar, and they bought me a fancy new bike, which I swore would never see the inside of a dump truck.

We had a good crowd and a great party. Ann and Frank, Randy and his wife, Al Thompson, and Roberta Reid, the elderly lady who had rescued me after I escaped from the truck, all came. The Steiners showed up. Mike Steiner followed Jenny around like a loyal puppy, keeping me at bay all night as he extracted sports story after sports story from her.

Jenny spends some time in Tennessee with her parents and some time in Boston now. She does some legal work for me on occasion, and also tries to capitalize, as my agent, on my minor celebrity. As of yet, she hasn't made much money off me. The latest pitch she wants to sell me on is from the biggest tire manufacturer in the country. The company wants me to do a commercial made in a real-life tire pile. Fat chance. It's bad enough I agreed to the damn book deal she negotiated.

• • •

Months later, on a beautiful, unusually warm day in March, I went back to Wettamesett with my bike. I parked at the cottage and took a walk on the beach. There were no people about. A heron patrolled the water's edge.

I took a long bike ride over the route Aaron and I had taken. I stopped twice, once where I passed Aaron when he'd been driven off the road, and once where his body had been left. Each time, I got off the bike and looked around for a few minutes. It was calm and peaceful. Only the birds and a few early bugs spoke out. Spring, not death, was in the air.

The trail to the tire pile was not far away, but I didn't take it. I'd been down there too often. I pedaled past it, pumping hard. I didn't bike as fast as Aaron would have, but I went as fast as I could.